LEGION OF HORROR

José crossed himself when he saw who it was—or, rather, what it was.

Now he knew what had happened to his missing patrols.

He heard a small gasp from Consuela, but he could not tear his eyes away from the shambling, decayed parodies of humanity that had lurched into view on the trail. Shreds of their uniforms hung off their twisted limbs, the wounds that had killed them clearly visible through the rags. Hoses from the dull metallic tanks on their backs circled their tortured bodies and entered their chests in several places.

"The dead have risen from the grave," he breathed.

VOR: THE MAELSTROM

Available from Warner Aspect®

HELL HEART

ROBERT E. VARDEMAN

ASPECT®

WARNER BOOKS

A Time Warner Company

WARNER BOOKS EDITION

Copyright © 2000 by FASA Corporation
All rights reserved. No part of this book may be reproduced in any form or by any electronic or mechanical means, including information storage and retrieval systems, without permission in writing from the publisher, except by a reviewer who may quote brief passages in a review.

Aspect® name and logo are registered trademarks of Warner Books, Inc.

VOR: The Maelstrom and all related characters, slogans, and indicia are trademarks of FASA Corporation.

Cover design by Don Puckey
Cover illustration by Donato
Cover logo design by Jim Nelson

Warner Books, Inc.
1271 Avenue of the Americas
New York, NY 10020

Visit our Web site at
www.twbookmark.com

 A Time Warner Company

Printed in the United States of America

First Printing: November 2000

10 9 8 7 6 5 4 3 2 1

For Fred and Joan Saberhagen

Words (and book dedications) are not enough
but it's a start.

Thanks to Mike Nielsen for loaning me such a
wonderful universe to play in.

Special thanks also to Donna Ippolito, Annalise Raziq, and Wyn Hilty
for the pep talks and support, and to
Jaime Levine for such good direction and outright
fine ideas on how to make this better.

And a tip of the hat to Mike Stackpole for the
recommendation and years of friendship.

HELL HEART

1

Brighter than a star it blazed, spewing out deadly radiation in all directions throughout the turbulent Styx Nebula. But the Pharon spaceship *Destroyer for the Faith* drove straight for its burning core, oblivious to the possible damage to its equipment and crew.

"Prepare to grapple," ordered the Death Priest in command of the vessel. Most of the control-room slaves hurried to obey, but one, more decrepit than the rest, did not move quickly enough for the priest's liking. Without warning, a wickedly sharp, meter-long devotional blade sliced through the air—and the slave's neck. A dust cloud rose where the curved diamond blade severed mummified head from torso, only to be quickly vacuumed away by the relentless flow of air through the control room—designed to prevent contamination rather than to hold down the ever-present, throat-tightening stench of death. The slave's carcass thudded noisily to the deck. Fluids dribbled from sundered life-support hoses until three other slaves stripped the corpse of its back tank and dragged the pa-

thetic remains out of the way. Another hurriedly took its
place at the control console.

The Death Priest sheathed his blade at his side, adjusted the greasy gray bandages around his head, and
turned back to the array of sensors in front of him, his
quick mind calculating the approach vector and the amount
of damage his ship might sustain in his quest to capture
this bit of errant matter.

It had to be a piece of the Vorack itself, that swirling
eye of bleeding energy responsible for their captivity in the
peculiar chaotic region surrounding it. Other races might
fear the power of the Vorack, but the Pharon reveled in it.
Their homeworld was located close to the energy vortex at
the heart of the Maelstrom, constantly bathed in the Vorack's erratic radiation. *Destroyer for the Faith* had picked
up the intense energy blasting outward from that speck of
strangeness several days ago, and the priest had ordered
his crew to follow.

The Pharon had detected such fragments of pure
power before, but never had a ship been close enough to
pursue them. Until now. With this incandescent tidbit harnessed to the will of the God-king, the Pharon would have
sufficient energy to do anything they liked: move their
planet freely throughout the Rings, a mobile fortress to
conquer all the other races; harness it as a directed-energy
weapon; even, perhaps, use its power to return them to true
life. It was the Vorack, after all, that had revived the
Pharon from their tombs after their homeworld had been
drawn into the Maelstrom. Who was to say that, tamed, it
could not do more?

The ship had followed the mote for days as the priest
studied it, trying to discover the best way to capture it. As

nearly as the sensors could determine, the energy source itself was microscopic. It was encased in a solid globe of some sort of crystalline structure that seemed to contain most of its immense power, allowing only enough radiation to leak out so that their instruments could detect it. But the Pharon knew he had to act quickly. The powerful speck might be a piece of the Vorack, but the crystal encasing it almost certainly was not. That could mean other races might be aware of it—might even have captured and then lost it—and could very well be in pursuit. Perhaps even the hated Shard, those crystalline abominations. The Death Priest had to capture the mote quickly, surround it with a force field to contain its deadly radiation, then return it to the homeworld for the glory of the God-king.

"Slayer!" barked the Death Priest. Immediately the enormously tall, prodigiously strong warrior, outfitted in shining, exquisite golden armor that contrasted horribly with the sickly gray of his skin, came to his side. The Slayer clacked his battle claw in anticipation of his orders, and the control room filled with the whine of the energy weapon at his right hand, charging to full capacity for even more widespread slaughter.

"At your command!" the Slayer snapped. His voice came out in a croak; the vocal cords had decayed. He nodded his small head once, then stood ready for orders. One baleful dark eye stared at the priest from between heavy wrappings.

"Assemble a squadron and launch them with force grapples," the priest commanded. "Fasten the cables around the crystal, then reel it close to *Destroyer for the Faith.* But do not bring it aboard until the hold is evacuated and ready." The Pharon chafed at the need to keep the inner force-shields lowered until the mote was aboard. Leaving them down rendered the ship vulnerable to attack. But they had to be lowered until the crystal was safely contained in the hold's internal electromagnetic field.

"At once," the Slayer said. The deadly soldier spun, knocking a too-slow control-room slave from his path, then hastened to the launch tubes amidships, where four small, torpedo-shaped vessels would be sent on their mission. It was possible that, once outside the protection of the ship, the slaves aboard the squadron would be crisped by the radiation emanating from the mote. But the Death Priest cared little how many of the crew were lost; the Slayer cared even less. Compassion was as extraneous to their makeup as life itself—and, with all the inferior races struggling to survive in the chaos of the Maelstrom, there were always new slaves to be had.

Confident that the Slayer would fulfill his mission with dispatch, the priest turned his attention back to the speck from the Vorack, the quintessence of death and power, and indulged in a small smile of triumph. He would return to the Pharon homeworld and bask in the God-king's favor. High Priests, soldiers, Slayers—he would be elevated above them all with this gift. How this treasure had come loose from the Vorack meant less to the Death Priest than how he could use it. Conquest. Pain to the living. Destruction to anyone or anything in his path. Glory to the God-king!

Turning his head slightly, the Death Priest glanced at the sensor screen centered on the Vor-stuff. The external polarizers strained to hold down its blinding, pure white light, and still the intensity was excruciating. Space bent reluctantly around the edges of the pellet from the heart of the Maelstrom, corrupting light and mutilating time.

"How can I use it fully?" the Death Priest murmured aloud, lost in contemplation of the mote's potential. Such a resource could not be squandered.

"We are ready for launch," came the Slayer's corrupt voice over the ship's communications system.

"Launch now," the priest ordered. He felt a moment of satisfaction as the four small ships blasted away from *Destroyer for the Faith* and went into tight orbit around the Vorack-stuff. Four force grapples would be positioned, each interlocked with the other three, their beams directed toward the incandescent speck. Then lines spun from single-crystal monofilament steel, almost impossible to break, would be woven through the rings mounted on the force grapples. The combination of the material with the energetic would ensure proper entrapment of the gift from the Vorack.

As the small ships jockeyed into position, an alarm clangor startled the priest from his intense contemplation. The Death Priest's head whipped around so fast that his elaborately crafted life-support tank shifted on his back, sending him reeling off balance. One hand shot out, hooked the edge of a control panel, and steadied him. His deep-set eyes widened in surprise. Then a gut-wrenching fury began to build.

As he had feared, he was not the only hunter in the cosmos with a hunger for a piece of the Vorack.

Without need of instrumentation, the Shard drove its vessel through the murky dust of the nebula filling this portion of space. It was difficult to tell where the sharp, curved edges of the alien's crystalline shell ended and the smooth walls of its ship began. The Shard itself lay motionless in the center of its tiny vessel. It needed no controls and wasted no physical movement as it speared through space toward the source of energy it had detected only a few hours ago. Piezoelectric nodules on the glassy surface of its body fed commands directly to the ship, which responded instantaneously to the Shard's desires.

Even the Shard's body felt the strain of the ship's intense acceleration. Ignoring the sensation and the warning signals from its vessel, the alien dispassionately scanned the data being fed into its body by the ship, calculating the best course to intercept the mysterious energy source, coolly weighing risks and alternatives.

The signal it thought it had detected earlier came again. It was not the only being to have discovered the powerful fragment, after all; a Pharon ship pursued it closely, and was in fact about to capture it.

That was impermissible. A bare flicker of anger touched the cool surface of the Shard's mind. Bad enough it was forced to exist in a universe filled with shambling hulks of flesh, the disgustingly biological organisms that infested the Maelstrom. But the Pharon were a double insult: once dead, now restored to a semblance of life they did not deserve. Their rotting flesh, their mockery of life, their very existence was an affront to the Shard that could not be borne.

And now they dared to claim a source of unknowable, immeasurable power for their own. A force so powerful it might even lead the Shard to the freedom they had hungered after for so long—escape from the Maelstrom, and from the loathed crystalline cells of their bodies. If this tiny shred of raw power really was from the Maw, perhaps it held the key to unlocking their prisons.

The cube-shaped hull of the Shard ship heated as the Shard raced through the inky black nebular gases, then slowed and masked its approach as it came within range of the Pharon sensors. The electrostatic charge on the hull oscillated to chaotically stir the nebular gases around it, shutting off direct visual observation. The Shard cooled the hull until it matched the temperature of the gases around it; EM pulses from sensing lidar were absorbed by the crystalline structure of the ship's shell. Then it lowered its internal voltage until even the most sensitive Pharon equipment would pick up only nebula-filled space. All this took place in a matter of seconds, the ship obeying the Shard's unspoken commands instantly.

The Shard lay quietly for a moment, its ship undetectable, sorting through its options.

Problem: The Pharon.

Goal: The Maw-stuff.

Solution: Destroy the Pharon.

The crystalline humanoid tensed and relaxed, generating electrical currents all over its quicksilver surface. The outer surface of the spaceship shimmered and transformed, turning pearlescent and highly reflective—and, the Shard knew, instantly alerting the Pharon enemy to its presence. One more command, and lasers lashed out from the side of its ship, blasting the four Pharon vessels attempting to capture the mote into dust.

From half a hundred ports on the Pharon ship lanced ravening beams of energy, licking tentatively at the smooth hull of the Shard ship before reflecting away. In its crystal cocoon, the Shard rocked only slightly from the impact. As the energy bounced off, superheating and ionizing the gases around the ship, the Shard had time for only one flash of apprehension as it detected one reflected laser beam's new course—aimed straight into the core of the Maelstrom-stuff.

Just as it had deflected from the crystalline surface of the Shard's ship, the laser bounced ineffectively off the globe surrounding the microscopic pinpoint of light. But it lashed back at the two warring ships with a thousand times more power, feeding off the unthinkable amounts of energy contained within the mote's crystal prison and sending a shock wave of pure destruction through the Shard and Pharon's battlefield.

The Pharon ship caught the brunt of the explosion, positioned as it was between the Shard vessel and the mote. It was hurled far off its original course, spinning and tumbling helplessly deeper into the nebula. The Shard was also buffeted by the wave front of radiation, but it was shielded from the worst of the blast by its hapless foe. The Shard struggled to regain control over its vessel, its body generating higher voltages to better command the ship's damaged circuitry. Slowly, the ship came under the Shard's dominion again, and it headed back for the mote from the heart of the Maelstrom. It noted with quiet satisfaction that the Pharon ship had come to rest deep in the Styx Nebula, lying silent and apparently dead in space.

The Shard stopped a few kilometers away from the fragment, its quick mind studying the emanations, calculating the best way to take the crystal globe into tow. The Pharon ship was no longer of concern; it had been badly damaged and was in no position to claim the potent speck for its own. Now it was only a matter of time.

The mote would belong to the Shard.

* * *

The Death Priest forced himself to stand. His senses were fogged, and the confusion in the control room further stunned him. *Destroyer for the Faith* had sustained incredible damage when the Vorack-stuff had unleashed its wave of malevolent energy. In that split second, the Pharon ship had suffered more destruction than any enemy vessel had ever delivered. Slaves all around the priest were dusty, smoking ruins. Corpses piled on corpses along the bulkheads until the few survivors could barely force their way back to their stations.

Somehow, this wall of charred, undead flesh had protected the Death Priest. His interleaved metallic armor had grounded more of the EMP burst, and his devotion to the God-king had sustained him even further. The priest survived. The lesser castes died. So it was written.

"Slayer, report!" barked the Death Priest. When he received no answer, he checked his few working sensors and saw that communications to the hold were down. He spun, lost his balance in the slippery life fluids on the deck, and went to one knee with a clatter that sounded louder than the alarm bells ringing throughout the ship. He refastened a vital hose that had come loose from his sustenance tank and took a moment to calm himself.

Regaining his feet, the Death Priest ordered a badly damaged slave to go to the hold and fetch the Slayer. The slave picked its way through the litter of bodies, trailing body parts and a long length of hose from its life-support pack. The priest did not care if the slave returned as long as it fulfilled its mission before it went to its final rest.

The few sensors still working on his control board showed that the Shard vessel had come to rest only a few kilometers away from the mote. The priest clenched his fists in impotent fury, his rage building until it could no longer be contained.

Screeching, wild with anger, the priest yanked his scythe from its sheath at his side and began hacking wildly at the pile of unfortunate slaves. Oily fluids spurted from hoses, and decayed bodies simply fell apart at the impact of the blade.

But his fury could not sustain itself for long, and the priest slowed and finally stopped, his wickedly edged scythe dangling forgotten from his hand. His rage had changed nothing. His ship was devastated, his crew was dead, and his mortal enemy was in possession of the greatest prize the Maelstrom had ever offered up. Defeating the Shard through force of arms was not an option. If he had any hopes of salvaging triumph from this defeat, he would have to calm himself and *think*.

"At your orders, Burning One!" barked the Slayer in his diseased voice, hastening into the control room.

"Preserve our inferiors aboard *Destroyer for the Faith*," the priest ordered with icy calm. "We will need them to defeat the Shard."

"They are not necessary," the Slayer said angrily. "Let *me* fight the Shard!" The Slayer brought up his battle claw and clacked it open and closed several times, undoubtedly visualizing what it would be like if a crystalline Shard were trapped in its savage jaws.

"We will get the Vorack-stuff," the priest said, beginning to regain control of the ship and get reports from all quarters. There was damage, substantial damage, but not so much that it could not be fixed. Unfortunately, most of the crew had perished in the battle. This would prolong the time spent repairing the ship. "You must have patience."

"The Shard has what we want," the Slayer said single-mindedly. "Kill the Shard, gain our reward."

"True," the Death Priest said. "What would you like to use to kill it?" He gestured at the smoking ruins of the control room, the heaped bodies of its trained slaves, and waited, eyeing the hulking Slayer with a certain degree of amusement. The Slayer had been trained for one task only: killing. The priest could consider the situation from other perspectives, ones subtler than a rapid-fire laser cannon or a head-removing battle claw. Engaging the Shard ship again would mean only their destruction—and the loss of their prize forever. There had to be other tactics than full-scale, all-out combat they could never win, no matter how determined or enthusiastic the Slayer might be.

"I will have the surviving slaves start repairing the ship. Then we can attack," the Slayer said.

"Begin the repairs," the Death Priest ordered. "I will let you know when to launch the attack. To do so before the ship is ready is to fail."

"I am pious!" the Slayer insisted.

"Defeat is blasphemy," said the Death Priest, reciting the God-king's Prime Dictum. "We will not stray from the path of righteousness. I will not permit it. Go—see to the repairs."

The priest turned back to his sensors as the Slayer swept out of the control room, attempting to analyze his enemy's next move. The area of space where the ancient enemies had vied was a desolate sector of the Outer Ring, the part of the Maelstrom farthest from the sustaining energies of the Vorack. Aside from the nebula in which his crippled ship now floated, the only objects of interest were a small moon and the greenish blue planet it orbited. The Shard ship, maintaining its proximity to the mote, was inexorably drawing closer to this insignificant orb. The priest began coaxing faint radio signals emanating from the distant planet, setting his computers to analyze the content and syntax of those primitive transmissions. Until his ship was repaired, he could do nothing but watch and wait.

Perhaps, if he was very lucky, the crawling primitives that infested the planet and its satellite would blow the Shard out of the sky for him.

2

Visual contact lost, Major," came the crisp report from *Battle Station Independence*'s command sergeant. "We have a full-spectrum report in the works, and it looks like a dandy."

Major Lenore D'Arcy looked over Sergeant Lewis's shoulder. Ever since the Change, nothing had worked quite right, but she'd never seen such sheer data overload, even when their instruments were pointed straight at the Maw. Meters had shifted to accept input several orders of magnitude greater than usual. Soon even that was not enough for some systems, and equipment began shutting down automatically to protect sensor elements. Being unable to spot visually the problem in the shifting, chaotic Styx Nebula was nothing new, but the rest was. Not even a proton storm could cause such a wild, wide spread of readings.

"What do you think it is?" D'Arcy asked.

"No idea. We've got rad shields up, Major. The gamma is within acceptable limits, but it spikes sporadically. Things are still within safety range across the board."

D'Arcy frowned. It was as if a new kind of pulsar had suddenly come into being in the Styx Nebula. Radiation levels rose and fell randomly. Just her luck it was happening now, with Colonel Custer on the moon at a high-level conference, leaving her in command of the *Independence*. The man's name and straw-colored hair always sparked comparisons with the boy general who'd gotten his clock cleaned so many years ago at Little Bighorn, but there the similarities ended. Colonel Max Custer was a no-nonsense, by-the-book officer, and the last time he had done anything spontaneous, Terra was still revolving around Sol and the universe had not been stood on its head.

Major D'Arcy was aware of her superior's distaste for the way she conducted herself. "Too sloppy, not up to the highest military standards and traditions," had read her last quarterly performance report, and all because of a single party she had attended. She sighed as she remembered it. Billy Newman had been rotated back to ground detail, and she was not likely to see him again anytime soon. If the colonel found her guilty of dereliction of duty because she was a half hour late and out of uniform after she'd taken the time to see Billy off properly, so be it. There was no chance she could rotate Earthside to be with him until her duty cycle was over in another eighteen months.

Unless, of course, this thing coming out of the nebula was more serious than she thought. Then they all might find themselves returning to Earth, in smaller pieces than they had anticipated.

"I'm picking up separate lidar returns now, Major," Lewis reported. "Could be two or three spaceships, or it might just be one really whacking big target. It keeps splitting and rejoining. It might even be one body rotating around two others, each occluding the other at points in the orbit. A real Lagrangian nightmare."

D'Arcy turned from the sergeant and called to her communications officer: "Get me a secure link to Earth. I need to talk with someone who can identify this mess."

"No can do," said Lieutenant Ng. "Laser comm is out. We can broadcast radio frequency to Earth, but any monitoring Neo-Sov station will pick it up."

D'Arcy swore under her breath. She had known the comm situation might get dicey if faulty equipment wasn't fixed soon, but spare parts from Earth had been slow in coming. The Neo-Sovs had recently made a devastating attack in Alaska, and spare parts were going to support the Union troops there, not to fix a station up in distant orbit.

"Any immediate threat, Sergeant?" she asked, trying to make sense of the flood of information on her control board.

"Above my pay grade to decide that, Major, but safety range has not been violated yet."

"We might try contacting Moonbase," suggested Lieutenant Ng.

"Let's wait a while before informing the colonel," D'Arcy said. "Try to get information from the database at Cheyenne Mountain that can identify this, uh, phenomenon. It'll be better to take something definite to the colonel."

"A big up-check on that, Major." The comm officer started working to plunder the Earthside computer database, using only radio in such a way that they could keep the brewing problems from the Neo-Soviets.

D'Arcy couldn't help wondering if she was doing the right thing by waiting for more information. She still had hopes of becoming the next commander of *Independence* if Colonel Custer received his expected promotion, but after her last fitness report, she would have to earn it. She dared not make a mistake now.

She pushed back her short, dark hair and focused on the sensors and the confusing readings they were spewing forth like demented bile. None of it made any sense. Then all extraneous thoughts were driven from her mind as the readouts suddenly spiked higher than any of the previous readings, straining the limits of her sensors.

"General quarters!" she bellowed, leaning over and hitting the alarm herself. Everything fell apart at the same instant. The quantum pilot wave had tickled the sensors, giving a split-second advance hint of more—and worse— to come. A wave front of intense radiation bathed the battle station, challenging the shielding to the limit of its design. It was a blast of physical intensity, shuddering through the station and sending crew members grabbing for handholds to keep themselves on their feet.

"An explosion?" she asked, clinging grimly to the arm of her chair as a final trailing wave of energetic particles gusted past the battle station. The rad shields had held— barely.

"Bigger than anything we or the Neo-Soviets could orbit," Lewis said. "Worse, it doesn't have the usual profile of a nuke. It peaked, then died down, but now it's increasing again, as if it is feeding on its own debris. Never seen anything like it—and it is big, really big."

"Bigger than a gigaton fusion bomb," she said, chewing on her lower lip. D'Arcy's brown eyes scanned the banks of equipment. She was no slouch when it came to analysis. She had tried out for R&D with her biophysics degree, but the

Siren's call of command had pulled her away from pure research into the labyrinth of telling others what to do in such a way that they believed in her.

Even if she didn't have a clue.

"Definitely bigger than a gigaton," came the confirmation.

"No immediate biohazard from the radiation," she decided. "Power up our weapons systems, in case those lidar returns are Neo-Sov spacecraft." She watched her sensors intently as the orders were passed along. Her mind worked overtime trying to fit this into an understandable scenario. Nothing seemed right. High pinpoint radiation source, strange sensor readings all over the spectrum, visuals gone, and possible Neo-Sov spaceships of unusual configuration in the middle of it all.

"It's coming out of the Styx Nebula," she said. "Any Cerenkov radiation showing in the nebular gases?"

"Nothing, Major. No evidence of anything ftl out there."

"Ng, forget trying to check dirtside data on this. Patch me through to Lunar Command," she said.

"That might take a few minutes, Major," Ng said, his sure hands darting precisely over the communications console. "That blast fried some of our radio equipment. I can reroute the signal to compensate, but it'll take time. Unless you want me to relay through an orbiting repeater to *Battle Station Freedom* on the far side of Earth. They have secure laser comm up and running."

D'Arcy considered that option for a moment, then discarded the notion. At every step along such an open relay, the signal might be intercepted—and not just by the Neo-

Soviets. The last thing she wanted to do was cause a panic for no reason.

"Negative, Lieutenant. Just give me as tight a radio signal to Moonbase as you can generate, and make it snappy," she said. Reporting to Colonel Custer was admittedly kicking the buck upstairs, but the anomalous readings worried her—and that wave front concerned her even more. If this whatever-it-was coming out of the nebula could pose a real threat to Earth, stopping it was more important than trying to look like a hero.

D'Arcy gnawed on a thumbnail and scowled at her sensors, trying not to let her impatience show. Ng was a good officer; if anyone could get the radio comm back online, it was him.

After a few minutes of intense activity over his board, Ng straightened up with a look of mild triumph. "Got it locked and scrambled the best I can, Major," he said. "The signal is getting chopped up by the nebular radiation."

"Comm for Colonel Custer, highest priority," she ordered.

"Need to boost the signal strength. Unknown cause is sapping the power," Lieutenant Ng said. "Don't know what could do it. Usually, the signal goes right through, and—" Ng shook his head, staring at the readouts.

"If you're going to do something, do it fast," said Sergeant Lewis. "Whatever it is in the nebula, it looks like it's headed this way."

One glance at her readouts confirmed his words. The mysterious signatures from the nebula were aimed straight for Earth.

"Readings have resolved a little better, Major," Lewis said. "Looks like two bogeys. The first is putting out an incredible amount of energy—I've never seen anything like it. The second—I can't tell. It doesn't look like a Neo-Sov design. I can't even determine what's powering it."

If D'Arcy had cherished some faint hope of contacting the colonel, that hope was now dead. Right now survival was looking like a higher priority than covering her ass.

"Laser cannon, charge and prepare to fire on my order," she said grimly, dropping into the command chair and working to home in on the incoming blips. "Missiles, arm and heat up the fuel for launch. All stations report!"

"Major, it looks like they're on a collision course with the station," Lewis reported quietly, the tension in his voice belying his calm manner.

"Then I guess it doesn't really matter what it is, does it?" D'Arcy muttered to herself. She raised her voice. "Ng, has either bogey made any effort to contact us?"

"Negative, Major," her comm officer said, his eyes intent on his board. "I'm checking the whole spectrum, and I'm not getting any kind of communications from either one."

Alarms flared as radiation smashed into their defensive shields at a level high enough to fry the battle station crew if they'd been caught unprepared. Through the rad assault they could now make out a distinctive shape, a massive cube with sharp edges.

"All lasers, fire!" D'Arcy snapped. "Missile batteries, track."

"Missiles locked and hot," came the report.

Major D'Arcy felt the battle station quiver as the laser cannons fired repeatedly. The air took on an electric feel as the potent weapons discharged and then struggled to replenish their capacitors for another blast.

"Negative damage sustained," came the laser-ranging officer's report.

"Missiles, fire. Full battery—fire, fire, fire!"

Battle Station Independence shook as the interceptor missiles raced from their launch tubes toward the unidentified blip. Major D'Arcy held her breath as she watched the slow progression of the heavy missiles snake toward the target. Lasers took seconds to reach their target. The nuke-tipped missiles took an eternity.

She let out the breath she had been holding at the same time a cheer went up around the room. Direct hits!

Then a new and powerful shock wave slammed into the station. To those inside, it felt as if a giant had picked up the massive battle station and shaken it playfully. Crew members were tossed like dolls against bulkheads. Equipment shorted out as the massive EMP blast tore through the station. Lieutenant Ng screamed as electricity volted through his board and into his body.

Then, as abruptly as it started, it was over. D'Arcy pulled herself up on wobbly legs, hanging on to her command board for support. "What the hell was that?" she demanded of the room at large. Absently, she wiped at the blood trickling into her eyes from a savage cut on her scalp.

"Unknown," said her missile-launch officer, his face drawn with pain as he wrapped one arm tightly around his cracked ribs. "I can tell you we got dead-on hits on that first bogey; it vectored off out of control. We didn't destroy it, but we hammered it so hard it must have been turned to jelly inside."

"Systems report," D'Arcy said. "What have we got left?"

"Communications are completely fried," said Ng, pale from the agony of his badly burned hand.

"The good news is life support is fully functional," Lewis reported. "But weapons, comm, propulsion—all dead. It'll take a lot of work to repair."

"Ng, is there any way we can get a report to the colonel or Earthside?" D'Arcy asked. To hell with radio secrecy now. They may have eliminated one threat, but the second blip—that incredible energy source—might still be out there, and still headed toward Earth.

"Negative," Ng replied. "All comm systems are completely out—my board's fused into a lump. It'll take days to repair—assuming we even *can* repair it."

"Not good enough," D'Arcy snapped. "I want a casualty report and a full systems check aboard the station. We need to know what still works. Aside from keeping life support functional, top priority is restoring communications. We have to get a warning Earthside that that thing is coming in."

She felt a momentary pride as her people—bruised, battered, and shaken—quietly got to work. But pride was quickly replaced by worry. Had that second bogey been responsible for the blast that had crippled her station? What damage might it do if it hit the Earth? And what could she do about it? She couldn't even warn Earth that big trouble was on its way.

Major D'Arcy clenched her fists for a moment in helpless fury, then got down to business.

For the time being, at least, Earth was on its own.

3

The Death Priest clacked his diamond-edged cere-
monial death scythes together high above his head
in triumph. Just when it seemed he had failed in his
mission to bring glory and power to the God-king, the
primitives' vessel had succeeded where Pharon weapons
had not—they had destroyed the Shard.

True, there was an element of disgrace in having his
quest salvaged by such inferior beings. The priest smiled
inwardly at the thought of how enraged the Slayer must be.
But he took a broader view of things. It would have been
pleasant to be the ones who blasted that diseased rock out
of the sky, but as long as the Shard was destroyed, that was
all that truly mattered. The prize he was after was too important to allow petty considerations like pride to stand in
his way.

The Pharon called up the recordings he had made
while the battle between the Shard and the primitives
raged. He made it a habit to gather as much information as
he could about any aliens he encountered. Such data

would be useful later, when it came time to conquer them. He watched again as the Shard vessel single-mindedly pursued the Vorack-stuff, ignoring all potential obstacles and dangers as it chased after its prize. He saw again how their puny lasers reflected off the surface of the Shard's ship—just as the Pharon's infinitely more powerful weapons had—but their second attack, made with ridiculously archaic missiles, had cracked the hard shell of the crystalline vessel and sent the Shard spinning helplessly out of control.

Unfortunately for them, the attack had also thrown a fragment of the Shard's ship directly into the heart of the mote, which had lashed back with an explosion even fiercer than the one that had disabled *Destroyer for the Faith*. The resulting shock wave had disabled the station— leaving the field free for the Pharon to swoop in and claim the mote for his own.

Assuming his ship was capable of swooping. The Slayer's report had been hopeful. The damage the Pharon spaceship had sustained was repairable—if enough slaves had survived. The priest was not sure they had. All the control-room slaves had been killed; the result of long months of battle, conquest, and enslavement wiped out in seconds. The Slayer had reported that the engines were intact, but radiation leakage had fried the slaves and soldiers in the aft section before baffles could be pulled into place. Most of the ship's energy cannon were fused and melted as a result of the back blast from the Vorack-stuff.

The priest cared about none of that. All he wanted was a functional guidance system and at least one working engine—and he had that. The result would have none of *Destroyer*'s usual grace, but it would be sufficient to recapture the mote and limp slowly back to the Pharon homeworld.

Unfortunately, when the Shard ship collided with the speck of the Vorack, the explosion had altered the mote's path—sending it directly toward the surface of the insignificant little planet that hung in the priest's viewscreens. That would make retrieval of the mote more difficult, but not impossible—and if the planet was as infested with the crawling little primitives as their orbiting station was, the priest might even find a way to replenish his decimated workforce.

For the moment, he and the Slayer would have to suffice.

"Track the course of the Vorack-stuff," the priest ordered the Slayer, who obediently turned to the control console. "When you have a precise fix on it, go find the surviving slaves elsewhere in the ship. We need them to man the control room."

The priest himself began gingerly coaxing his battered ship back to life. As he worked to plot a course that would take him into an undetected orbit around the planet and eventually follow the mote down to its surface, his mind turned inexorably to thoughts of the raw power contained in that microscopic speck. What did it matter if his possession of it was delayed for a short time? Soon it would be back within his grasp, and then all enemies of the Pharon would be destroyed by the fist of the God-king.

Slowly, haltingly, *Destroyer for the Faith* began to cruise toward the little blue world.

4

Sir, here are the latest intel reports." The stolid lieutenant dropped the folder onto the desk of Colonel Diego Villalobos, head of the Chiapas command center at San Cristóbal, and glared at him as if accusing him of some treachery.

"And?" Diego asked, looking up from the book on tactics he was studying. His thin face was drawn with fatigue, his forehead creased with intense concentration. Lieutenant Betty June Travis, otherwise known as BJ in the too-small officer corps, never failed to make her displeasure with him known. She hailed from Houston and, like most Texans, considered duty at any post south of the Rio Grande a hardship assignment. Chiapas, Mexico, had proved especially onerous for her; she considered her fellow soldiers inept and often dangerously incompetent. More than once he had pointedly instructed her to keep her feelings about the Mexican Contribution Force to herself. More than once Diego had had to keep *his* opinions of Texans to *himself*.

Still, for all the attitude, she was a decent field officer who always pulled her own weight. BJ was built like a bulldog—short, squat, and physically powerful. In a way, she even resembled one, with her undershot jaw and fierce expression. And he needed a bulldog to keep his post running. She was a good XO and an even better field commander.

"*And*, your brother's at it again," she said in an accusatory tone. "We got good intelligence he's going to hit Puerto Madero at dawn. We have three hours. We can use antigrav transports and get a rifle company there and catch the son of a bitch red-handed." She cleared her throat and glowered at him, her deep-set black eyes hard as marbles. "If you're up for it. Sir."

"Enough!" Diego snapped. He shot to his feet and glared down at her, using the power of his rank and his thirty centimeters of additional height over her. All his life he had lived in the shadow of his older brother. They had both graduated from the Union Academy, José first in his class while Diego barely scraped by in the lower quintile two years later. Then they had held neighboring MCF commands for years: José brilliant and decorated and always the talk of their superiors, Diego doggedly doing his duty but never reaching the heights José scaled. Always it was so.

Until three years ago.

That was when José had refused a command to attack a guerrilla camp because he thought it would endanger a village in the Lacandon jungle. Diego, however, had judged that a strike would not put civilians in jeopardy. He executed the mission and captured four guerrilla captains without damaging the village. It had been the fifth—and unknown—guerrilla leader who had blown up the village to cover his escape.

Ninety-seven *campesinos* had died, and José blamed the Union—and Diego—for the unfortunate deaths. Nothing Diego said could convince his older brother—lovingly called Viejo until that moment—that the Zapatista guerrilla chief had been responsible. All José saw was the death, the destruction, and the remnants of the Union blockbuster bomb that had wrought them. It had taken Diego weeks to locate the arsenal from which the powerful explosive device had been stolen, but by then José had been branded an outlaw, a traitor, a guerrilla who had turned against the Union.

In a way, Diego thought it was inevitable that his older brother had followed the path of earlier Chiapas rebels. Their mother had been deeply involved in the EZLN, the Zapatista National Liberation Army, and a ranking member of the ruling Zapatista Consulta for years. Women had always been politically active in Chiapas, and José had been very close to their mother, especially after government troops had murdered their father during a search-and-smash raid. The rise of the Union and the absorption of the old Mexican government into a true North American alliance had seemed a godsend, with promise of much-needed reforms in government policies.

But José, for all his success in the Union military, had always felt his true roots in the countryside, among the *campesinos*. Perhaps it *had* been inevitable that José would become the leader of the Zapatistas, even though it meant consorting with the Neo-Sovs.

Whatever the reason, José's turning against the Union had been doubly hard on Diego, who now had to deal with the loss of the only family he had left as well as the suspicion and distrust of the High Command in Mexico City. Where one brother could betray them, Diego's superiors reasoned, why wouldn't the other?

So for the past three years, Mexico City HQ had been seeking an excuse to get rid of him. But Diego had given them no opening; he might not be as brilliant as José, but he was methodical and diligent about fulfilling his duty.

His main regret was that some of his soldiers, including some officers like Lieutenant Travis, shared HQ's dislike of him. They saw his caution, his reluctant responses to raids, his unwillingness to commit troops as signs that he was soft.

But Diego Villalobos was not soft. His superiors and his men simply failed to understand that traditional Union tactics were useless against an enemy that raided and killed and then faded back into the jungle—a jungle riddled with traps and snares for the unwary. He would have to use a different strategy if he were to have any hope of defeating his brother.

He just didn't know what that strategy was yet.

"What's at Puerto Madero?" he asked, picking up the report BJ had dropped in front of him and leafing through it quickly. He had seen everything in it before, except the IR aerial recon photos showing movement a few kilometers to the east that might indicate a staging area for Zapatista guerrillas.

"A hundred soldiers, a supply depot for the region a hundred klicks up and down the coast, a—"

"Supplies," Diego said forcefully. "We cannot spare the troops to protect a few kilos of rations and a handful of weapons. Let them have the food. At least it will go to the *campesinos*."

"You sound like a Zapatista yourself," BJ said bitterly. "Sir," she added belatedly.

"My loyalty is not in question, Lieutenant," he said coldly. "It is your grasp of tactics that is lacking." Diego shoved his book toward her. His eyes were bloodshot from reading all night, and his strong, blunt-fingered hands shook slightly because he had forgotten to eat again. He had opposed the guerrillas for years and had never fought a satisfying battle. Always the firefights were on their terms. A man killed here, another ambushed there. A powerful bomb that destroyed equipment in the dead of night. Vehicles sabotaged. Nothing and no one to fight against. It was like grasping a handful of the ocean and squeezing. All that remained was a faint salty dampness, the real cause of the moisture draining away unnoticed.

BJ looked at the book. "General Giap, sir? I don't—"

"No, you don't know him. He fought a guerrilla war and won it. Just as José is winning this one."

"That's because—" BJ clamped her mouth shut as his fierce gaze pinned her in place.

"How do we fight an enemy that fires a single sniper round and fades away? Blow up entire villages in retaliation? If so, we lose. We either win over the *campesinos* or José wins. At times, it is as if even our own side works against us. If we train a company well, HQ transfers it to more active combat fronts. I hardly dare to admit we have any veterans out here." They would just get transferred away like all the others. If HQ would only let him keep his good men, Diego thought he might actually succeed.

"We have equipment, but it is the wrong equipment for our fight," he added.

"Sir, are you referring to the three Ares heavy-assault suits we just received?"

"Just what we need to go crashing through thick jungles. *These* are the tactics we should be using to fight my brother and his guerrillas," Diego said, slamming his hand onto Giap's book.

"We aren't authorized to become guerrillas ourselves," BJ said. "We don't fight that way. We don't have to."

Diego wasn't going to waste any more time arguing with her. José might indeed be planning a raid on Puerto Madero, but there were other intel reports that worried him more. Shuffling through the disks and hardcopy on his desk, he pulled out the single EYES ONLY sheet he had received from the Union Command at Cheyenne Mountain and passed it to BJ.

"Sir, I'm not cleared for this."

"Read it," he said wearily. She picked up the sheet and scanned it. She frowned, then reread the warning.

"I don't understand. Are we going to face Rad troopers?"

"No. The Neo-Soviets have sent mutant soldiers—Cyclops—for my brother to use as he sees fit. Why they did that is a mystery. Union Command did not share its suppositions with me."

Diego leaned back in his chair, infinitely tired. Although only thirty, he was getting too old to fight all day and work all night. The ideas in Giap's book were important, though. Something there could tell him how to fight José, if only he could piece it all together.

"The guerrillas might use the mutants as shock troops against an outpost," BJ said, her words becoming a slow drawl as she began to consider what had worried him all night long. "That's a waste, though. José does a good job without them big-footed mutants clomping through the jungle."

"This is not the best terrain for using Cyclops Fs," Diego agreed. "I think these are new mutations, ones better suited for jungle warfare. The Neo-Soviets might be trying them out before launching a new assault on our position. It wouldn't be the first time they've tried to attack here."

He didn't mention what worried him the most: the vulnerability of the fiber-optic lines running through his command post at San Cristóbal. Shortwave radio communication had been chancy ever since the Change—the day when all hell broke loose and the Earth got sucked into the Maelstrom. The Heaviside layer was in constant turmoil, scrambling and scattering even the strongest signals. Reaching any of the remaining battle stations with laser comm often proved difficult. Worse, many of the comsats that had carried most of the world's electronic commerce had been blasted out of orbit during the Change, leaving only landlines intact. If communications between the two segments of the Union should get cut off, the Neo-Soviets would gain an immense advantage.

Diego didn't intend to go down in history as the commander responsible for allowing the Neo-Soviets to gain a foothold—or even a secure position—between North and South America.

"There are other considerations," he said. "God only knows what hideous bioweapons the Neo-Sovs may have

cooked up and sent over. And the fact that they're now supplying my brother with mutant soldiers worries me—it
might mean they're shifting from simply supplying the
guerrillas with weapons to outright war."

"We don't have much in the way of experienced soldiers," BJ said. Her lower jaw thrust out even more, and
she looked more like a bulldog than ever. "For every squad
of veterans, we've got two that get scared when they see
their reflections in their own boots."

Diego said nothing. His XO was right. HQ had raided his
best companies only last month, once again making it necessary to train new recruits. His troops were well armed but
with so little practice time on the range that they couldn't hit
a target even using laser sights. Worse, he had no idea how
they would fare in combat. Too many of them were villagers
from the surrounding pueblos, drawn by the promise of regu-
lar meals. They had no real desire to fight José's guerrillas—
who might well be their own relatives.

There was also the chance that some of the newest recruits were Zapatista agents sending stolen supplies to the
very guerrillas they were supposed to be fighting.

"Who do you want to send against José?" he asked.

"Sergeant Suarez did well in the firefight last week,"
BJ said, warming to her recommendation. "And Sergeant
Baca deserves a brevet commission. She held together the
troops during the 16th of September attack, when they
wanted to turn tail and run. If it wasn't for her, we'd've lost
a passel of good soldiers."

"Two squads out of seven?" Diego saw the danger in
risking his veteran soldiers in a mere skirmish when Cyclops mutants were roaming the countryside. His comm officer had just reported that a Cyclops had been sighted

south of the central command post there in San Cristóbal. If it attacked, he would have only his greenest recruits to counter it.

"We stop Viejo, we stop the rebels," insisted BJ.

"There'd be someone else. There always is. No one thought Subcomandante Marcos could be replaced, but he was. We cannot win a guerrilla war by chopping off the head. We must go to the guts of the rebellion and pull them out whole."

"You going to sit and do nothing, then? Sir." BJ's lower lip thrust out truculently.

"Not at all. You like the way Sergeant Baca fought? *Muy bien.* She's in charge of her own squad and two of the recruit squads. She's to go after the Cyclops working its way south of San Cristóbal and destroy it. Have her deploy in such a way that the new soldiers gain confidence while the Cyclops is neutralized by the veterans." Diego sounded sure of himself, as a commander should, but his thoughts continued to turn in agonizing circles. What did José really have up his sleeve? Why would the Neo-Sovs send him Cyclops? And how could Diego hope to fight them both?

With a mental shake, he turned his attention back to BJ. "You'll be in charge here, Lieutenant Travis, since I'm going along on this mission," he said. "Keep Suarez to be sure our backsides are well protected if Puerto Madero turns out to be merely a feint and the Cyclops attack nothing but a diversion. I've got a feeling José is planning a more substantial attack elsewhere."

The intercom buzzed. Diego flipped it on, and said wearily, "What is it, Private?" His orderly usually fielded most problems before they reached him. Private Murdo ought to have sensed his mood and put off annoying details until later.

"Sir, Captain Allen is here to see you."

For a moment, Diego's exhausted mind refused to summon all the information he needed. Then he remembered the memo that had crossed his desk a week earlier while he had been preoccupied with more important matters—like two firefights, a guerrilla attack on a supply truck delivering medical supplies to San Cristóbal from the major Union seaport at El Manguito, and worrying over what his brother might come up with next.

Yes, Captain Alex Allen. Sent as a liaison by Union Command at Cheyenne Mountain to observe and report back on military readiness in the Chiapas region, so that the Union military could better allot supplies and troops where most needed.

Translation: Someone in Mexico City—probably General Ramirez—had complained loudly enough and often enough about Diego Villalobos that Union HQ had sent someone down to spy on him, preparatory to removing him from command.

Diego knew the ice under his feet was thinner than it had ever been. One little misstep, one failure, one bungled engagement while Allen was looking over his shoulder, and his career was over. Just what he needed right now.

"Send him in," he said resignedly.

BJ stepped to one side as Captain Allen came in and snapped a smart salute.

"Welcome to Chiapas," Diego said without sincerity.

"My apologies for my late arrival," the captain said. "My flight from Mexico City was delayed. Here are my orders."

He thrust a packet at Diego and stood braced at attention. He was a tall man, fit as most Union officers were, but there was a petulant air about him that was anything but reassuring. He wore the expression of a perpetual martyr, and he was clearly resentful about being sent to a backwater like Chiapas.

Diego flipped the top thin plastic sheet onto his reader and dutifully watched the decoded pages unfold in 3-D projection a few centimeters above his desk. "I see you have combat experience," he said. "Tell me about it, Captain."

"I was in command of J Company, sir. First Alaskan Arctic Scout Battalion."

"What fights were you in, sir?" asked BJ. Judging by the flash of fury on the captain's face, she had broached a touchy subject. As quickly as it appeared, it was replaced by a poker face even more curious than the anger.

"I was in the first wave against the growlers when the Neo-Sovs released them on our position."

Diego waited for Allen to go on, but decided not to press the matter when the captain didn't elaborate. He filed the detail away, however, thinking it might come in handy later.

"Welcome to our happy little home down here in San Cristóbal de las Casas," he said ironically. "It must be quite a change of climate for you."

"You can say that again, sir."

"At ease. Experienced officers are scarce in the MCF. With the action you've seen, you're exactly the man I need to go after a Cyclops F."

"Here? I thought there were only native guerrillas. You mean we might actually get to face a real threat?"

Allen's lips twisted contemptuously on the word *native*, and Diego briefly closed his eyes in irritation.

"We face everything, Captain," he said with exaggerated patience. It was probably a mistake to antagonize Allen, but Diego already had enough to do just dealing with BJ's bigotry and resentment. He didn't have the time or the energy to coddle another sulky northerner.

He pushed back from the desk. "Let's both go into the field for a training maneuver. We have a target identified." Diego made a point of putting aside the intel brief BJ Travis had given him regarding the possible guerrilla attack on Puerto Madero.

"Sir, we can't do this. We ought to—" began BJ.

"Notify Puerto Madero of your concerns, then muster the troops for a skirmish, Lieutenant. Against the Cyclops south of here."

BJ obviously wanted to continue her protests, but one look at Diego's expression warned her off. Instead, she spun on her heel and stomped out of Diego's office.

"We have three brand-new Ares assault armor units," Diego said, taking his uniform jacket off the back of his chair and pulling it on over his lean torso. "You familiar with them, Captain?"

"Yes, sir."

"Power one up and stay in reserve, should we need you. This will give you a chance to observe and get your bearings."

"Yes, sir. Thank you." Allen saluted. Diego returned the salute, wondering what he was getting himself into. Baca was a good sergeant, but he did not consider her officer material, no matter how desperately he needed more leadership in the field. He wanted to observe her in action, but with Allen peering over his shoulder, Diego was not certain he could give Baca his full attention.

Regardless, he had to stop the mutants and stop them decisively; if they proved successful against his forces, Mexico might soon be overflowing with them. That was a threat greater even than that posed by his older brother.

He smiled ruefully. It was hard enough fighting guerrillas—guerrillas led by his own brother, at that—but now he had to fight inhuman monsters created by the Neo-Soviets. Colonel Diego Villalobos hurried to his quarters to get into jungle camo and secure his weapons. It was not even dawn, and already he was juggling more than he cared to.

5

D iego Villalobos stared up at Captain Allen, already outfitted in one of the Ares assault suits, with mixed feelings. He just didn't think the man could be trusted, but with Neo-Soviet mutants and guerrillas roaming the countryside, Diego needed every experienced combat officer he could lay his hands on. If Allen acquitted himself well enough on the battlefield, perhaps Diego could recommend him for a medal. Maybe *that* would get a decent evaluation for the San Cristóbal garrison and its commander. Diego grumbled at his own cynicism and began inspecting the Ares.

The heavy attack weapons, a Lucifer plasma cannon and a Harbinger rail gun, hung at the ready on either side of the massively armored suit. Diego walked around it, examining the latest the Union had offered him in the way of combat gear. The shiny metal armor had to be camouflaged to prevent detection in the jungle, but there hadn't been time to paint it. The grinding sounds the suit made as Allen shifted its weight also posed a problem. The noise carried and would alert any guerrilla on patrol; rather than engaging, the enemy would simply vanish into the jungle.

Diego completed his circuit of the Ares and stared up at the brilliantly shining faceplate. Captain Allen had it set to full reflectivity, as if he expected to meet heavy laser fire or brilliant detonation flares—neither of which was likely here.

Diego settled his battle helmet to a more comfortable position and activated his helmet commlink. "How's comm?" he asked Allen.

"Coming in five-by-five, Colonel." The captain bent slightly and reached out a massive gloved hand.

Diego was not sure if Allen expected him to shake it, so he stood still. Allen brought the hand around into an awkward salute. Diego returned it.

"You will hang back and give support, should it be needed," Diego said. "This is both a training mission for two recruit squads and an exploratory engagement of the Cyclops. We need to probe their strengths and find weaknesses to exploit later—and we need an opportunity to test the Ares's capabilities in a jungle environment."

"Affirmative," Allen responded. "I am patched into your command circuit, sir, and I have a full battle map of the area in front of me."

Diego could picture the ghostly green VR display and the pale orange heads-up controls floating like fireflies in the captain's field of vision. A look, a blink, a twist of the head, and incredible weaponry would come into play. He had trained in an earlier-model Ares but had not liked it. They might be useful for massive army movements, fighting growlers, Rad Troopers, or death hounds, but in the jungle they seemed . . . excessive.

"I'll rely on that map, Captain," Diego said untruthfully. He had long since etched the topography of the region into his mind and rarely used maps in the field.

He switched his helmet radio to the private frequency he shared with the squad commander, and said, "Sergeant Baca, report."

"Ready, sir, all three squads," Baca responded. Her voice was slightly tentative, belying her words.

"Keep to the battle plan and don't improvise, Sergeant," he told her. "Do that and we'll bag this Cyclops with no trouble."

"Sir," Baca said hesitantly, "am I in command or are you? Or is the captain in the Ares?"

"Captain Allen is our backup," Diego assured her. "I'll watch for trouble, but you're on the hot seat when the shooting starts. If you want, I'll take command of one of the recruit squads."

"That's all right, sir," she said. "I can handle it. I just wanted to find out how involved you were going to be."

"Rest easy, Sergeant. If you need help, I'll give it. Otherwise, ignore me. My mission is to observe so we can plan better campaigns against the Cyclops in the future, if necessary. Yours is to destroy the mutant."

"Yes, sir," she answered, still skeptical. Diego knew why she was concerned. Too many commanders or a confused chain of command in combat meant casualties. Baca was taking three squads of untrained soldiers against a mutant man-machine of unknown capabilities. Any hesitation could bring disaster. Diego knew Baca was a good sergeant. If she said jump, none of her people would come back down until she gave them permission. But when the shooting started, even the best training-range trooper could fall apart and endanger them all.

He briefly considered sending Baca alone on the mission to remove any potential command snarl, but he knew he had to see the Cyclops in battle personally. And if Baca got into trouble, he wanted to be there to make the best possible extraction.

Ultimate command responsibility had to rest on him—especially with a Union liaison officer spying on him. He couldn't afford to show any weakness or make any mistakes.

"Move out, Sergeant," he ordered. The three squads, two commanded by brevet corporals, piled into the trio of Hydra antigrav transports. Diego had decided to keep his force divided rather than huddled together in one vehicle. Larger troop transports made too-convenient targets for guerrillas.

"Grab hold, Captain," Diego radioed. Allen reached up, caught an exterior rail, and swung around so his back flattened against the Hydra's outer hull. There was an audible click as magnetic grapples clasped the Ares firmly in place, turning the armored captain into a temporary captive.

"Ready to roar, sir."

Diego climbed into the lead Hydra and motioned the pilots to proceed from the heavily protected command post and into the dangerous jungle. It was two hours before dawn, and buried sensors had relayed seismic activity matching a Cyclops in precisely the region he had anticipated. Diego leaned back and turned off his radio for all frequencies but Baca's, which he switched to receive-only. Let the soldiers chatter about going into combat—many of them for the first time. He wanted to listen to how Baca handled them, psyched them up, got them into fighting prime. He needed to decide whether he should follow BJ's recommendation and give Baca a commission.

The battle would be time enough to evaluate the sergeant. Diego also needed time to think: to figure out how to handle the Union spy, to speculate about José's larger strategy—and to wonder if he was going after the Cyclops because, deep down, he was afraid to face his brother at Puerto Madero.

To that question, he had as yet no answer.

José Villalobos gazed up through the sparse, leafy gray-green canopy of the jungle just outside Puerto Madero. He was stockier and shorter than his younger brother, his face fuller, but they shared the same intense brown eyes and strong-looking hands. He touched the silver crucifix given him by his mother, dangling inside his shirt where it wouldn't get caught on the thick jungle undergrowth. It was two hours before dawn. The Maw, which had replaced Sol as Earth's sun, had not yet risen. He must strike now to have any hope of winning this endless war against the Union.

First supplies, then he would hit Revancha. And Consuela Ortega—clever, dependable Consuela—would damage the Union forces enough to ensure the success of this raid. How well José's strike on Puerto Madero went depended on her deployment of the Cyclops south of San Cristóbal and how many soldiers the Union sent after it. He knew his younger brother. Diego was a competent commander but no match for José. Time and again, José's tricks, traps, and diversions had cost Diego men, supplies, and weapons. The potential threat of the Cyclops was enough that his brother wouldn't be able to resist trying to defend against them.

Hunkered down at the edge of the clearing, José held his Neo-Soviet-made Kalashnikov tightly. The weapon was inferior to the sleek Union Pitbulls, but he carried it as a symbolic gesture, to remind his soldiers who they fought against. The sight of it reassured them of his commitment to their cause: to rid Chiapas of Union occupation and return the land to its rightful owners.

It was a grand dream, but he wasn't sure the men and women gathered around him could pull it off. Many of them were half-starved farmers, *campesinos* who hated the Union as much as he did. He wished he had a real army, but in Chiapas that was not possible. The Neo-Soviets' repeated attempts to invade had proved as much, but that made José more glad than otherwise. He might accept weapons and supplies from the Neo-Sovs, who were eager to see the Union's vast territories split in half by an independent Chiapas, but he had no desire to drive out one oppressor only to replace it with another. From what he had seen in his years with the Union military, the Neo-Soviets were even more ruthless with the unfortunates they ruled than his former allies.

But José needed all the help he could get to rid his land of the parasites who fed off it. Too often the Union bled the people of Chiapas with its oppressive taxes, money that went to fight its political wars to the north. Too often the Mexican Contribution Force swooped down from its safe garrisons in Mexico City looking for "recruits." To the poor people of this region, it was little more than the MCF hunting for slaves to fight their wars on distant continents. The Mexican Contribution Force had to supply a certain percentage of troops to the Union military, though it could never quite meet its quotas.

Except by enslavement.

Forever it had been so. Before the Change, before the Union, before the old, corrupt Mexican government, before . . . But José Villalobos would end the chain of *patrónes* and finally give his people the self-government they deserved.

"Is all ready?" he asked, looking around. The expressions he saw were always the same. The new soldiers were uneasy, some hiding their confusion behind a mask of machismo and others looking like frightened rabbits. Those who had raided with José before showed a curious mixture of anticipation and wariness. They knew the danger but had judged it worth risking their lives to win their families' freedom. They knew that José would not allow a single excess drop of their blood to be spilled. But those José was most concerned about were the ones who were eager to kill. They stroked their AK51s as they would a lover's cheek, and ecstasy built in them as the attack neared. They fought not because of devotion to family and land or for a cause or even to avenge wrongs, but because they enjoyed killing.

They made him truly afraid.

"This raid will be a quick one: in, steal what supplies we can carry, destroy what we cannot, then fade back into the jungle. Kill only those who try to stop you," he said.

The frightened novices clutched their guns nervously, doing their best to understand his orders. The kill-crazed were already ignoring him. "We must preserve our ammunition."

"What of the Neo-Soviet supply ship?" asked one of the veterans, a trusted lieutenant ironically called Flaco. He was not thin; he was too well fed. How he got so many rations was something of a mystery, but José did not suspect him of trafficking with the Union or even of dealing on the sporadic black market. Flaco's skill at obtaining supplies was so great that José was considering making the man his quartermaster. "Did it not bring us weapons we can use?"

"Nothing that could help us here," José said in a neutral tone. He had looked over the three-meter-long canisters in the Neo-Soviets' latest shipment to the guerrillas and found not rifles or ammunition or even the nauseating freeze-dried *mierda* that passed for Neo-Soviet field rations, but mutant soldiers, all in suspended animation cryotanks and ready to pop out into battle.

He would permit none of his guerrillas to touch the plastic cylinders, outfitted with spray nozzles, that had accompanied the mutants. Those were the true weapons; the giant sleeping monsters were just for show, a distraction from the real menace contained in the shipment.

José had spent a few days considering how best to use this strange shipment. The Cyclops were only a nuisance—a smash-and-grab operation such as he was engaged in now was beyond their capabilities. One day he might use them for a frontal assault, but not now. He needed real arms and provisions, not cannon fodder for the Union lasers.

As for the other weapons—well, after today he would know how useful those would be.

"Consuela has deployed one of the mutants as a diversion," José said. "She will not fail us. We will find only the hundred soldiers in the Puerto Madero garrison waiting for us."

He looked around and saw his lieutenants nodding. They were good, all of them, but he wished Consuela could be there.

He sucked in a deep breath and without conscious thought sorted through the myriad scents reaching him. Such a bewildering avalanche of odors would overwhelm a city dweller. José had been in the jungle long enough to appreciate even the fetid smells—all normal, expected, and reassuring.

He let the ragtag guerrillas settle down for a moment, then motioned his lieutenants to join him for last-minute instructions. He had learned not to amend his plans at this point. If anything changed, he would cancel the attack, but never confuse the guerrillas with a new target. They were humble farmers, not dedicated soldiers, and he would rather see them returned to their villages and families than buried in an unmarked grave.

"Flaco, go to the north of the garrison and lay down all the fire you can deliver. Follow a few seconds later with the smoke grenades."

Flaco nodded, his double chins bobbing. He grinned, showing a missing tooth in front as he reached into his pocket and pulled out a string of firecrackers.

"These will add to our attack."

"*Muy bien*," José said, matching Flaco's smile. The man's brother Estéban was as good at scrounging odds and ends as Flaco. Those firecrackers were left over from *El Día de los Muertos*, the celebration of the day of the dead. It was appropriate to use them today, though only for the Union soldiers who would die.

"You want my squad to the south?" asked Mary Stephenson, a onetime missionary turned freedom fighter. She was short, petite, almost fragile-looking. Her dark hair had been hacked in a mannish fashion, and the black streaks of camouflage grease on her face looked like a mustache and beard.

José thought that she came from somewhere near Cheyenne Mountain, where she had learned to hate the Union arrogance, but he had never asked. She spoke Spanish like a native and had never given him a moment of doubt concerning her loyalty to the Zapatista cause. She looked delicate, but he had seen her kill a Union soldier twice her size in hand-to-hand combat. It was easy to underestimate Mary, and if you did, you died.

He nodded once in her direction, his mind racing ahead to the plans for Gunther Gonzáles y León. The man's ancestry in the region went back only fifty years, his grandfather a German immigrant and his mother one of *los ricos*, the rich ones who usually sided with the Union. That did not worry José as much as Gunther's fervor for killing. He was one of those who enjoyed the battle for its own sake and undoubtedly hoped that the killing could go on forever.

José sometimes worried that Gunther would get his wish.

"Gunther, we go in together, your squad to the left of mine. We wait for Flaco's opening fire, then I go in. You follow and support me. Do not stray to the south, or Mary's squad will cut you down. She is to fire at anything and anyone there."

"Why must my men follow you in?" Gunther complained.

"Because those are my orders," José said flatly, holding the other man's gaze with his own until Gunther looked away. These incidents had become more frequent in recent weeks. Gunther chafed at the restrictions José placed on him; he wished only to kill, while José wished only to win. The man's defiance had not yet become overt, but it was only a matter of time before Gunther directly challenged his authority. If the man were not such an effective soldier on the battlefield, José would have already dismissed him. As it was, he needed his experienced soldiers; he would deal with Gunther's lust for power after the greater enemy had been defeated.

"We will drive them into Mary's guns, or toward the ocean," he emphasized. "If they flee, let them go. We aren't looking for a high body count. We only need supplies."

José gripped his Kalashnikov a little tighter. Unlike him, many of his guerrillas carried Union-issue weapons, stolen from armories and dead Union patrols that had ventured out too far into the jungle. If his plan was to succeed, they needed more ammunition for those stolen weapons.

José's only concession to the superior Union weaponry was the Pug pistol he wore in a cross-draw holster at his left hip. His standard-issue Neo-Soviet Viper had been irreparably damaged by a fragmentation grenade. José had used the ruined weapon as bait in a trap to blow up a Union private more interested in collecting trophies than in his own safety.

One useless gun for one Union soldier. It had been a good trade.

"To victory!" cried Gunther, holding up his Pitbull and brandishing it as if he were posing for a propaganda poster.

"To victory," José said more softly. His fingers traced the outline of the crucifix under his cotton shirt. Already he was sweating like a beast of burden. The cloth outlined the cross as he pressed it and said a quick prayer. José was at a loss to know which saint to pray to for victory in battle; the last priest in the area had been killed by MCF recruiters three months ago.

He checked his radio commlink with his three lieutenants. For the moment, the radio worked. In combat that would change. It always did. Then he had to rely on their quick wit and hand signals. Today even those might be out of the question after Flaco laid down the line of smoke grenades to cover their attack.

He motioned the guerrillas off the footpath and into the heavy undergrowth of the jungle. It made for slow going, but the Union had booby-trapped many of its trails; it had taken them two years of lost patrols and damaged vehicles before they had learned from José's example.

José couldn't afford to lose any of them. He needed every one of his forty soldiers to arrive at Puerto Madero if his daring dawn raid was to succeed.

The three Union Hydras slowed and then sank silently to the ground. Diego Villalobos checked his chronometer. Less than an hour before dawn, and they had penetrated fifty klicks into guerrilla territory. If Union intelligence was correct, the Cyclops had only recently arrived on these shores. This was the best time to take them out, before they learned the harsh lessons the jungle had already taught him.

"By squads, off-load!" came Sergeant Baca's sharp command over the common frequency shared by all the soldiers. "Squad One, left flank. Squad Two, take the right. Squad Three, on my orders, advance!"

Diego hung back as Baca and the twenty-four soldiers worked their way into the jungle. Allen's Ares was also making its way more slowly through the undergrowth, and Diego frowned, unsure if the captain was being delayed by the terrain or was for some reason reluctant to face battle. He shrugged and turned his attention back to his sensors. Unless Allen did something incredibly foolish, like fall on a squad, Diego believed his people would be able to eliminate the Cyclops on their own.

According to his remote sensors, the seismic disturbances were increasing. The Cyclops was rapidly approaching their position. He found a secure spot, unlimbered his Bulldog rifle, and peered down the length of its barrel at a likely area in the overgrown jungle. Diego turned on his scope and went up and down the spectrum, hunting from IR into UV for the human/robotic horror concocted by Neo-Soviet scientists.

The three squads had gone to earth on either side of the crude trail and had fallen so silent that the usual jungle sounds were quick in returning. Baca had deployed them well. Diego glanced back over his shoulder toward the Ares, but Allen had somehow managed to hide the massive assault suit in the undergrowth, so he turned back to the hardest part of any jungle combat: waiting.

Diego wasn't one of those soldiers who got fired up on the adrenaline rush and fear and heightened senses of combat. Just the opposite. His pulse barely accelerated, and he remained as cool as if he sat behind his desk in San Cristóbal. Only after the fight did he finally react—usually thrilled that it was over and that he was still alive. But now, nothing. His breathing even, his eyes clear, he waited and watched and waited some more.

He checked his remotes again and blinked at the readings. "Baca," he said over the commlink, "be ready. The Cyclops is almost on us."

Then the Neo-Soviet abomination burst from the sheltering jungle, barely visible in the pale light of dawn. It towered above them, easily two and a half meters of steel and mean. Diego tried to make out what weapons it carried but could not. It was coming at them too fast—and it spotted them even faster. This was a man-machine combination designed for speed—and killing.

The Cyclops's arms rose from its sides, a faint blue discharge around the tube in its left hand betraying a charging energy weapon. Diego gave it no chance to power up. His Bulldog assault rifle spoke, hitting the thing's left wrist. Firing steadily, he began to blast away at spots along the armored side, trying to break through the steel and reach the flesh beneath. Then a half dozen Pitbulls from Baca's squad of veterans fired, the high-pitched whines echoing as the rounds bounced off the Cyclops's armor.

The plasma gun in the left hand of the Cyclops exploded as a grenade caught it. The blast finally shook the other two squads out of their shock, and they opened fire. Bullets spanged off the heavy armor, staggering the mutant. It recovered, spun around, and, using the weapon in its right hand, sprayed full-automatic explosive slugs into the jungle. The vegetation blew apart in miniature detonations all around the Union troopers. Several of the recruits, their nerve broken, fled their hiding places. The Cyclops cut them down within meters.

"Enough of this," Baca snapped over the commlink. "Everything you've got. Take that thing out."

Diego's bullets were having no effect. He switched to the grenade launcher and fired one frag grenade after another at the Cyclops's left leg, trying to bring it down. For one heart-stopping moment, he thought he had succeeded as the Cyclops dropped to one knee, but the thing was merely assuming a better position to fire more exploding rounds at the squad on its left flank. The Cyclops's offensive flushed out two more troopers to their deaths. Diego missed with his next two grenades.

Baca's voice crackled into his ear from his helmet speaker. "Private Valdez, use the Rottweiler," she ordered. "Take out that monster!"

"The Rott jammed, ma'am," came the panicky voice of one of Baca's soldiers. "And Private Limón is wounded—it looks like she lost an arm."

Diego raised his Bulldog once again. He had one grenade left, and with the high-powered Rott out of commission, he had to make it count. He wasn't certain, but he thought he saw the malevolent glare of too-human eyes through the Cyclops's face mask. Motor-driven limbs gave the creature incredible strength, but the real menace came from its human brain.

He focused his sights on the Cyclops's bent knee, where it met the jungle floor, and fired. The grenade exploded on contact, knocking the mutant onto its side and—Diego hoped—shattering its knee. If he had managed to render it immobile, his soldiers could easily take it out.

As if the Cyclops sensed the danger it faced, it struggled back upright, lowered its right hand, and fired a burst of exploding rounds into the soft earth at its feet, effectively digging itself a protective trench. If they wanted it now, Diego's force would have to advance and dig it out.

Diego was between a rock and a hard place. If they attacked, the Cyclops would cut them to bloody ribbons before they could take it out. If they retreated, the mutant was free to fire on them at will. Of course, if the Cyclops tried to flee, its damaged leg would give them the chance to hit it with enough lead to bring down a herd of elephants.

But the Cyclops was burrowed in, damaged, wary, and willing to outwait them.

Quieter than a Union patrol but still noisy enough to worry José, the guerrillas approached the seacoast garrison of Puerto Madero. The lazy Union soldiers were sleeping late, as they always did, feeling secure behind their electrified fences and surveillance devices. Only now was the far horizon tinged with dawn.

José dropped belly down in the brush and slowly wriggled forward, infiltrating the outer defenses with ease. He knew from his time in the Union military that Union radar detectors were usually set slightly above ground level to keep small animals from setting them off. If a snake could wriggle in without triggering the alarms, so could his guerrillas.

And they did.

The next ring of defense electronics presented a more difficult barrier. Cameras monitored the perimeter just beyond where he lay, checking heat signatures as well as the visual spectrum and radiation levels. As if he could smuggle a nuke this close—or even a Neo-Sov rad grenade. José had wondered at this gratuitous waste of matériel until he realized the Union did not customize its equipment. Their production lines turned out vast quantities of military gear, all interchangeable, whether sent to the Siberian front, Chicago, Cheyenne Mountain, or some insignificant supply port in Chiapas.

Ignoring the radiation detectors, he fixed his Kalashnikov's sights on the ceaselessly rotating cameras. José tipped his head to one side to activate his helmet radio and whispered, "Report."

"In position," came Mary's terse response. She had undoubtedly been ready for long minutes. She was efficient and deadly in battle.

"Twenty meters to your left," came Gunther's husky voice. He sounded as if he was breathing heavily in anticipation of the fight.

"Just tell me when," Flaco said.

"Let's celebrate," José responded, and gently squeezed the trigger on his Kalashnikov. Knowing where the camera's protection was weakest, he fired at the armored casing directly under the lens. From all around the perimeter of the post came more fire, as the best shots in each squad aimed at the weak spot José had told them to look for. Most if not all of the cameras would be out of commission now, preventing the confused Union soldiers from learning exactly how many enemies they faced.

Gunfire erupted from Flaco's position, and José flinched at the sound, though it was not unexpected. A few seconds later came dense clouds of white smoke. It would take the Union sentries precious seconds to analyze it. Was it a poison gas? A mutagen? Something worse? Those seconds must be well used.

"Attack!" he ordered.

"Degüello!" cried Gunther so loudly that José did not need his radio to hear it. No quarter!

José scrambled to his feet, kept low and ran for the garrison, the radiation detectors basically useless now that it was obvious the post was under attack. To his right screamed a grenade launched directly at the gate. He lowered his head and took the force of the explosion on the top of his helmet and along his back without stopping. By the time he reached the gate, it hung on one hinge. He kicked at it, climbed over, and rolled into the compound, his Kalashnikov firing full-auto.

Several soldiers emerged from the barracks building directly in front of him, half-dressed and calling out in confusion, their weapons held loosely at their sides. José killed them, not without a measure of regret. Most of the soldiers at Puerto Madero were fresh recruits, inexperienced and ill trained—certainly not equipped to deal with his military expertise. They were not much different from the guerrillas now pouring in through the shattered gate.

He ejected the spent clip and slammed in a fresh one as he glanced left and right to be sure the rest of his force was not running headlong into a trap. His lips twitched in a smile as he realized they had hit at the precise moment most of the Union garrison was rising to greet another day of tedious duty. Many were in the shower, wasting hot water. Others were at breakfast, their weapons back in the barracks. Most of them, as he had expected, hid rather than risk death. Those few who tried to resist died.

It was a slaughter, and he took no pride in it. This was war, and he did his job well. Nothing more.

Just past the barracks, he could see the squat shape of the supply warehouse that was their goal.

"There," he radioed, only to realize he spoke into dead air. The radios had failed once again. José lifted his Kalashnikov and fired a quick double burst to get his people's attention. He pointed to the supply warehouses, and his squad immediately set off for them. But Gunther's men continued to fire, seeking out and slaughtering the unarmed, cowering Union soldiers.

"Get your squad in there. Get us ammo!" José shouted at Gunther. Reluctantly, his lieutenant obeyed.

José ducked into the warehouse and surveyed the scene as Mary's squad took position to guard the cache of supplies. Most of his guerrillas were, as he had instructed, loading up on ammunition for their Pitbull rifles, grenades, and other armaments. José pulled a few men aside and had them begin collecting food and medical supplies instead. They needed weapons to carry out his plan, yes, but they also needed to feed the people if he was to enjoy their continued support.

Or the support of his guerrillas, for that matter. Too often of late, they had been forced to live off the unforgiving land. They were tired of snake meat and boiled weeds—and they would fight better on full stomachs.

Setting his rifle aside, José grabbed a nearby pack and began stuffing grenades into it. When it was as heavy as he could safely carry, he slung it over his shoulder and picked up his Kalashnikov. Many of his people had already loaded up and retreated from the warehouse.

He looked out the warehouse door and saw the Union soldiers finally beginning to shake off the shock of the surprise attack. The few experienced soldiers stationed at the garrison were harassing and chivvying the others into small, effective fire squads. But it was too late for most of them—Gunther's and Flaco's squads, even burdened as they were, had already made it to the safety of the surrounding jungle. José's squad was retreating steadily under the covering fire laid down by Mary's team. That left only Mary and her soldiers—and José himself.

José reached into the bag over his shoulder and pulled out a grenade. Popping the pin, he threw the grenade in one easy motion. It arced high, a bright orange against the morning sky. José wanted this "pineapple" to be seen—and feared. It landed with a couple of bounces and then exploded, making the Union soldiers near it turn and flee, as he had hoped. This mission was meant to sow terror in the hearts of his enemy, not to slaughter them. Any Union soldier who survived today's raid would fear the guerrillas. That was more effective than slaughtering them all, no matter what Gunther thought.

He pulled another grenade from his bag and tossed it at a small squad of Union soldiers, knocking them about like bowling pins; perhaps killing some. José finished off two others with well-aimed rounds.

"Retreat," he signaled with his hand, and the few remaining guerrillas headed for the gates. Mary methodically destroyed Union vehicles as she went, to slow any pursuit. Flaco's and Gunther's squads were now laying down protective fire from the cover of the jungle, further pinning down the Union troops.

José fixed a grenade in his Kalashnikov as he backed toward the gate, counting his guerrillas as they left. Two hobbled along, wounded in the hip or leg. Another was a bloody mess after taking a round in the chest, but he was still walking—and dragging a case of field rations behind him.

The rest were none the worse for the fight. José made sure the last of them had started across the field outside the garrison walls. Then he fired the grenade into the Union magazine, turned and ran as if the devil himself nipped at his heels.

José was halfway to the jungle when the grenade exploded. The munitions cut loose with a secondary, bigger explosion that knocked him to the ground. He kept scrambling, his feet pistoning in the soft dirt, the sanctuary of the jungle fifty meters in front of him.

From all sides came rifle fire, and he was not sure if it was aimed at him or poured into the compound by his forces. Speed was his only ally now. He dug in and sprinted to the edge of the jungle. Once shielded by the thick vegetation, he turned and brought up his field glasses to assess the damage they had done to the garrison.

Mary appeared silently at his side, her face even dirtier than before but her expression serene. "How's it look?" she asked.

"We have been very successful this day," José said. "I think we can say Consuela's plan worked perfectly. My brother could have had no idea . . ." And then, overhead, he heard a shrill whine, and he realized that the Union must have lured him into a trap.

"Incoming!" he cried to no avail.

In the dawn light, ripping apart the heavens, raced a thin silver streak that screamed deafeningly and then struck with devastating effect. The earth shook, and the overpressure from the monumental blast swept José Villalobos off his feet and flung him mightily through the air. He landed on his back, stunned by the impact, unable to breathe or move, staring for long seconds at the morning sky until it—and everything else—faded to black.

Diego checked the seismic sensors to see if the Cyclops was waiting for reinforcements. But if anything was moving along the trail hacked through the jungle, Diego could not detect it.

His radio crackled as Sergeant Baca accessed their private frequency. "I know I'm in command, sir," she said, "but do you have any advice here? Should we outwait it?"

"No, Sergeant," Diego responded. "It might maintain its position for a week. I don't know about you, but I don't want to wait that long for breakfast."

Diego switched to Captain Allen's frequency. "You there, Allen?"

"Yes, sir."

"Get that Ares in motion and take out the Cyclops. It's burrowed down only a couple of meters. Blow it out with the rail gun. Using the Lucifer this close to our soldiers might be too messy . . . for us."

"Understood, sir."

Diego heard the powered armor even before he felt the *thud-thud-thud* of the approaching Ares. He waited calmly, ready to fire the instant the Cyclops showed itself. The Ares's rail-gun ingot would blow open even the Cyclops's armor—and if it did not crack the thick skin, it would rattle the human brain inside into a stupor. Either way, a few well-placed grenades from his soldiers could then take it out.

The Ares crashed through the thick undergrowth and burst onto the field, its rail gun humming and ready. A depleted-uranium ingot whined out of the Harbinger and sped toward the Cyclops.

But the noise and vibrations had alerted the mutant, and anticipating the attack, it had begun wiggling away, using explosive rounds to cut a channel through the jungle floor ahead of it. A second ingot missed but did flush the Cyclops. It scuttled along like a crab, faster than any man even with its damaged leg. Captain Allen chased it down the path, firing as he went.

And then everything happened at once.

Allen finally scored a direct hit on the fleeing Cyclops, blowing it into a thousand pieces of flesh and steel. As he passed under a tall tree overhanging the path, a greenish mist sprayed down from its branches, coating the bright armor of his suit. At the same moment a sudden screaming high in the dawn-lit sky pierced Diego's brain like a hot needle. Clearly the Cyclops was not José's only weapon. Once again, it looked like Diego had miscalculated his brother's strategy.

"Take cover!" he shouted, unable to hear his own voice. "Incoming!"

Then the impact came. The ground rose under his feet and threw him ten meters through the air. He slammed into the trunk of a tree and crashed to the ground as the shock wave slashed through the jungle, stripping towering trees of leaves and bushes of small branches and passing over him like a hurricane.

But Diego Villalobos was not aware of it. He was already unconscious.

6

For long minutes after it came to rest, the Shard simply lay, stunned, at the bottom of the long, narrow tunnel it had cut through the dense vegetation overhead. Shard did not feel pain in the same way as their biological inferiors, but injuries to its crystalline shell transmitted themselves as a sense of wrongness. The Shard remained prone as it scanned for fractures and other dislocation damage to its crystal lattice. It found internal cracks along shear planes it had not known it possessed, but nothing that could stop it from achieving its goal.

The alien knew it had a limited time before the natives of this world came to investigate the explosion of the mote's landing, but it calculated it could remain a while longer in the shallow trench its landing had carved in the earth. The speed of its descent through the planet's atmosphere, unprotected by the tough shell of its ship, had raised its body temperature higher than it had ever experienced, and although the Shard knew its shell was in no danger of fracturing, it needed a few moments to recover from the stress of its landing.

And from the shock of having its ship destroyed. The battle station orbiting this murky planet had fired primitive energy weapons that had been easily nullified. It had not expected a missile attack to follow and crack the structure of its vessel.

The Shard's body had survived, but its ship was vaporized, blasted into meteoritic dust cascading downward to the planet. The piezoelectric currents the Shard used to command its ship would never again produce the familiar, instantaneous obedience it was accustomed to.

Slowly, the Shard had reasserted order, one lattice plane at a time, until it was once more in control—as much as it could be—of its body. With command reestablished, the Shard focused all its attention on the planet whose gravity well had captured the bit of Maw-stuff. It slipped into the soupy atmosphere. The mote had come in fast and hard, and the ionization trail it had left in the air was clear to the Shard's visual sensors.

The Shard's ability to control its descent was not as finely tuned as its ship's had been, but it was capable of some maneuvering. It had extended its arms and legs, using them as lifting surfaces to skim through the thick atmosphere. It felt its body exterior warming, from cherry to yellow to blue to white-hot, but it ignored the risks, totally absorbed in following the energetic piece of the Maelstrom down to its projected landing place—a narrow neck between two larger landmasses.

The mote's impact with the earth had sent out a shock wave that the Shard could see from its vantage point still high in the air. The explosion expanded in a circle, flattening vegetation and raising a huge cloud of dust as the mote buried itself in the ground. Then the Shard had to turn its attention to its own landing, struggling to come to rest as close to the Maw-stuff as it could.

And it had. The Shard finally levered its body upright, moving with only a trace of its usual grace and speed. Its shell was still cooling, and it moved with care to prevent any of the stress fractures lacing its body from growing large enough to cause a problem. It could already feel the crystalline lattices flowing and knitting together, morphing the structure of its body to repair the damage.

The Shard climbed easily out of its landing crater, using its razor-sharp arms to punch handholds in the earthen walls. Once it was on the surface, it scanned its surroundings briefly to orient itself. The world it had landed on was absolutely teeming with life: the plants that towered over it, the small forms that scurried and flew and hopped past it. But even the unrelenting swirl of movement could not disguise the immense pulsations of energy coming from the crater just a few kilometers away. The Shard could not see the mote through the thick vegetation, but it did not need to; sensors on the surface of its shell could detect radiation across a broad spectrum.

The Shard sped nimbly in the direction of the new pockmark on this world's ugly face. In spite of its injuries, it lithely dodged around tangled undergrowth and thick-boled mahogany trees at more than thirty kilometers per hour, soon coming to an abrupt halt at the edge of a smoking, obsidian-glassy crater. The Maelstrom-stuff had come in so fast and so hot it had buried itself deep in the earth. All around the crater, for tens of meters in every direction, trees and undergrowth lay shredded on the ground. Here and there, the small bodies of animals lay tangled in the destroyed jungle growth.

But the Shard ignored its surroundings, all its attention focused on the object dimly visible at the bottom of the crater. It moved with caution, unwilling to approach too closely until it could determine whether the radiation leaking from the mote posed a threat. The radiation seemed stronger there, which could be due to the fact that it was no longer being filtered through the thick skin of the Shard's now-destroyed ship. At any rate, the incredible power of the Maelstrom-stuff seemed largely contained.

Slowly, cautiously, the Shard lowered itself down the smooth walls of the crater until it stood on the bottom. It gingerly approached the smooth, glowing ball of energy that lay half-buried under a cascade of dirt. This close to the energy source, it could feel the radiation pulsing through its body, but it judged that the damage sustained would be minimal enough that it could convey the globe away from its landing place. Perhaps the Pharon ship had been destroyed—but perhaps it had not. At any moment, the Shard's mortal enemy could come seeking to reclaim its prize. There would be time enough to plan an escape from this backwater world after it had retrieved the mote.

The Shard bent with liquid grace and brushed the dirt away from the glowing globe. It worked the spikes of its hands into the earth under the mote and strained to leverage it out of the grave it had dug for itself. Slowly, as if reluctant to leave its prison, the globe came out of the ground.

And as it did, the Shard heard a cracking noise, and knew it had miscalculated horribly.

From the top of the globe, from a hairline crack that had been too small to detect, shot a beam of pure, intense

white light—a beam that shone directly into the Shard's inhuman face.

Overwhelmed by the surge of raw energy it could feel
pouring into its body, the Shard dropped its prize. When
the globe hit the ground, the crack widened even farther,
saturating the Shard's body with radiation. Instinctively,
the Shard threw its arms over its face, trying vainly to
shield itself from the waves of energy battering its shell. A
strange, mewing sound came from its throat.

And then the Shard began to change.

Consuela Ortega lay unmoving behind a fallen tree.
The screaming from above had been worse than a stricken
angel's death cry, and the explosion that followed had
briefly plunged her into darkness. She sat up, her head
throbbing, and pushed her thick black hair away from her
eyes. She waited a few seconds for the world to stop spinning, then began to take stock of her injuries.

Her head ached, but she didn't think she had suffered
a concussion, and when she touched her forehead, her fin-
gertips came away unstained by blood. She was covered
with cuts and bruises, but none of them was serious.

But when she levered herself to her feet, she let out a
gasp and sank down again. Her left ankle had flared with
agony as soon as she put any weight on it, and she could
see that it was swelling rapidly. She didn't think any bones
were broken, but it was, at the least, a severe sprain.

Some, finding themselves alone and crippled in the
depths of the jungle, would be afraid. Consuela Ortega
wasn't one of them. She was a soldier, a soldier in the fight
for liberation. She had seen injuries much worse than
this—some of them her own.

Working as quickly as she could, she ripped fabric from the bottom of her coarse cotton shirt and tied the rags as tightly as she could stand around her ankle, hissing through her teeth at the pain. When finished, she made another attempt to stand, bracing herself on the trunk of the fallen tree, and gingerly tested her weight on the injured leg. This time, the ankle held—painfully, but she could walk.

That was all that mattered. She did not know the source of the explosion that had injured her, but she knew she had to get back to José and make her report. The attack with the Cyclops had gone better than she had dared to hope, and the other weapon—the one José trusted only her to handle—had deployed perfectly. José would need the information she carried to finish planning his attack—assuming he had survived.

Slowly, carefully, using her Kalashnikov rifle for support, Consuela made her way through the jungle, away from the Union patrol. She doubted they would come after her even if any of them could make it through the green mist that had sprayed from the Neo-Soviet cylinder she had hidden in the tree before the battle.

She was tired and in pain, but she was used to that. She was not used to how slow her progress through the jungle was. She had been making her way toward the rendezvous point, cutting north and east to avoid the Union troops, for three hours before the pain in her leg finally forced her to rest. She lowered herself carefully to the ground and blew out a breath in frustration. At this rate, it would take her forever to make her way back to the others.

Despite her injuries, despite her concern abut rejoining José, curiosity got the better of her as she took a deep sniff of the air and found strange odors mingling with the more usual ones she had known all her life. José had to know of the Cyclops's success, and he must also know what had caused the sonic blast and aerial explosion that had injured her. Had the Union countered the Neo-Sov terror weapon with one of its own?

The stench of burned plants gave her a clue as to the location of the blast. When she spotted scorched leaves in the jungle canopy high over her head, she deviated from her trek to the arranged rendezvous and instead went due east, toward the evidence of destruction.

Consuela limped down the path, holding the Kalashnikov in her right hand rather than using it for support. If it was a Union weapon responsible for her injuries, she might have to defend herself against the soldiers who had deployed it.

Consuela was short at a bare 158 centimeters, but she was sturdy and carried her fifty-five kilos like a dancer. Even hobbled by her ankle, she moved gracefully through the jungle, her dark eyes missing nothing. Here and there she saw increasingly singed vegetation, giving her a road map more precise than a GPS. Her nose wrinkled at the pungent, charred odors from blackened vines dangling high up in the towering jacaranda trees.

Consuela's progress slowed even further as she came to the edge of a clearing in the jungle—a clearing that had not been there before. The destruction stretched for meters in every direction, the flattened trees and bushes pointing like blackened arrows away from the pit in the center of the blasted field. She looked up and saw where the missile—or bomb or ag plane—had come down, searing the vegetation as it crashed into her jungle. The absence of a secondary explosion made her even warier. She had once found an unexploded Union missile burrowed into the ground. José had dropped a grenade into the hole to set it off and had barely escaped with his life, but the risk had been necessary. What if a curious village child had accidentally detonated it instead? She could hear faint noises coming from the pit—Union personnel, examining the aftereffects of their weapon?

Somehow, she did not think so. Whatever had caused this destruction, it felt alien, beyond the scope of anything she had seen in her years of fighting the Union oppressors. Cautiously, her rifle at the ready, she approached the pit. Lowering herself to her belly, she crawled to the edge of the blackened crater and raised her head just enough to see to the bottom.

She fell back immediately, blinded by the intense white light blasting from the bottom of the pit. Her eyes watering, she could think of only one thing: radiation. Consuela rolled to her side and fumbled at her vest strap, pulling around a dosimeter. Blinking fiercely, she peered through its microscope-like end, fearing what she would see. If she had been exposed to a lethal amount of gamma radiation, the indicator would have spiked into to the red zone. But it remained in the yellow, where it had been for months after she had blown up a Union convoy carrying uranium fuel pellets to the CANDU reactor in Revancha.

For the moment, she was safe, but she had no desire to remain in the crater's vicinity any longer than necessary. She had to gather as much data as she could for José. Was this some new threat to her land? Even the *campesinos* in the depths of the jungle had learned of the dangers of radiation poisoning in the years of nuclear war that had followed the Earth's capture by this strange space in which they struggled to survive.

Her mind retained only confused impressions from her split-second glimpse over the edge of the pit: a single figure, pitch-black against the blinding glare. Some kind of struggle was going on at the bottom of this wound in the earth, but it was something she had never encountered before. She slowly scrabbled backward from the edge and made her way cautiously around the crater, hoping to find a better vantage point. The ground had turned to glass-slick slag, and any miscalculation would send her plunging downward. The crater walls were too steep for her to have a prayer of escape on her own—assuming the radiation didn't kill her immediately.

Whatever was in the pit made the noise she had heard before—a faint mewing sound, but with a harsh undertone that scraped at her nerves and set her teeth on edge. And this time it was accompanied by another noise: a kind of wet sizzling that sounded as if blobs of molten glass were falling to the earth just below her feet.

At the far side of the crater she stopped and fished silently in the pouch at her belt. What she thought she had remembered was there: a pair of full-spectrum binoculars she had liberated from a Union soldier several days before. He would not be needing them again. Holding them up to her eyes, she adjusted them to filter out the maximum amount of light and once again peered over the edge.

What she saw was something entirely outside her experience, something she instinctively recognized as alien. At the bottom of the crater, still bright enough to bring tears to her eyes despite the heavy filtering of the binoculars, was a round, glowing globe, small enough for a man to lift. From the top of the globe shot a beam of light—and bathed in that light was a figure. Consuela did not know what it had originally looked like, but she could tell that what she was seeing now was unnatural.

From the crystalline figure dripped globules of what looked like liquid glass. As they touched the ground, the tendrils connecting them to their parent broke away, and they wriggled toward the walls of the pit with a horrible purpose. There were only a few now visible, but from every part of the creature, new glassy tumors were bulging from all over the smooth crystal surface of the creature.

The monster at the bottom of the pit looked like a malformed ice sculpture as it staggered away from the light source, still making that strange mewing sound. But now the sound was quietly echoed by the monster's unnatural children. The creature's movements grew even wilder and more uncontrolled. It lost its footing and crashed heavily to the ground, a crystalline cancer grown out of control.

"*Madre de Dios*," Consuela muttered, crossing herself. She knew she had to find José and tell him of this . . . thing. But she was hypnotized by the spectacle of unbridled crystal growth and the way the sharp-edged beast thrashed and rolled on the ground, trying to crush and destroy what had once been parts of itself. What remained of the creature's once-symmetrical body sickened her with its ugly pseudolife.

And beyond the monster, trapped in a crystal globe, glowed the pinpoint of brilliance in the depths of the pit.

"*El corazón del infierno*," she gasped. "Hell heart!"

Consuela used the Kalashnikov to push herself to her

feet, took one final look at the crater, then limped as quickly as she could into the jungle, more determined than ever to find José Villalobos and tell him of this new and terrible invader.

7

"Report!" Diego Villalobos shouted to his people, not realizing he was still deaf from the concussion of the impact. He could not tell whether the explosion had been a large blast far away or a smaller one nearby. He was even less able to explain the nature of the explosion. But since the Change, there was not a lot he could explain about the universe. He simply accepted what was and did the best job he could.

"Sergeant Baca?" he called out. From the far side of the clearing, a figure raised a hand in acknowledgment and began the arduous task of regaining command of the confused soldiers. Most of them sat with their heads cradled in their hands, more shaken than he had been. If the guerrillas attacked at this instant, they would find easy pickings.

At least the Ares assault suit was still upright, although it wasn't moving. That could mean the explosion had disabled it or that the pilot inside was hurt. Or dead. Diego felt a twinge of guilt as he realized the prospect of

Allen's death brought him more pleasure than pain. It would solve at least one of his problems.

"Captain Allen," Diego radioed. Dead air greeted him, so he ripped off his helmet. He checked what remained of his instrumentation and verified that the concussion had been caused by something falling from space. He made a mental note to contact Major D'Arcy once back at San Cristóbal and ask what the *Independence*, with its top-of-the-line equipment, had detected.

It was not likely to be anything launched by the guerrillas, but he could not rule out a chunk coming loose from one of the battle stations and crashing to Earth. It might even be some Union missile test gone awry. He would have been the last to know of any launch.

"That rattled me a little more than I like," came Allen's shaky voice. He had opened the Ares assault armor helmet and was gasping in the fetid jungle air. Diego guessed the powered suit had lost some systems, possibly including life support. Without compressors pumping air throughout the Ares, a man could suffocate in a few minutes unless he popped the sealed face protection.

"How could the concussion disable your suit?" Diego asked. The Ares was tough. Enough firepower to cause failure of its internal systems should have leveled the jungle.

"Sure wasn't a grenade. No grenade is *that* powerful," Allen said. "I got some anomalous radiation readings as the bogey streaked down. Do you know what it was? The cause of the shock wave?"

"Can you still uplink?" asked Diego, ignoring the man's questions. He looked around and saw that his sergeant had finally gotten her soldiers up and moving; the activity was enabling them to shake off the worst of their shock. Perhaps Baca had what it took to be an officer after all. He still had his doubts, but beggars could not be choosers, as his mother had always told him.

Diego touched the crucifix that hung around his neck at her memory and then turned back to Allen.

The captain was panting harshly, but the color had returned to his face, and he no longer seemed in danger of suffocating.

"Sorry, sir, but I'm not getting anything from the *Independence*," Allen reported. "I can't tell if it's my equipment or theirs, but I've got dead silence on all frequencies."

"Keep trying," Diego said shortly.

As Allen worked, Diego turned away to see to his soldiers' injuries. Most of the casualties appeared to be minor, although several of his people had been seriously injured in the battle with the Cyclops, and the explosion—whatever it was—had done none of them any good.

"Sir!" Baca said abruptly. He turned to face her, but she was looking beyond him toward Allen, who was still absorbed in his suit controls. "Captain Allen!"

Allen looked up, startled.

"I'd button that thing up fast, sir," Baca snapped. "The rest of you, don't go near it."

"He can't close it up. His life support's out," Diego said. He stepped away and took a longer look at the once-shiny exterior of the Ares suit—and went cold inside when he saw what Baca already had.

"Allen!" he bellowed. "Can you shift power to your life support?"

"I think so, but that's going to mean no more comm.

The battle station's secure laser link is out. I was just trying the radio—"

"Seal against atmosphere and use only internal systems," Diego said. "You've got some green gunk all over your left side—and it's spreading."

"What!"

Allen stood clumsily and swatted at the kelly green splotches creeping up his left arm. His left leg was already a fuzzy mass that undulated like wind through tall grass. The growth must have started slowly and was now accelerating to engulf him.

"Sir, I think we walked into a trap, one set specially to put the Ares out of action," Baca said. "The captain triggered the trap by chasing the Cyclops and got sprayed with that gunk. The Zapatistas would think nothing of trading a Neo-Sov mutant for one of our suits."

"Get your face covered," Diego shouted at Allen, wishing he had never set eyes on the man's face at all. "The goo is spreading."

Allen's face was pale with panic as he whirled around, as if bedeviled by a mosquito just beyond his reach. All his earlier composure was gone—the man looked positively frantic. The gyros in the Ares overcorrected and sent him crashing to the jungle floor. Until the suit recovered, he was pinned down by the gyroscopic action—but at least he had finally gotten his faceplate sealed. Diego wondered if the green fuzz had eaten into vital controller microchips or if some other malfunction had caused the Ares to react so erratically to ordinary movement. His money was on the goo.

Baca backed away even more, staring with wide eyes at the Ares. "This isn't good, sir. What is that stuff?"

"Something toxic as hell," Diego said. "It's gnawing

away at the metal, but it seems to be leaving the plastic fittings alone. For now." Louder, he called, "Who's got a working radio? Nobody? Sergeant, double-time a courier back to the Hydras. Call in airborne extraction. Get something heavy with an isolation cargo hold to remove the captain and his suit. *Fast!*"

Diego's fingers tapped the stock of his Bulldog as he considered whether firing a grenade against the Ares's goo-covered left flank would be at all useful. His stomach turned as the sludge's feathery tendrils rose up and wrapped around Captain Allen's plasma cannon, turning it into Swiss cheese. He doubted they had anything outside the repair depot that could decontaminate the Ares without killing Allen. And as much as the man's death might benefit Diego personally, Allen was still a Union officer, and the Union did not leave their men behind. He was no José, to turn his back on his loyalties.

The whir of an antigrav Hydra commanded his attention. Diego got the more seriously wounded soldiers loaded and signaled the virtually inert Ares that help was on the way. The suit nodded its massive head in response. Diego was sure Allen wasn't happy with the situation, but he would live—assuming they could get him safely out of the suit.

The Hydra carrying the wounded whirred away, and the other two arrived almost immediately after. Diego climbed in with Baca and the others and smiled grimly. At least now Allen had something to report to his Union bosses, even if it wasn't likely to be too complimentary of the MCF.

"That's the worst four hours I ever spent," Allen said, wiping rivers of sweat off his forehead with a soggy uniform sleeve. His shirt clung tenaciously to his body as more sweat formed. "I thought I was a goner."

Diego had also doubted Allen would survive the trip back to the repair bay. Of the soldiers who had gone into the field, Allen was the only one not sporting some wound, either minor or major, yet he had been in the most danger of dancing with the dead.

It had taken three of his biotechnicians—fully encased in plastic environment suits that seemed impervious to the bioweapon—and liberal applications of disinfectant to carefully pry the captain out of his suit without coating him in the slime. Those same technicians moved cautiously around the remnants of the Ares, now lying in a jumbled, molten heap in the middle of the room, safely isolated behind plastic.

"Have they identified the green slime yet?" Diego asked.

"Your bio team says it's something new and toxic," Allen said. "The suit's got to be decommissioned."

"I expected as much," Diego said glumly.

"It's history, a complete loss," Allen said, and Diego looked at him sharply, reacting to the hint of satisfaction in his voice. Perhaps it was just the man's relief that he was still alive while his suit was not. Still, it showed an astonishing lack of empathy for his fellow soldiers—six of whom had not survived their encounter with the Cyclops. It was hardly appropriate to gloat over one's own survival when one's comrades lay dead just a few rooms away. Perhaps it was his brush with death in Alaska—the one he refused to talk about—that had made him callous.

"Carry on, Captain," Diego said, carefully keeping the

distaste out of his voice. "I'll take charge of the decontamination."

"Yes, sir. Will there be anything else, sir?"

"No, Captain. Find your quarters and settle in. This has been a trying day for us all. Report to me when you're ready."

Diego watched Allen walk off. He was just as glad to see the man go. While he was certain Allen had been sent to spy on him, in response to Mexico City's complaints, he still had no idea what the man's private agenda was. And he had no time to worry about it now. Diego turned back to his bio expert, a warrant officer.

"What does it do?" he asked without preamble.

"Never seen anything like it, Colonel. The slime feeds on metal and, given enough time, chews right through it," the man replied. "It looks as if aerosol delivery is necessary. The spray hits the air and activates. Finds metal, eats, and grows in those fuzzy green patches." The gaunt warrant officer pointed to areas visible through the thick, clear plastic quarantine vessel holding the suit out of which they had so laboriously pried Allen. "I never expected the Neo-Sovs to come up with anything so nasty or dangerous. God knows how they came up with this stuff."

"What happens when it runs out of metal?" asked Diego. "It doesn't seem to like plastic."

"No metal—that is, no food—and it dies quick. There's a kicker, though, Colonel. When it dies, it's poisonous to anything living. Very toxic."

"For how long?"

"Not too long—maybe a few minutes before it dissipates. It's hard to remove from metal while it's fuzzy and growing, but after it dies and begins exuding poison, standard disinfectant works okay."

"So it's under control?"

The words had hardly left Diego's lips when alarms began to ring. All around the building doors slammed shut, automatically sealed and locked. The bio officer cursed and snapped a demand into his radio for his staff to report.

"What's wrong?" demanded Diego.

The warrant officer held up a hand, obviously listening to someone speaking over the radio, then took a deep breath and said, "Part of the captain's suit brushed a steel doorframe when we were bringing him in. The green goo started eating there. We isolated it—thought it was contained."

Diego waited for the rest. He would have a hard time with his report to HQ on this one.

"But a speck must have gotten onto the other suits. The goo is eating at both of the other Ares."

"Both? Get them decontaminated! Stop the spread. Get the entire area hosed down with disinfectant." Diego barely held his anger in check.

"Doing it all, sir. Spraying plastic over the green spots to see if that works as containment."

"Get repair crews to work on the suits. We might need them. And try to find a countermeasure for the goo while it's still on metal. You know the drill."

"Yes, sir, of course. Sorry about this, but it's a new one on all of us."

"Try to keep it *off* all of us," snapped Diego. He went through decon, double-checked any metal he carried, and returned to his office to begin a report he was loath to make.

8

The Death Priest prayed to his God-king and wished he had time to perform a suitable ritual sacrifice. But there was none. After his spacecraft had tumbled out of control following its encounter with the Shard and the Vorack-stuff, he had painstakingly nursed it into orbit, skipping along the upper planetary atmosphere, and then dipping lower with each orbit until the hull began to shriek with the heat of its descent.

"Do not leave your stations!" the priest snapped. The Slayer nodded brusquely and patrolled behind the few remaining slaves. After its violent encounter with the Shard, the *Destroyer for the Faith* had barely retained its atmosphere. The priest cared little about that. His elaborate life-support system sustained him whether air stayed within the ship or leaked into the energy-swirled vacuum of the Maelstrom. What he did require was for all systems to work well enough that he could follow the piece of Vorack-stuff to the planet below.

The Slayer had forced the few surviving slaves to repair some of the equipment. But the priest could see leaking hoses running from the slaves' life-support packs to their torsos. None of them could survive for long. The Death Priest knew he would have to replace the workers, possibly with primitives on the planet below. But to get to his slave-replacement pool, he had to execute a decent landing. Already he had spent half a planetary rotation braking in the atmosphere and working to repair the damage well enough to land. That was far too long.

"You will burn forever from the God-king's wrath if you do not execute a proper landing," the Death Priest told his slaves encouragingly. He rested both hands on the scythes sheathed at his waist to reinforce the need for efficiency. The Slayer performed adequately, as always. The severely damaged slaves worked more slowly as the atmospheric braking forces mounted on the spacecraft. But they retained enough control over the ship to home in on the fallen Vor-mote's landing site.

One by one the slaves collapsed or simply fell apart under the stress of the landing. The Slayer kicked the mummified debris from the vacant posts and ordered replacements forward. But before the ship had even reached the thick lower troposphere, the Slayer had run out of control-room slaves and had taken over the controls himself. The Death Priest worked alongside him, the two Pharon striving frantically to hold their ship together.

"Yes, there, now, now!" the priest barked over the patched-together comm system. The handful of survivors in the depths of the Pharon ship strained to obey his orders. Braking rockets fired and dug hard into the atmosphere, slowing the ship to subsonic speeds in the wet blanket of noxious, oxygen-laden air.

The Death Priest's ship came in at a steep angle and kicked up a tall plume of shredded vegetation and dirt behind it. The craft touched down on its landing tripod, prow to the sky, then teetered and crashed onto its side, staggering the survivors inside. The ship was sturdy, and such a tumble would not impair it unduly. But the Death Priest would have to undo all the damage the battle with the Shard had inflicted on his vessel before he could lift off from this pitiful world.

Lift off—with the mote from the Vorack.

"Organize the remaining slaves into work parties. Repair the ship immediately," the priest ordered the Slayer. When the gold-armored Pharon warrior did not immediately move to obey, the priest turned to face him fully.

"You refuse my orders?" he asked softly.

"Holy one, never! But there are no slaves left intact anywhere in the ship!" The Slayer clacked his battle claw in his agitation.

"Get more," the priest said. "This world teems with life. Kill enough to repair the ship." A curious weakness suddenly seized the priest. He sagged slightly, caught hold of a stanchion, and then straightened. Recognizing the effects of a life-support malfunction, he ran a quick system check and saw the trouble: the back tank that maintained his life-in-death was dangerously close to empty.

"I will go immediately," the warrior declared.

"I accompany you," the priest said. "Rites must be conducted."

The warrior bowed his small head and waited to follow the priest out of the control room. On increasingly shaky legs, the priest picked his way through the toppled corpses of slaves to the airlock and out into the fetid jungle. His filters removed much of the stench of life that surrounded him, but the priest still recognized the disagreeable odor of undisciplined, rampant growth. Where were the priests to discipline this planet? Did this ugly world lack a God-king or lords and ladies to impose structure?

"Inferior," the Death Priest mused as he forced himself to stride commandingly from the downed spaceship, showing no weakness, not even bothering to survey the external damage. There was no point in determining what repairs needed to be made until he had the slaves to make them. And he needed more than dead bodies to reanimate as slaves—he needed life-preserving gel to ensure his own continued existence.

"There," the Slayer said, pointing into the dense curtain of jungle vegetation. "Primitives."

"Kill them," the priest said. He had not detected the local inhabitants, another sign of diminished capacity. The warrior blasted a portion of the jungle with his plasma weapon, leaving behind a body too charred for use either as slave or nourishment. The other native screamed and ran deeper into the jungle.

"Stay here," the Death Priest ordered irritably. He activated his phase-shift generator and began to flicker in and out of sight as he raced to the jungle edge with the last of his strength. The remaining primitive froze at the tachistoscope image of a demon coming at him and started to shriek. The priest did not allow him to finish. One strong, bandage-swathed hand shot out to grip the native by the throat.

From his belt, the Death Priest pulled a special gauntlet with a huge, rounded knob. A thick syringe protruded from the middle. With practiced ease, he impaled his victim's chest on the spike, which sank deeply into the man's flesh. A monofilament line unspooled into the human's chest cavity and began lashing about, turning his innards to a viscous liquid. The priest pinned the thrashing, dying human to the ground and expertly reached behind his back, finding the correct hose leading from his life-support unit. The hose clamped onto the gauntlet, and the feeding began.

The jellied nourishment that had once been the man's internal organs flowed through the syringe, into the gauntlet, and back into the life-sustaining pack. As the man's body slowly collapsed inward, the Death Priest felt a renewed surge of strength.

"For the glory of the God-king," the priest said, beginning his prayer ritual. As he strengthened, his mental powers were returning to their usual acute levels. He had not realized how dangerously weak the battle had made him until this moment.

"Slayer!" the priest called. "Do not kill any more of the natives!"

With a dry rustle, he pulled the gauntlet and its syringe free of the husk that had been a human being. The Death Priest looked around, his senses sharper now.

"Holy one, why not? You ordered me to get slaves to repair the spaceship."

"We must act slowly," the priest stated. "These two were easy kills, but above us orbits a battle station that was strong enough to destroy a Shard. We must proceed cautiously until we determine how strong these natives are."

"At your orders, holy one," the Slayer rumbled.

The Vorack was setting on the distant horizon, plunging the overgrown land into darkness—a darkness suitable for what the Death Priest had in mind. He had railed at the time it took to land his damaged spaceship, but now he saw how the God-king's blessing followed him.

Priest and Slayer moved quietly through the night, alert for any movement. The few animals they encountered were inadequate for the priest's purposes, and he skirted more than a dozen villages, certain the jungle held smaller bands of primitives who would not be immediately missed.

And he found them.

"The entire patrol searching for Consuela?" José Villalobos's eyebrows rose. When she had not returned to the rendezvous point by noon, José had become worried. He had sent most of his soldiers back to the rebel headquarters in the city of Comitan but had continued to wait until well past dusk, occasionally sending out a small patrol to sweep the jungle for any signs of Consuela. The raid on Puerto Madero had been successful, but he had to know to what extent that was due to Consuela's decoy attack with the Cyclops and how well the Neo-Sov bioweapon had deployed. But most of all, he could not afford to part with his most valued lieutenant. To gain supplies and lose Consuela would be a Pyrrhic victory indeed.

"We have not lost an entire patrol to the Union in months," he said.

"It couldn't be to the Union soldiers," Mary Stephenson stated. "They are pigs. They root about, make too much noise, and then fall out among themselves over the spoils. They could not possibly take an entire patrol without leaving any sign of struggle. No, this is something more, a greater threat. I just wish I knew what it was."

"If a Union patrol did not kill our people, what did?" José asked, perplexed.

"Maybe one of the Cyclops turned on Consuela, then went on the rampage after *our* patrols," suggested Gunther. "Let me go hunt it down."

"Consuela took only the one mutant," José said. That wasn't entirely true, of course. She'd also taken the demon weapon.

"We have to move on soon," Mary said. "Flaco is almost finished camouflaging the booty from the Puerto Madero raid, and it's too dangerous for us to stay any longer."

"Consuela knows where to find us," José said, still worried but knowing Mary was right. "Come. Let's return to Comitan and continue preparations for the big attack."

"Revancha?" Gunther smiled wickedly.

"We must plan every detail of that raid," José said. "If we succeed, we can wrest control of Chiapas from the Union once and for all."

"We will kill all of them!" cried Gunther.

"To Comitan," José said, repressing a sigh. Gunther hurried off, but Mary hung back. "What is it?" José asked her.

"The missing patrol, the one sent to look for Consuela. What are we to do?"

"Rest and regroup, prepare for Revancha . . . and pray that Gunther does not jump the gun. We cannot spare men to search for the patrol. If they still live, they will meet us at Comitan."

Mary nodded, her lips tight, and faded into the jungle. José waited a while longer, despite the risk of being discovered by Union patrols—and whatever else was out there—hoping Consuela would miraculously appear. But he was not surprised when she did not.

War was hell, and living with the consequences was even worse.

José started through the jungle toward Comitan, wary of the animals and the Union—and whatever it was that had prevented Consuela from returning from her mission.

9

Alex Allen stopped just outside the garrison gate and tightened the handkerchief around his forehead in a vain attempt to stop the perspiration from running into his eyes. He wondered how the MCF soldiers managed not to sweat to death in this sultry jungle. It was still early morning, and already the heat was boiling the flesh off his bones. The induction of the Earth into the Maelstrom had resulted in dramatic weather changes, causing the jungle temperatures to soar, but the heat of this place must have been unbearable even before the Change.

It was almost enough to make him reconsider his mission, but he knew he was doing the right thing. After all, the colonel had told him not to report until he was ready, and he would not be ready until he had tracked down the chunk of space debris that had crashed the previous day. His repeated attempts to contact the battle station had failed, but some quick work with the reconnaissance display in his Ares—before he'd had to switch all available power to maintaining life support—had given him a fix on the landing site. Villalobos had thought it might be a bomb, but the radiation signature was like nothing Allen had ever seen on earth—which to him meant an alien genesis.

And, possibly, a ticket out of this tropical hellhole. Allen was no fool. The Union brass might have told him the purpose of his visit was to evaluate Villalobos's competence, and that was probably true, but he knew the real reason for sending him down here: punishment duty after the debacle in Alaska.

If he ever hoped to remove the black marks on his service record, he would have to produce something truly spectacular—like some exotic new energy source, something the scientists at HQ might find valuable.

He hefted the Pitbull rifle he had finagled from the corporal in charge of the armory and then checked his battle vest to be sure he had all the equipment essential for a successful scouting mission. He had tried to get an Aztec cycle, but the motor-pool sergeant assured him they were easy targets for every guerrilla in the jungle. The man could not be talked into releasing a Hydra or any other vehicle, so that left Allen on foot. He certainly didn't want to get into any more of those Ares suits!

He had slung so much water in his backpack that he gurgled loudly as he walked. He would need a lot to replace the moisture he was sweating away. An automated first-aid kit, a GPS so he could find his way through the alien jungle, some food, ammo, the battle vest, and boots designed to slog through mud and heavy vegetation—with all this, he could probably take on the guerrillas single-handedly and win. Not that that would take much effort—anyone who would bother to fight over this worthless piece of land was almost too stupid to be any threat.

Like the colorless Colonel Villalobos. Now he understood why Mexico City disliked the man so much. Allen, like most soldiers in the former United States, had a pretty low opinion of the Mexican forces; coming to Chiapas had, if possible, lowered it even further. True, Villalobos had acquitted himself reasonably well against the Cyclops, but his post was sloppy, underequipped, and undermanned. Worse, his soldiers were incompetent; and the man himself was dull-minded. Why, he'd been so obsessed with the green goo that had disabled Allen's Ares that he hadn't even asked if the suit had picked up anything on the explosion in the jungle. And that was just fine with Allen.

All day he hiked, until the afternoon sunlight slanted down and seemed to boil the life out of him. Now he understood why everyone, including the enlisted men out on punishment duty, took their precious siestas until the worst of the heat had died away.

But he was above such malingering; duty required him to be alert every minute of the day. Allen knew about slovenly soldiers who did not share his commitment. He had commanded a company of them in Alaska, and they had let him down. His men could have held the line against the growler attack as the creatures came rushing across the glacier, but they had turned and run at first contact. That was the only possible explanation for how quickly the growlers had ripped through the defensive line and penetrated to his command post. He had barely had enough time to find the Aztec and beat a retreat before the growlers exterminated him. To stand and fight was futile after his soldiers had failed so miserably.

Every man and woman in his command had been slaughtered—everyone but Captain Alex Allen, thanks to his uncanny knack for survival. The board of inquiry would have loved to court-martial him for deserting his post and leaving his men to die, but with no survivors to contradict his testimony, the evidence had been too sketchy. Allen growled deep in his throat at the notion that *he* was somehow at fault for retreating when all those under him had failed. Just like these indolent MCF troopers. Fools. Idiots. Incompetents.

He had to show Union Command how capable he was if he was ever going to get reassigned to a decent post. This was exile, Allen knew, until his superiors could figure out what to do with him. He had to use this opportunity, this fugue in his career, to win approval, or he would be buried forever in dead-end garrisons.

Allen had only to look at Diego Villalobos's career to know what lay ahead of him if he failed.

He drank more water than anticipated and seemed no closer to the crash site in spite of hurrying and taking only short rest breaks. With his legs and back killing him, Allen sank down and rested against a tree to reassess his mission.

He fiddled with the GPS, knowing it did no good to take new readings every few minutes. That only made the hike seem longer. But he was certain he would discover something so spectacular the brass would have to sit up and take notice of him again, and this made him overly eager. This time it would be done right. He would be the hero because he had done it all on his own and had not depended on lesser soldiers who betrayed his trust in them.

"Incompetents, all of them," he grumbled, then took one last drink of stimulant-laced water. Allen let the drinking tube slip from his fingers as he reached for his rifle beside him on the ground, ready to move on.

"You have nothing to fear from me," came a soft voice by his side. Allen yelped and shot to his feet, fumbling to get his rifle at the ready.

A tiny peasant girl stood by the tree, gazing up at him. The urchin had slipped up on him, and he hadn't even noticed her until she spoke. Allen hesitated, then lowered his rifle. He felt foolish holding a gun on a child who barely came up to his chest.

Besides, a native guide might be useful in this hellish jungle. He gave the girl his best winning smile and motioned her to come closer. But as she limped toward him, he revised his estimate. She was a woman, and she was injured. Bruises and cuts covered her face, and rags were wrapped tightly around her left ankle, which was swollen to twice its normal size.

"What happened to you?" he asked, indicating her leg.

"It was awful," she said in a tiny voice. "I . . . I do not know what happened. There was a terrible screaming in the sky, and then—this." She gestured at her injuries, then reached up and tentatively touched the drinking tube at his left shoulder that led to the water in his pack. "Please, sir, I have had no water for so long. I am *very* thirsty."

"Go ahead," he said, offering her the tube of a medicine-laced bottle. With the condition she was in, it looked like she needed the antibiotics fast. She drank greedily, giving him a chance to study her up close. Allen decided that under the dirt and blood she was not bad-looking. She was young, perhaps in her early twenties, with a submissive manner that appealed to him.

She wiped the last drop of water off her lips and limped back a few paces, studying him as carefully as he had studied her. He offered her some of the stimulant-water, and she drank that bottle dry as well.

"You are a very important man, no?" she asked. "I can tell. And kind. You are kind to share your water with me."

Allen puffed up a little at the notion that even a native scrabbling out a pathetic living in this jungle could see how important he was.

"Let me see if I can fix that ankle of yours," he said avuncularly. "There's a good chance of infection setting in, you know."

Consuela held still, breath hissing through her teeth, as he carefully unwrapped the rags, which had cut deeply into the swollen flesh.

"Hmm, yeah, I can do something," he said. "I've got an auto-med kit that can take care of most of this swelling."

Allen pulled out his first-aid kit and broke open the seals on the small device before strapping it to Consuela's ankle. "This will hurt a little, but it will really help," he explained carefully. She flinched, then settled down as the auto-med worked to repair what it could. In a few minutes a tiny beep signaled the end of its duty cycle.

"It . . . it feels better," she said, flexing her foot. She looked into Allen's eyes and smiled shyly. "I feel stronger. There was medicine in the water? And a pick-me-up drug?"

"Glad to help," Allen said. She was a clever girl to understand exactly what he had given her.

"How can I repay you?" Consuela said. "I have no money, and you are a rich, powerful Union officer with marvelous machines to help you."

"I can think of one way," Allen said. "You know your way through the jungle?"

"Of course. And I can help you stay away from the guerrillas. They are not so far from here."

"Where?" Panic seized Allen. He could not allow those unwashed, uncouth animals to steal his secret. Whatever had crashed into the jungle had been tiny, and yet it had radiated more energy than he would have thought possible. To harness that would mean an unlimited supply of power in the field, a gift to be cherished by any combat officer.

"Not so far. You can avoid them. I can help." Consuela lowered her head demurely. "I do not even know your name. I am Consuela."

"Captain Allen," he said.

"*Un capitán*," she said, her dark eyes wide. "You are a very important man. I knew it. And you are kind."

"How many guerrillas were there?"

"Oh, not many. No more than fifty or sixty. They move entire companies through this region. They are so powerful—it makes us all afraid."

"I can imagine," Allen said. "Look, I've got a GPS fix on a site not more than two klicks from here." He showed her his handheld GPS unit. "Can you help me get through the guerrilla patrols so I can reach this place?"

Consuela studied the GPS and the compass setting, frowned, and then brightened and nodded slowly. "I know the place well. Something fell there from the sky yesterday morning. Is it one of your powerful missiles?"

"Uh, no," he said. "That's why I'm investigating."

"You do not command other men?" Consuela asked.

"Not this time," Allen said hastily. "Let's go."

"Come, and stay low," she cautioned. Together they moved off the trail and into the jungle, her ankle obviously well on its way to recovery. Consuela slipped easily through the thick vines and tangled undergrowth while he blundered along as if he had one foot in a bucket of concrete. More than once she motioned him down, often into anthills or other exasperating spots where bugs or nettles stabbed and gnawed at his flesh.

At last she held out her hand to slow his advance but did not call out a warning of nearby guerrillas.

"There," she said in a whisper. "I have never seen anything like it before."

Allen double-checked his GPS. Consuela had led him directly to the impact spot. He thrust the compass into his vest pocket and unlimbered his Pitbull rifle. If he ran into any guerrillas, he would eliminate them and claim the prize for himself—and for the Union.

"What's that sound?" he asked. He looked around the small clearing where the jungle had been blown away by the impact, hunting for the source of the crunching sound. Or was it a crumbling noise? He couldn't quite make it out, but it was like nothing he'd ever heard.

Consuela shrugged. "I see only what you see."

"Stay here. I'll check it out." Allen advanced in a crouch, his Pitbull swinging to and fro in a short arc in front of him. He emerged from the thick jungle and stepped onto a glassy, dark plain.

He whirled as he caught a flicker of gold just out of the corner of his eye. He scanned the jungle, hands tight and sweaty on his rifle, but saw nothing. Then his attention was claimed entirely by the crater, and the brilliant beam of energy emerging from it. Whatever was the source of those noises, he had to get closer to the energy source, to examine it and figure out how to transport it safely back to the base.

He took one step toward the pit, and then another, moving carefully as he neared the slippery edge of the crater. Then he froze as a huge glass arm, its smooth surface bulging with crystalline tumors, reached up over the side of the pit and sank sharp, lethal claws into the hardened surface of the soil. Slowly, a face rose into view over the lip of the crater, and Allen knew suddenly that the guerrillas were the least of his problems.

The creature might have been humanoid once, but no longer. Now it writhed and bulged with nodules that swelled rapidly and fell off, forming crystalline snakes with razor-sharp spikes erupting from their sides and backs. They hit the ground and rapidly wriggled toward him. The creature looked up for just a moment, its eyes— if it could be said to have such things—locking with Allen's briefly. He was unsure whether it even saw him. Then its grip on the soil slipped, and it plunged back into the pit. Allen winced at the sound it made when it hit bottom.

Hastily backing away, Allen leveled his rifle at the half dozen creatures coming at him. Their speed was astonishing. His Pitbull spat a heavy slug, and then he went to full automatic fire. One of the monstrosities exploded into a million pieces, drifting down around him like a jeweled rain. Allen backpedaled and kept firing at the other crystal snakes. He ejected an empty clip, rammed in a new one, and kept firing until the rifle barrel turned cherry red from the friction of the slugs ripping away at the creatures.

Allen blew apart his six attackers, but another one

popped from a bulge in the ground at his feet just as he ejected an empty clip. With no time to reload, he swung the butt of his rifle in a short, vicious arc and knocked off the eyestalks growing from the center of its head. That killed the thing as surely as the slugs that had blown apart the others.

He took another step backward, caught his heel, and sat down heavily. If Allen thought he was sweating profusely before, now his body was almost washed away in the torrents pouring from his skin. His mouth was dry with fear, and his heart hammered until it felt like a grenade ready to explode.

"What *are* they?" cried Consuela.

"I have no idea," Allen said, "but they aren't very friendly."

For a moment Consuela stared at him and then laughed and shook her head. "You are not like other men, Capitán Allen. Not at all."

"Thanks. I think," he said, wondering if she was mocking him. But that was crazy. Consuela was only a poor ignorant country girl who'd wandered out in the jungle.

She quickly helped him to his feet. He rammed in his last clip of ammunition and knew he couldn't hope to fight these monstrosities, more of which were now wriggling and tunneling up from the bottom of the pit. Whatever was down there, it was a breeding ground for other hideous, dangerous *things*. He had to find out what they were if he was to have a hope of retrieving his prize.

"Help me get that one into my pack," Allen said, indicating the monster whose eyestalks he had bashed off. He pulled off his backpack and saw that his water was nearly gone. Opening one empty plastic bottle, he handed it to Consuela and indicated that she should put the glassy creature into it.

"You do not do this yourself?" she asked, recoiling from the task.

"I'll cover you," he said, damp hands tight on the Pitbull.

Consuela shrugged, then used a small stick to maneuver the dead crystal thing into the empty water bottle. She handed it to Allen, who carefully screwed on the cap.

"What will you do with this?"

Allen had no idea, but someone back at San Cristóbal might. This was not the real menace; that still crunched and lurched at the bottom of the pit, sucking up energy from whatever had crashed there. To get to the energy source, Allen knew he had to destroy the quartz humanoid brute, and he lacked the firepower for that. He didn't think anything short of a SPEAR missile could kill it—and, unfortunately, that meant he would have to talk Diego into authorizing the strike.

"I'm going to take it back to the post and examine it," he said more confidently than he felt. "Thanks for helping me."

"Oh, Capitán Allen, if I can ever help you at any other time, please do not hesitate to call on Consuela," the girl said. She came closer and rested a hand on his vest.

"I won't forget your service today," he said, his mouth even drier than it had been a few seconds earlier.

"You are so good to me," she said, standing on tiptoe and kissing him fleetingly on the cheek. He felt a kilo lighter as Consuela slipped into the thick green barrier of jungle surrounding the crater and disappeared.

Allen started to call after her to ask how he could find her and then bit his tongue. It would not pay to announce his presence in a jungle filled with guerrilla patrols.

Not to mention whatever it was he had killed and stuffed into the plastic bottle. With the keening sounds and radiance from the pit at his back, Alex Allen headed back for the garrison, victorious.

From the edge of the jungle, crouched behind the sheltering vegetation, the two Pharon watched him go.

"Why would you not allow me to kill them?" the Slayer asked, perplexed. "They would have made fitting additions to our crew." He gestured behind him, where a number of natives stood—fresh wounds gaping from their torsos, heads caved in, limbs missing, but somehow horribly still upright. They staggered under the weight of the life packs strapped to their backs, the hoses containing the essence of their former comrades plunging into their chests.

"I wanted to see what they were capable of," the priest replied dismissively. "One primitive more or less makes no difference, but now we have information. We know that the Shard survived"—one hand clenched convulsively on a scythe at his waist—"and we also know that the Vor-stuff has somehow changed it."

"And now we can kill it," the Slayer said eagerly, his battle claw tensing in anticipation.

"Not yet," the priest said, glaring at the pit that held the prize he had chased for days. He longed to race over to the crater and claim it for his own, but the Shard's terrible transformation made him wary. "Caution is needed. Take the slaves and begin the repairs to our ship while I ponder how best to retrieve the mote."

"But the Shard—"

"Is no threat to us," the priest interrupted. "It has enough to concern it for the moment."

The Slayer reluctantly retreated into the jungle, herding ahead of it the shambling monstrosities that had once been José's missing guerrillas. The priest watched them go, then turned his attention back to the desperate struggle taking place in the crater. He had learned his lesson in the earlier encounter with the Shard. This time he would wait, and watch, and learn. And at the end of the day, the power would be his.

On the other side of the clearing torn from the jungle, Consuela was testing her ankle in preparation for the long trek back to the guerrilla headquarters, unaware of how close had been her brush with death. All in all, she thought, the day had gone extremely well. She could have simply killed the Union man—could have snapped his neck before he even realized she was there. But by leading him to the crater, she had gained much valuable information about what the alien was capable of. The delay had been worth it—now she had a healed ankle, her thirst quenched, and much more data to bring to José. As for the gullible Union captain, she did not think he would be reporting back to his people anytime soon—if at all.

She headed deeper into the jungle, moving easily now. As she went, she casually dropped something shiny on the ground, where it disappeared into the undergrowth: Allen's GPS.

10

José Villalobos found it hard to concentrate, even in the safety of his headquarters at Comitan. He stared out the window at the bustling, prosperous city, its bright lights holding the darkness of the night at bay. In all Chiapas no city held the Zapatista guerrillas in greater esteem. Union forces avoided the town, and in return, José kept order in the city. It was a peculiar standoff, but one that suited both sides. The Union would kill thousands of innocents if they tried to ferret out the guerrillas there, and José constantly reminded them of that. Guerrilla war was as much about propaganda as it was about killing—maybe even more.

But it would change soon, this standoff, once he seized the nuclear reactor at Revancha. If the source of power for the entire region came under Zapatista control, José could pick and choose which villages received electricity. His hold on the countryside would strengthen, even in the cities, where the Union currently held greater sway. He would become a force to be reckoned with—and the

Union would be forced to deal with him. It was a blow with the potential to win the war in one stroke. Even if he failed to seize the CANDU reactor, he would disable it and blame the Union for the subsequent loss of power. Propaganda did not have to be true to be effective.

He needed to put some last-minute touches on the plan, but his mind kept drifting to Consuela and her mysterious disappearance after the Puerto Madero raid. Mary had reported that two patrols hunting for Consuela had also vanished without a trace, something that should be impossible in guerrilla-controlled territory. Worse, intelligence from the entire region had turned spotty. Without decent intel, how could he plan? How could he fight the Union's superior weapons?

"You look like you need a friend," said Flaco, coming into the room with two bottles under one pudgy arm. He dropped one on the maps and documents that littered the table and uncorked the other for his own sampling. "Tequila, José, fine tequila. Just what you need."

José stared at the bottle for a moment before trying some. The bite was worse than he had anticipated. Vices required practice, and for this one he was out of shape.

"Good, eh?" Flaco worked on his own bottle with a vengeance. "I see you plan for Revancha. I have all the arms. Supplies, food, water, it is all ready. There is only one thing lacking."

"What's that?" José asked, startled. "We got everything we needed at Puerto Madero."

"To pound some sanity into Gunther's head. He trains his men like the Japanese. What were they called?"

"Kamikaze," José said. "It's true what you say. We

don't need suicides. We want victory and the guerrillas alive for the celebration afterward."

"He is a strange one. I try to get him to relax, but he is so . . . so determined. Gunther is like a train that runs only on his own odd gauge of track."

José nodded, smiling wanly. "I will redirect him."

"You need Consuela. She is the only one who can convince him to do the proper thing—and sometimes even she does not succeed." Flaco tipped his head to one side and peered at his leader. "Any word?"

José shook his head.

"A pity. She would get my vote for the Consulta any day."

"I will hold you to that, Flaco," Consuela said, coming into the office. "First, give me some of your tequila. I am thirsty and tired and need it!"

José heaved a huge sigh of relief on seeing her; he had feared she was lost permanently. He pushed his barely touched bottle across the desk to her.

"All yours—in exchange for a report. You had us worrying that you had gone over to the Union, seduced by their fine clothing and ample food," he teased.

"Bah," she said, taking a pull on the tequila. "Abandon good tequila for that? Ahhh!" Consuela put the bottle back on the desk, settled into a chair, and seemed to deflate. As worried as he had been, José had not realized until this moment how much he had feared losing her. Without her, he would have been like a man without eyes or ears. None of his soldiers produced more useful intelligence than Consuela.

"You have been hurt," he noted, seeing the bruises and

scratches that covered her skin. "You should rest. There will be time enough for you to make your report . . ."

"No!" The sudden flare in Consuela's dark eyes told José he had misjudged the level of her exhaustion. "There is too much to tell. I should not have wasted time with this." She waved dismissively at the bottle.

"Waste?" protested Flaco. "Never. Not good tequila!"

"What kept you so long, *chica*?" José asked gently.

Consuela took a deep breath, and José could see her mentally sorting through all she had to tell him. If nothing else, he wanted her report on how the Cyclops had fared against the Union forces. The Cyclops—and the demon weapon he had sent with it.

"There is so much, José," she said wearily. "I made contact with a Union captain from San Cristóbal, a foolish man we might use later for information—assuming he survives. I took his GPS from him. Without that, he is either dead or lost in the jungle. But that is not the biggest thing."

"The Cyclops," José said, gently steering her toward the important details of her adventure.

"No, no, not that. The mutant obeyed commands, used the aerosol weapon, and destroyed an Ares suit with it. The metal on the assault suit was beginning to erode by the time I retreated. The Union soldiers destroyed the Cyclops, but not before it killed at least four of them. Perhaps more."

"And this is not the *big* news?" asked José. "What could be better than that?"

"Not better, but bigger," Consuela said. "I was stunned by the fall of a thing from the sky."

"After the Puerto Madero raid, we were hit by a shock

wave, also," José confirmed. "I thought it was a Union weapon, but they never followed up."

"I saw where it crashed. Where the *monster* crashed!"

"Monster?" José asked skeptically. Consuela had been through a lot in the past two days, but he placed tremendous faith in her abilities. What she told him, he believed. But monsters from the sky?

"Don't say it like that, José," she snapped. "I am no fool. I did not imagine it. There is a crater in the jungle, and in that crater is something . . . I do not even know how to describe it. It is like a creature made of glass."

"Perhaps it is what has been killing our patrols," Flaco suggested, half-joking. He raised his eyebrows when Consuela stared at him. "You had not heard? Two patrols hunting for you, Consuela, both vanished. Gossip in the villages says they were stolen away by a *chupacabra*."

"A goat sucker?" José laughed. "That is a myth, a story to scare small children."

Flaco shrugged eloquently and took another long drink of the potent tequila. "*Something* killed them. A small boy from a village near Teopisca, just south of San Cristóbal, claimed he saw a wild tall creature all in golden armor attack a patrol. Quickly following the attack came the *chupacabra*. It flickered in and out of sight and moved fast, very fast. And it wore a cleric's chasuble, only it was metallic."

"There is more, I suppose," José said, amused at the tales spun by the *campesinos*. Only last month, he had been hearing reports of ghost demons stalking the countryside; now the long-mythical *chupacabra* was back. If Consuela told him she had seen a monster, he would—however reluctantly—believe her. But that did not mean he was forced to accept the locals' stories as well. Two different monsters, both attacking at once? It defied belief.

"It wore a headdress, larger than any Mayan priest's and with lenses and glass focusing devices," Flaco said doggedly. "On the *chupacabra*'s back hung a large backpack with hoses coming from it and running to its chest and arms."

"Quite an imagination, this *muchacho*," José said. "Anything else?"

"He said it punctured its victim's chest and drank his blood."

"So young," said José, "so young to sample tequila." Flaco shrugged again as José turned to Consuela. "This was not your monster, was it?"

"No," she said positively. "It was nothing like that. *My* monster is of crystal and changed form as I watched. It burrowed down to the thing that crashed and—"

He held up his hand. Even if what she was saying was true—and he couldn't help but wonder if she was exaggerating slightly to convince him of the magnitude of the threat—he could not deal with it now. The raid on Revancha needed all his care if he was to succeed, and he could not afford to divide his attention this close to the attack.

"Consuela, I promise you—as soon as we have seized power at the reactor, I will look into your report," he said. "But for now, let us concentrate on the danger that we know."

"With all respect, José, you are wrong," she retorted. "This is a greater threat than the Union soldiers. If you had seen it . . ."

"*After* the raid," José repeated firmly. Consuela

opened her mouth to argue further, but then seemed to realize it was a hopeless battle.

"Find the *curandero, chica,*" José said gently. "He will tend your wounds and give you something to make you sleep."

"But—"

"You will not miss the raid on Revancha. I promise. Now go," he said, shooing her out.

When Consuela had gone—slowly, reluctantly—José turned angrily to Flaco. "She has been injured. Why should you taunt her with myths and legends?"

"I only tell you what I hear. It is nothing that is not being passed from lip to ear even now," Flaco said.

"Bloodsuckers, monsters in golden armor, monsters of crystal. The real monsters are the Union soldiers! You, too—go, get your squad ready for Revancha. It will not be an easy fight."

"You will use the Cyclops?" Flaco asked as he pushed himself to his feet, swaying slightly from the tequila.

"No," José said. "Not at Revancha. We cannot risk having them turn on us at a critical moment." As for the demon weapon, José did not want to use it at all, even if it could bring down an Ares. He wished he could leave the two remaining cylinders of the deadly green aerosol in their jungle hiding place forever. Some weapons were too dangerous to be used.

"Be careful, José," said Flaco. "Be careful of *not* believing."

José watched his trusted lieutenant disappear. For months he had concentrated all his hopes and attention on the Revancha attack. If he could cut off power to Union sympathizers, give electricity to those loyal to the Zapatistas, his movement could take control of all central Chiapas without having to fight the current war of attrition. If the Union tried to retake the CANDU nuclear reactor, they would pay a high price. Recruitment for the Mexican Contribution Forces fell off with every Union defeat, no matter how small.

Revancha would dry up all volunteers.

So much rode on this victory, and here were his aides, obsessed with monsters. José forced himself to look away from the window to the maps spread on his desk. Time grew short, and he had so much to do.

"*Chupacabras*," he snorted. He took one last drink of tequila and returned to his planning.

11

The Shard staggered and collapsed against the wall of the crater. Its once-smooth surface bulged and writhed with glassy tumors, and with every passing hour more of its unholy spawn broke free of their parent.

Earlier in this sundering of its self, the Shard might have recognized what was happening to it. It might have sensed the disintegration of its finely tuned control over the precise internal structure of its shell and that its ability to morph its physical form at will was burgeoning out of control. Somehow the radiation from the mote had caused the Shard's body to mutate horribly.

But the Shard was no longer capable of thinking anything. Its once cool, sharp mind had been reduced to a level of mindless, animal rage. For as its traitorous body had broken apart, pieces of itself dropping loose and wriggling away, to its horror it had felt its consciousness fracturing along with its crystalline shell. Where once it had relied on precise data from its surface sensors, now it was receiving a confused jumble of impressions from dozens of viewpoints all at once. It was still in the pit, but it was simultaneously wriggling into the jungle in a dozen directions, overwhelming the Shard's splintered mind with a barrage of sensations until it felt all knowledge of its consciousness, its self, slipping away. The Shard tried to order its shear planes, to eliminate dislocations in its structure, to return discipline to the crystal husk that kept its energy from being sucked into the Maw.

It failed.

Yet another growth swelled from its side and dropped to the ground. The Shard fell to its knees and used its fist to crush the creature, but try as it might, it could not destroy all the growths. They sprang up fast, too fast even for a swiftly attacking Shard.

Somehow, without even knowing how it had happened, the Shard found itself on the surface, rolling on the ground to crush the errant growths under its bulk. It remembered nothing of scaling the shaft to reach the surface, but with each mutant offspring it destroyed, it felt a slight semblance of order return to its mind as another channel of impressions was closed.

In a frenzy, the Shard leapt at the growths now surrounding the pit, crushing them in its hands and under its feet. When it had destroyed every crystalline snake it could see, it paused for a moment, trying desperately to regain control over its shredded consciousness. Shard felt neither physical pain nor exhaustion, but they were not immune to mental anguish.

It could feel other pieces of itself, ones that had thus far escaped it, receding from it into the jungle, and it knew what it had to do. Only when it had destroyed every last cancerous growth would it regain its self. On clumsy feet, displaying none of its usual quicksilver grace, the Shard blundered into the jungle in search of its mutant offspring. One by one, it tracked them and killed them, each tiny death bringing slight relief to its fevered mind.

It scarcely noticed when its rampage sent it staggering into a village, just beginning to stir in the morning light. Several humans failed to get out of its path quickly enough, and the Shard killed them without slowing, with efficient slashes of its razor-sharp talons. The few bullets bouncing off its tough crystalline exterior, fired in desperation by the village's protectors, only helped propel it on its mission.

Had the Shard still been capable of reason, it would have known this was madness. But it did not care. It only knew it had to destroy the pieces of itself and restore its mind to normality. Only then would it be able to claim its prize, which it dimly recalled had been important.

But for now, it roared, it slashed, and it killed as it raced across the countryside.

The Death Priest stepped out of his hiding place and watched the Shard crash through the vegetation on the other side of the clearing in pursuit of he knew not what. Nor did he care. His long hours of patient waiting had yielded victory. The field was now open. The Vorack fragment was his!

With caution, phase generator fully activated for whatever protection it might offer, the priest approached the pit that had been the Shard's prison. He circled the edge of the crater, keeping well out of the path of the radiance that blasted upward from the mote buried at the bottom of the hole. The radiation readings from the mote were much more intense than they had been during the Pharon's pursuit of it in space. Perhaps the violence of its landing had cracked the protective globe surrounding the pinpoint of light, unleashing its deadly energy to such devastating effect on the Shard.

No matter. The priest was confident he would be able to cobble together sufficient equipment from the ruins of his ship to surround the globe with a force field. That would be sufficient for the trek back to the ship and the hold prepared and waiting to receive the mote of Vorackstuff. The temporary field would not be sufficient to stop all of the radiation, but what of it? Some slaves would undoubtedly die along the way, but what of it?

After all, as long as there was life on the planet, there were always more slaves to be had.

12

Diego Villalobos rubbed his bleary eyes and tried to concentrate. He had been awake half the night once again, trying to decide what his brother might be planning to do next. The attack on the Puerto Madero supply base two days ago was only the beginning of a new guerrilla campaign, of that Diego was now sure. He'd feared as much at the time, but with his limited resources, the Cyclops had been too great a threat to ignore. Still, it was obvious José wanted the ammo stored at the Puerto Madero outpost for something else.

What would it be?

His finger traced along the ancient, cracked, yellowed map spread on the desk in front of him. He had found it in a trunk of his father's belongings after José had angrily renounced the Union and disappeared into the jungle.

"Where are you going to strike next, Viejo?" Diego wondered aloud.

He knew he should no longer be thinking of his brother as "the Old One." It lent him an air of honor and dignity—even wisdom—but old habits died hard. "Co-mandante" was what the *campesinos* called him, revealing that the Zapatista guerrillas had wormed their way into the power structure of the villages and turned the *alcaldes* against the Union. Diego seldom went into the villages anymore—places where he had been born and raised—without wearing his Kevlar vest and carrying a weapon. This obvious mistrust turned many against him and the Union, but more than once a guerrilla sniper had almost taken his life.

José always claimed those were instances of Union soldiers turning against their oppressive military ruler, that he would never attack his brother in so cowardly a fashion. Diego knew better. José might not have ordered the assassination attempts, but he did nothing to punish them.

Diego believed his brother had loved him, but he had never respected his abilities as a military commander. And Viejo's contempt for his younger brother deepened when Diego refused to renounce his allegiance to the Union. What festered in Diego's soul was the worry that José might be right.

"Another guerrilla trick," Diego muttered. Find the enemy's weakness and exploit it. He still loved and even admired José, despite all that separated them now. It was foolish, but blood was blood.

He turned back to the map and studied the points where Viejo had attacked recently. Supply depots, from which he'd carried off ammo, explosives. In preparation for what?

Perhaps he would attack San Cristóbal because the fiber-optic cable that was the backbone of communications between north and south ran through the garrison? If José could cut off the Union's communications, he would have an enormous advantage. Or was he planning something even larger, something involving mutants and the deadly bioweapons the Neo-Sovs had supplied him?

Diego tipped his chair back, bracing himself against the wall and chewing on his lower lip as he thought. Viejo was a traditionalist in many ways. That tied him to the *campesinos*, who would never allow the Neo-Soviet mutant soldiers into their villages. More, Viejo couldn't use the twisted DNA disasters to full advantage in battle anyway. He had perfected guerrilla tactics, not the straightforward battlefield sweeps and counters the Neo-Sovs favored.

So, where would he be most likely to strike?

Diego's eyes drifted to a crease in the map, a spot where the disintegrating paper had almost deleted an entire town. He ran a hand over the yellowed sheet to smooth it out and noticed that the town blotted out was Revancha. There had been no CANDU reactor there when this map was first made, but there had been a town. Everything he'd been thinking and pondering suddenly came together, took shape, fitting together like the notches of well-honed gears.

"Here," he said softly. "Here is where you will attack, brother. Revancha. You want to seize the old CANDU reactor. With it, you become the one to give power to the countryside."

Diego considered what it would take to launch a guerrilla assault on the Canada Deuterium Uranium reactor. A major offensive, Viejo's most ambitious attack in three years and one designed to turn the people against the Union in several ways.

Showing that the Zapatista guerrillas were a force to be reckoned with might cut off the trickle of recruitment now enjoyed by the MCF. The increase in forced impressment that would follow would drive more *campesinos* into José's camp. If he kept a stranglehold on the reactor, Union-controlled towns in the region would be forced to find alternative power sources. With the heavy cloud layers seldom breaking apart over the jungle, solar power was more a fantasy than a workable scheme.

It was so obvious. José intended to seize the reactor, force the Union to fight to get it back. The CANDU used ordinary uranium, which would not contaminate the countryside too seriously should the pressure vessel be breached in the battle, but the *campesinos* were terrified of radioactivity. Viejo could play on that, blaming the Union for any contamination, turning even a defeat into a propaganda triumph.

If José managed somehow to hold Revancha against the Union, he could expand his influence quickly in many directions by distributing power to his supporters and denying it to his foes. The more Diego thought about it, the more he realized his brother had decided to step up from small acts of sabotage and pointless jungle skirmishes. The war had been fought that way for too long. Viejo wanted to win, and Revancha was the key.

So how could Diego stop him? A preemptive strike against Comitan would never work. José was safely garrisoned in the center of the city, shielded by Zapatista sympathizers. An attack there would result in an unacceptable amount of collateral damage—both from a propaganda standpoint and from Diego's own conscience.

He would have to defeat José even before he got there.

Diego knew that the Revancha garrison consisted of some of the best soldiers in his command, reflecting the key importance of the reactor. But Viejo could have attempted an attack there at any time. What made the reactor such an attractive target now?

The mutant soldiers, Diego decided. They had changed the odds, and made Diego think he could succeed in storming Revancha. Diego's mind spun through supply problems, getting the ag vehicles on the way with sufficient reinforcements, figuring out how to counterattack the guerrilla force. It was at this point in his thought process that Betty June Travis burst into the office.

He glanced up at his XO and saw that she looked distraught. It was unusual for her to be up at this hour of the night—early morning, Diego corrected himself. She enjoyed her rack time.

"Got a bad one, Colonel," BJ said without preamble. "Your brother's launched a major offensive."

"The reactor at Revancha?"

"No, not there. He hit the port of El Manguito."

"What?" Diego dropped the front legs of his chair to the floor and stood, bracing himself on stiffened arms above his map. El Manguito was fifty klicks along the Pacific coast from Puerto Madero. Could he have misjudged José's intentions so completely?

"He hit five minutes ago, using those damned Neo-Soviet mutations. The garrison was still asleep and didn't have time to respond."

"Didn't the alarms function?"

"Every last one of them," BJ said. "It didn't matter. The first wave of mutants came straight on, full frontal assault, no slowing. Just a flat-out attack."

"How many did he use?"

"The mutants? No idea. The battalion major was killed, and the chain of command is re-forming. No one's sure what's going on, other than we're getting our butts whipped good."

"Why El Manguito?" Diego murmured, shaking his head. It made no sense. The port was important, granted, but why would José endanger civilians in an attack that, even if successful, gave him only a marginal advantage? El Manguito was not a main supply depot, and even if it were destroyed, it would not significantly diminish the Union's fighting capabilities. It had to be another diversion, like the Cyclops attack south of his garrison. One way or the other, he again had no choice but to respond.

"Don't know," BJ said, "but the locals have their underwear in a knot over it, sir." She stood with her feet shoulder width apart, looking as stolid and immovable as a granite statue. "Let me take the reinforcements, sir. I need to get into the field again."

"The Ares suits," Diego said, coming to a speedy decision. "Commit the assault suits. Get Captain Allen out."

"No can do, sir."

"Haven't they cleaned them up yet?"

"It's not that. Well, not only that," BJ said. "Nobody's seen Allen in nearly forty-eight hours. He took a rifle, and the armory corporal thinks he lit out for the tall grass."

"He went into the jungle alone?" Diego had thought he was past being shocked by soldiers doing stupid things. He was wrong. Even the best scouts went into the jungle in pairs—and Allen was totally unfamiliar with the terrain. Ordinarily he would rejoice at the spy's absence, but not now—not when he needed every trained soldier he could get.

"Hasn't seen fit to come back, either. Can I put him down as AWOL?" BJ took great glee in the idea. She didn't like Allen any better than Diego did.

"No, don't. Our best course of action is to defend El Manguito and forget Allen even exists. If he's still alive, that is." Diego fumed at the man's stupidity. "What about the Ares suits?"

"When they popped Allen out of the Ares day before yesterday, they contaminated the entire bay. All the assault suits have that green slime on them."

"I was told that. But they still haven't decontaminated?" Diego was startled. His biowar officer had left him with the impression that the suits would soon be clean as whistles just a few hours ago.

"They tried everything, but the damned stuff keeps coming back. Radiation doesn't work, heat doesn't work, and they're trying acids now that damage what they're supposed to be cleaning."

"The Neo-Soviets aren't stupid. They wouldn't use a weapon they didn't have an antidote for. Or whatever you'd call it."

"It's probably a gengineered bioagent. Finding and concocting a counter for that witch's brew will take a spell," BJ said, her Texas drawl heightening as her emotions rose. "There's no time to get the suits into the field. We have to act now, sir."

"Or we lose a port city to the guerrillas," Diego finished for her. He kept thinking of Revancha, where the nuclear reactor quietly and efficiently churned out power for the countryside. He couldn't let go of the thought that it was José's primary target, but he couldn't allow his brother to destroy El Manguito either.

"Forget the suits, Lieutenant," he said, coming to a swift decision. "Take a dozen Hydras and two Aztecs. Stop the attack, kill as many of the mutations as you can, and *do not allow El Manguito to fall.*"

"Your orders are as clear and refreshing as spring rainwater, sir," BJ said, smiling widely. She hated garrison duty and was raring for the chance to get back into action.

"I want results, not to hand out a bunch of posthumous medals. No heroes. That includes you." He fixed her with a cold stare, knowing she was likely to be at the front of any counterattack. That was one of the things that made her such a good officer, an officer soldiers would follow into the worst battles imaginable without flinching.

"You'll get results, sir."

"Get your force organized," he said, "but wait a minute while I see how much backup I can give you." BJ began shouting orders into a small radio as Diego keyed into his secure link with command and control in Mexico City. He braced himself for yet another unpleasant conversation with his superiors. But at this point, getting more men was more important than any bruises to his ego.

At this time of night it took several minutes for the duty officer to respond, and when he did it was not cheerfully.

"This is Colonel Villalobos," Diego said. "I need support troops at El Manguito, at least a battalion. A major guerrilla assault is in progress, threatening the city. Mutant Neo-Soviet troops are being used."

"Have you been smoking hemp again, Colonel?" came

the insulting response. "The guerrillas do not attack cities. They are cowards who fight from ambush."

"I repeat," Diego said through gritted teeth, "El Manguito is under heavy attack and will fall if you do not authorize reinforcements. Both ground troops and aerial support are needed."

"Use your assault suits, Colonel," said the duty officer dismissively.

"They were taken out by the guerrillas," Diego said, beginning to lose his temper. "They have new weapons we are only beginning to encounter."

The duty officer snorted in contempt. "I cannot authorize such engagement, but I will place it before General Ramirez immediately."

"When can the forces arrive if he gives immediate approval?"

"Oh, it might be some time. There is the question of mission authorization, financial approval from the governor, and adequate supply for the troops. We do not want them stranded without food, water, and enough ammunition, should this prove to be a lengthy battle. Then there is the matter of mission statement, extraction contingencies, and many others you are well aware of, Colonel."

"This is of highest priority," snapped Diego. He felt as if time had run out—for him and for the entire region.

"I'm sure it is. Colonel Villalobos, Mexico City depends on you to maintain order in Chiapas. We're talking about a handful of underfed, undertrained guerrillas, after all. I'm certain that if the burden of command is too much for you, General Ramirez would be happy to send a replacement," the officer said sarcastically. "I will get back

to you soon." The secure link went dead before Diego had
a chance to respond.

"Well, that went worse than I had expected," he said
bitterly to BJ. If relations with Mexico City HQ were moving into such open hostility, his command—and his career—was in greater jeopardy than he had believed. But he
had no time to worry about that at the moment.

"Stop them, BJ," he said, staring at the map, his mind
racing through all the possibilities. "Stop the mutants dead
in their tracks. And take *Second Lieutenant* Baca with
you."

"Yes, *sir!*" Betty June Travis spun and ran from the office, still barking orders into her handheld.

Giving BJ the privilege of promoting Baca showed his
trust in her decisions and made her look good in her subordinates' eyes. That would make her even more determined. She would command a force sufficient to repel any
invasion Viejo was likely to mount, even one spearheaded
by mutant soldiers. She would have fifty percent of his
best-trained troopers. She would stop José.

Diego knew he dared not leave the San Cristóbal command post undefended. With fully half his forces going to
El Manguito, he had to defend the seat of his power. But he
couldn't stop looking at the torn spot on the map where
Revancha ought to be.

Even as BJ prepared to move out for El Manguito,
Diego began assembling his senior enlisted personnel for a
desperate gamble. He would move the remainder of his
troops to Revancha and leave San Cristóbal with only a
skeleton force.

If he was wrong and José attacked San Cristóbal,
Diego's court-martial would become the stuff of legend,

the tale of the foolish commander who fought on two fronts—both wrong. One mistake at this point, and Diego knew it would be the end of him.

But he also knew it was a risk he had to take.

13

13

José Villalobos smiled when he received the first reports of the attack at El Manguito. He had committed every one of the mutant creatures given him by the Neo-Soviets. This freed his full force of more than two hundred guerrillas for the real attack on the Revancha CANDU nuclear reactor.

This time he had sent two eager young soldiers to deploy the mutants instead of Consuela. The chore was simple, after all; once pointed in the direction of the enemy garrison, the Cyclops would continue to attack until the Union soldiers were killed or the mutants were blown apart.

Either outcome suited José.

If his foolish brother remained occupied with other concerns—like the port of El Manguito or hiding with his men in the garrison at San Cristóbal—the Zapatistas would soon be triumphant. The Union would never pry the guerrillas loose once they gained a foothold in the cities. Taking control of the power supply from Revancha was the key in the lock.

Now all he had to do was turn that key.

"Consuela," he greeted, pleased to see her as she hurried up. "Have you heard the news?"

"Of the El Manguito attack, yes," she said, breathless. She hunkered down beside him. "But José, I must speak with you about the monster from the pit."

"So?" José said without interest. He could not be bothered with such things, not when he had to concentrate his full attention on the Revancha campaign. It marked the crossroads of his efforts against the Union. Win, and he would be able to build legitimate political power—a presence powerful enough to make even the Union think twice about eliminating him.

True power would be his, buoyed by the people themselves. Then he could see that their lives would change for the better. No more oppressive taxes, no MCF recruitment—only cooperative effort to live and prosper.

What was one monster, measured against all that?

"José!" Consuela said angrily. "Pay attention. This is important."

"So is the attack on the nuclear power plant," he retorted.

"We might not live to enjoy our victory if we do not deal with this monster," Consuela said earnestly.

José had learned to listen to her—she had often saved him terrible losses—but her obsession with this creature worried him. She seemed to have lost all perspective. Instead of staying focused on their true enemy—the Union—she was concerned about this thing, whatever it was.

He needed Consuela's considerable combat skills more than ever. Failure was not an option in the Revancha campaign, but if she continued to be distracted by this beast, José wondered if he could win. He did not doubt the creature's existence—since the Change, he had seen enough peculiar sights that he now disbelieved nothing, on principle. But this was one being. The Union forces numbered in the hundreds. Which was the greater threat?

"What should we do?" José asked her impatiently. "Abandon the attack to hunt down this crystal beast? Undo all the plans we have laid so carefully these past months?"

"We must do *something*," Consuela insisted. "Have you not heard about the attack on La Presa yesterday?"

José sighed. "Yes, I heard about the attack. All in the village were killed, torn to pieces."

"Then you know I am not exaggerating about this monster! About what it can do!"

"Consuela," he said patiently, "we have no way of knowing what killed the people at La Presa. There was no one left alive to reveal the truth to us. You know the Union soldiers have struck out in anger in the past. They torture, they maim, they kill wantonly. The true monsters wear Union MCF insignia. And the sooner we seize the power plant, the sooner we can be rid of them."

"José, I—"

"Consuela, please." He sought the right words to calm her and found nothing that might sway her from her purpose. He simply could not be distracted from Revancha. The war could be won, but not by going in different directions. Force the Union to split their forces, concentrate his. In that lay victory.

"We march for Revancha," he said decisively, almost daring her to object. Then he threw her a small concession.

"As soon as we have tightened our grip on the power plant—as soon as our battle there is won—we personally will lead a force to hunt down and destroy this creature. But surely you see that we cannot afford to divide our forces now—not when we are so close to our goal."

Consuela started to protest again, but then stopped and nodded slowly. "I do see that," she said, her voice wretched. "You are right—if we falter now, we risk losing all. But I tell you, the monster is the greater threat. And I worry that the longer we delay, the worse the danger to our people."

"Then we had better get moving," José said, hefting his rifle. "The sooner we have captured Revancha, the sooner we can destroy this monster of yours."

Consuela nodded, her mouth set in a grim line. "I am with you," she said. "As always. But I pray we are not making the biggest mistake of our lives."

"This is the correct path," José assured her.

He rose from his squatting position and let out a soft whistle. From out of the jungle the other guerrillas came, seeming to appear from thin air. All were weighed down with the matériel Flaco had so painstakingly assembled over the past few months: rifles, grenades, extra clips of ammunition. He could tell they were nervous, but not panicky. Even that had been part of José's plan. The raids they'd been carrying out over past few months had won them arms and ammunition. They had also boosted the guerrillas' confidence, all in preparation for this final strike.

José felt no need to make one last speech. They were ready—he could see it in their eyes, in their stance, in the way they clutched their weapons to them. Instead, he moved quietly through them, meeting one's eyes for a brief second, clapping another on the shoulder, trying by his presence and his touch to instill in them some of his confidence in their mission. Mary Stephenson shook his hand warmly, her petite features as calm as ever before heading into battle. Flaco gave him a gap-toothed grin. Even Gunther accorded him a grim smile, his hostility briefly suspended in anticipation of the coming bloodshed.

When he had finished circulating through his troops, José turned and surveyed them one more time, and then nodded. As one, they melted back into the jungle, breaking into squads and heading toward the reactor exactly as he had planned.

José watched them go with pride and turned to Consuela, as always, by his side.

"To Revancha?" he asked.

"Revancha," she said, and if doubt and worry still shadowed her eyes, she gave no outward sign of it as they moved off through the jungle toward victory.

14

The Death Priest lay in wait on the night-cloaked trail, the primitives unaware that they were coming directly toward him. Fewer of them ventured into the jungle at night, but his chances of detection were greatly diminished in the darkness.

The pair of natives were almost upon him when he stepped out of the greenery surrounding the crude path and revealed himself, his metallic armor making soft clicking sounds as he moved. He was accustomed by now to the primitives' response: blind terror, followed by a pathetic attempt to flee. But instead of panicking, these two launched an attack so fierce it startled the priest. The one in the lead whipped up a projectile weapon and fired, the bullet hitting the solar focusing device just above the Death Priest's bandage-wrapped head.

The impact knocked him about but did no real damage. As he spun with the impact of the bullet, he activated his phase generator. Winking in and out of sight, he darted toward the native, who was still firing blindly, confused by his adversary's disappearance.

The priest dodged to the left and attacked from the flank, knocking the rifle from the native's hands, then expertly used a stun-rod. Greenish electronic haze formed around the tip of the dual-electrode weapon before leaping forth to engulf the victim. The primitive shrieked, stiffened, and toppled rigidly, every muscle frozen and the neurons of his brain permanently burned out.

The Death Priest swiftly changed his angle of attack and struck the other native with one powerful blow of his fist. The female crashed to the ground and lay unmoving. Leaving the first primitive where it fell, the priest stared down at his most recent capture. He and the Slayer had worked assiduously to capture natives singly and in pairs. Twice they had tackled entire columns of well-armed creatures. Every attack had been as successful as this one. He had quickly learned these creatures' weaknesses, and their enslavements grew increasingly efficient.

The priest retrieved two life-support packs from his cache beside the trail, setting one on the ground beside each native. He knelt, and was rapidly lost in ceremony, his mind reaching out to the unconscious native. As before, he found no resistance as his mental tendrils insinuated themselves into the woman's mind and found the proper limbic regions to bring under his aegis. Prayers were recited. Invocations to the God-king's puissant presence were made. The female native's brain was imprinted with the need to obey the Death Priest in all things. He had recruited a new worker for the greater good of the Pharon.

As the Death Priest fitted on the life-support unit, the woman feebly began to stir. Leaving her to regain her bearings and balance, he turned his attention to the other one, the one he had brought down with the neural weapon.

This slave proved even easier to instruct.

Once both were on their feet, the priest ordered them to follow him down the trail. Their progress was slow at first, as the slaves adjusted to their new existence, but gradually they became steadier on their feet, and their pace quickened. The priest was pleased with their progress. He and the Slayer had recruited no fewer than twenty slaves for the repair work on the ship; the Slayer was there now, supervising their work. The Shard had abandoned the crater where the Vor-stuff had landed, leaving the priest free to claim the errant bit of the Vorack for his own.

And for the God-king's glory!

By now, the Slayer was undoubtedly close to finishing his final preparation of the ship's hold; that was the priest's primary concern. The interior of the hold was lined with a force field that the priest was confident would be able to contain the power of the energetic mote. The field had been in place for days, ever since the Pharon had first detected the mote speeding through space. The crash landing on the planet had slightly damaged the field's equipment, but the hold was in the best-protected part of the ship and damage was minimal.

The battle with the Shard that had sent the mote hurtling down to the surface of this forsaken planet might have temporarily delayed the priest in his quest, but he was close to victory. He could feel it. All that remained was for him to transport the Vorack-stuff back to the ship, oversee final repairs to the vessel, and depart.

"Halt," he ordered the slaves as the three of them emerged from the jungle into the blasted clearing surrounding the Vor-stuff's crater. A half dozen slaves were already hard at work digging a sloping tunnel down to the bottom of the pit to make it easier raising the mote to the surface. The bodies of another half dozen lay scattered around the edge of the crater, their corpses twisted and blackened by the fierce radiation blasting from the virulent globe at its bottom. Their work was illuminated by the glow from the pit, bright enough to see even in the predawn darkness.

The Pharon wished there were some way of shielding the slaves from the lethal radiance—it was so inefficient having to replace them so often!—but he had no time to jury-rig any sort of protective shielding. He had taken readings of the radiation blasting from the pit; the mote was sending out rays a thousand times more powerful than they had been able to detect in space. The Pharon suspected that the protective globe around the mote had cracked during its violent landing. The enormous power contained within was leaking out, bathing anything nearby in a lethal dose of radiation.

The danger lent the priest an extra impetus to finish his work quickly. He had no idea how extensive the damage to the globe was—it could be so fragile that it would crumble at any time. Once the mote was safely in *Destroyer*'s hold, the danger was over. Until then, it was a menace to every living thing on the world—including the Pharon. If the globe broke completely, the resulting power surge could easily destroy the planet, and the Pharon did not intend for that to happen while he was on it.

He sighed as a slave emerged from the tunnel, dragging the twisted remains of another one that had succumbed to the power of the Vorack. He motioned the replacements forward. At this rate, he would have to acquire dozens more—which meant attacking a larger settlement and perhaps bringing unwanted attention to his activities or finding a large supply of freshly killed corpses. Alive, dead—it made no difference to the Pharon. Either way, the lesser beings served the God-king.

The Death Priest left his slaves hard at work and headed back out into the jungle. The tunnel to the bottom of the crater was almost complete. It was time to check with the Slayer on how the repairs were progressing. Then he would see about locating a supply of slaves to transport the mote back to the ship. A large supply.

15

"On the road to glory, sir!" radioed BJ Travis, obviously eager to see action again.

Standing just inside the gate of the San Cristóbal compound, Diego Villalobos checked her progress on his portable display, estimated Hydra transport speed and distance, and saw that she would arrive at El Manguito within the hour. This was as swift a response as he could muster to meet the threat of the attacking Neo-Sov mutants. His latest reports from the officer in charge of the post there had heartened him. The mutants had killed several ranking officers, but the junior officers had rallied quickly and forced the Cyclops back beyond the post's defensive perimeter. They would hold out until BJ arrived to catch the Cyclops between the El Manguito post and her larger, well-armed mobile force.

"Sergeant Suarez, front and center!" Diego called. The sergeant hurried across the command compound and tossed him a salute. Diego considered how desperate his scheme was, how fraught with danger, how much he risked if he'd guessed wrong on any element of it. His career would be destroyed, and many lives would be lost.

"You feeling lucky today, Sergeant?" Diego asked Suarez.

"No, sir. I don't believe in luck."

"Good. I like a man who depends on skill. That's what is needed in a new second lieutenant."

"Sir?" Suarez frowned, not understanding.

"You just got promoted. And your first assignment is going to be hellacious."

"You want me to support Lieutenant Travis, sir?"

"No. I'm placing you in command of the garrison."

"Where, sir? El Manguito?"

Diego heaved a sigh. To him everything was crystal-clear. It wasn't to his subordinates, however, because he dared not share too much with any of them. The last mutiny in Union ranks had been years ago, in Cuernavaca, but that did not mean it couldn't happen again. "San Cristóbal," Diego said matter-of-factly. "You are the officer in charge here while I'm in the field."

"You're going to back up Lieutenant Travis, sir?"

"I'm going to reinforce the garrison at Revancha, because that's where the Zapatistas are going to launch their next attack." Behind Sergeant Suarez—Lieutenant Suarez—Diego saw the remaining vehicles assembling. He had to rely on the broken-down Pegasus ag transports, the ones named Coffin Wagons by his troops because they were so easily ambushed. With luck, they wouldn't encounter any guerrillas in the jungle, because the guerrillas would all be assembling to attack the reactor at Revancha.

With luck.

"How many troops are you taking, sir? It looks like most of them."

"That's right, Lieutenant. Most of them. You'll have twenty soldiers to defend our honor here."

"Twenty?" Suarez asked with disbelief. "I couldn't hold back a blind leprous beggar if he got cranky, not with only twenty soldiers. Sir."

Diego almost laughed. Suarez sounded like BJ. But this was deadly serious.

"We've got no choice, Lieutenant," Diego said. "Revancha is too important to risk losing it to guerrillas. I've got to head out right away if I'm going to reach Revancha in time. I've radioed the garrison commander and alerted him. If I'm right, the Zapatistas will hit the nuclear reactor just at dawn." Diego glanced at his chronometer. "That's in two hours, so I have to make good time. Any questions, Lieutenant?"

"Uh, I don't know, sir. This is all happening so fast."

"Work on it. If you have any big problems within the next hour, contact me. After that I'm going to full comm silence. We can't risk the guerrillas intercepting our communications. It's crucial that our arrival at Revancha be a surprise."

"What if someone from HQ wants to talk to you?"

"Make up something," Diego said brusquely. He put his hand on Suarez's shoulder. "You've got what it takes, Lieutenant. Make me proud. Make everyone in your family and village proud."

"Sir, yes, sir!" Suarez snapped the best military salute Diego had seen in weeks. He returned it and climbed into the Pegasus transport he intended to use as his command center. It took several minutes for him to interface his battlefield display unit with the Pegasus's circuitry, then he issued orders on a scrambled, encrypted band even as he felt the ag lifters begin to quiver. The Pegasus cleared ground, and the column moved out toward Revancha.

Toward Revancha—and destiny.

16

Alex Allen struggled back to the empty road leading to the front gate at San Cristóbal just as the Maw was breaking the eastern horizon. How he had lost his GPS was a mystery. He was always careful with military-issue gear he might have to pay for if lost. It must have fallen out of his belt pouch during the battle at the meteor crater. Explaining to Diego Villalobos how he had wandered around in the jungle for almost two days was going to take some doing. The colonel ought to give him a medal for surviving in such a terrible environment. He was trained for the icefields of Alaska, not the jungles of Chiapas, yet he'd survived on a single liter of water, avoiding guerrilla patrols and the terrifying creature he had seen at the bottom of the pit.

Allen frowned, remembering his meeting with Consuela. It had almost seemed that she'd wanted him to encounter the pit-thing, as if she already knew of its deadly existence. He couldn't shake the thought even though he knew it was absurd. She was merely a simple peasant he had rescued. For *that* he ought to get a commendation. After all, wasn't it the stated goal of the Mexican Contribution Force to give aid and assistance to the natives?

Feet sore and muscles aching, Allen finally reached the gate. He was surprised to see no sentries in the guardhouse on either side of the gate. What was this? A ghost town?

He jumped when a loudspeaker blared, "Recognition code!"

"This is Captain Alex Allen, and I've returned to report to the colonel on a recon mission. I don't know what the daily recognition code is. I've been gone almost two days."

There was a lengthy pause, and then, "ID verified. You may enter, Captain."

"I should hope so," Allen said testily. The gate unlocked. He stepped through, then it closed and locked behind him automatically. His mouth dropped open when he saw the empty garrison. Ghost town described it perfectly.

He wondered what had happened for Villalobos to move out so many of his soldiers, leaving his command post bare. If some crisis had occurred during his absence, it might reflect badly on him, unless he revealed all of what he had seen at the strange impact crater. Allen didn't really want to do that. Villalobos might steal his discovery to win some points finally with the MCF and Union brass.

Allen fumed, but there was nothing he could do. Before he could get to the object in the crater, he would have to take care of the whatever-it-was rampaging at the bottom of it. He had seen how useless standard armaments were against it; he didn't think anything short of a SPEAR missile could take it out. And, unfortunately, the only person who had the launch codes for the post's missiles was its commanding officer: Colonel Diego Villalobos.

Allen decided he'd first check out what Diego had done, then worry about forking over what he'd found. He hefted the rucksack holding the portion of the alien creature he had killed. Or almost killed. Even after hitting it with his rifle, stomping on it, and sealing it in an airtight bottle, he wasn't sure the crystalline tendril was dead. He swung the rucksack off his shoulder and peered inside.

The piece did not need air. That much was obvious, since it still fitfully kicked about inside the plastic bottle. As he watched, the tendril sprouted spikes that tentatively probed at the sides of the bottle, testing its strength. The faster he got it away from him, the happier he'd be. It was alien in a way he couldn't even begin to define, which made him profoundly uneasy.

"Hey, Cap'n!" came a shout. Allen looked up from his rucksack to see a private waving at him from across the compound. "You better get your butt on up to the colonel's office. The boss wants to see you *yesterday!*"

Allen growled at an enlisted man daring to speak so informally to him, then hurried up the stairs to Villalobos's second-floor office in the sprawling command and control building. The door to the colonel's office stood partially open. Allen sidled closer and eavesdropped for a moment, just to be on the safe side. Then he knocked boldly.

"Come!"

Allen breezed in past the vacant orderly's desk to the colonel's office, trying to look confident. Victory through arrogance. But all of Allen's simulated brashness died when he saw a sergeant sitting behind the colonel's desk, just as if he were in charge.

"Where's Villalobos?" Allen demanded.

Suarez looked up. "Where have you been, Captain? Things have been jumping here."

"Sergeant, I—"

"Lieutenant."

"*Lieutenant*," Allen said sarcastically. "Brief me on what's happened." Allen listened in dismay as Suarez told him about their split forces, half under Travis going to defend El Manguito and the other half with Villalobos at Revancha.

"The man's crazy!" Allen exclaimed. "He can't leave San Cristóbal undefended like this. How many troops on post?"

"Counting you, sir? Twenty-one."

"It's a good thing I returned when I did. Contact Villalobos immediately."

"Sorry, sir, he ordered complete comm blackout."

"I need to assemble all the officers for an immediate appraisal if I am going to properly command. I—"

"Sir," Suarez interrupted firmly. "Technically you are not my superior officer. You are an observer, not a member of the colonel's staff. Colonel Villalobos placed me in charge. I command here."

"I outrank you, Sergeant," Allen snapped. "Even if your claim to be a second lieutenant is valid, I still outrank you."

"You are on TDY while at this post and out of the chain of command," Suarez said, his expression darkening and his tone increasingly less polite. "Colonel Villalobos was wondering whether you had gone AWOL, since you did not formally report back to him as ordered. When I heard you had finally shown up, I sent word for you to come here. To *my* office."

"I was on a secret mission for Villalobos," Allen lied. "He would not take a lieutenant—let alone a sergeant—into his confidence about such an important mission."

He swung his rucksack off his shoulder and opened the top. He had hoped to avoid revealing his discovery, but it was clear that the time had come to play his trump card. Gingerly, he grasped the bottle containing the glass snake by its edges and set it on Villalobos's desk.

Suarez stood up from behind the desk and went pale. "What the hell is that?"

"*That* is what the colonel sent me to find," Allen said. Both men edged slightly away from the desk as another questing tendril from the snake rocked the bottle. "We need to get it into quarantine as quickly as possible. We don't yet know what its capabilities are."

Suarez reached for the comm unit at the side of Villalobos's desk but yanked his hand back as a fresh attack from a tendril tilted the bottle even closer to him. He pushed his chair back and edged carefully around the desk.

"Wait here," Suarez said. "I'll go get the biotechs to put that thing in isolation." He hurried from the room, and Allen could hear him shouting orders all the way down the stairs.

As soon as he was out of sight, Allen snatched his rucksack, pulled it over the furiously rocking bottle, and scooped it up, dexterously pulling the top closed without ever touching the crystal's prison. He carefully laid the bag on the floor and darted around to the other side of the desk, where he found the encryption code for the day and contacted the duty officer in Mexico City.

"Who am I speaking to?" Allen demanded.

"Major Ortiz, if it is of any importance to one so rude."

"Sorry, Major," Allen said insincerely. "This is Captain Alex Allen at San Cristóbal. I was sent here at General Ramirez's request, and I need to speak to him right away. Emergency."

"Does this have anything to do with that tedious problem at El Manguito? Where is Colonel Villalobos?"

"The colonel has abandoned San Cristóbal, sir," Allen said, his voice oozing concern. "He left a staff sergeant in command."

"You are joking."

"Afraid not," Allen replied, keeping a wary eye on the door. This was taking too long, and he was afraid Suarez might return too soon. "Let me speak to General Ramirez."

"One moment." The comm unit hummed, and then a deeper, more authoritative voice echoed from the speaker.

"General Ramirez here. What is this about Villalobos going AWOL?"

"This is Captain Alex Allen, TDY from Union HQ. I went on a scouting patrol into the jungle, and when I returned, Villalobos had left for Revancha."

"And you say a sergeant is in command?"

"Sergeant Suarez," Allen said. "Villalobos took all the soldiers, leaving San Cristóbal with only twenty men. Twenty-one, counting me now."

"We have reports from El Manguito of the mutant attack," Ramirez said. "Villalobos had no reason to have sent reinforcements. The garrison commander has the situation in hand. But you say he went to Revancha?"

"That's what the sergeant said, sir. What are your orders?"

"I'll have Villalobos's ears on a plate for this," Ramirez said. "He's deserted his post. No excuse for that. *You* are in command, Captain. If Villalobos returns, have him call me immediately, and I will repeat this order for him. Then you can clap him into the guardhouse!"

"Yes, sir, understood," Allen said. "*If* he returns." Allen clicked off the comm unit and turned to face an infuriated Suarez, who had burst back into the room during his final exchange, followed by two biotechs.

"I trust the general's orders were clear," Allen said, smiling. "There should be no more questions about the chain of command, I think?"

Suarez swallowed his fury with difficulty and spoke through clenched teeth. "What are your orders? Sir."

"First, get that thing down to an isolation chamber," Allen said, pointing at the rucksack on the floor. Suarez moved aside so the two technicians could get at Allen's find. "Then get me some maps of the region. We may have a bigger problem on our hands than a few poorly trained guerrillas, and I need to decide what to do about it."

As Suarez left, every step radiating rage, Allen sat down in Villalobos's chair and put his feet up on Villalobos's desk.

This had worked out even better than he could have hoped. Villalobos was gone, he was in command of the garrison, and he now had access to the missile-launch codes. As soon as he planned his best avenue of attack, the meteorite in the jungle would be his. Promotions and fame would follow.

Perhaps he should get lost in the jungle more often.

17

D awn. Time to attack Revancha.

José Villalobos touched the contact stud on his radio, then pulled back. The Union had too much electronic equipment monitoring all frequencies for any trace of guerrilla activity. This raid was too important to risk them intercepting his orders. He instead lifted his hand high over his head and squeezed it into a fist, signaling Flaco and Gunther on his right and Mary on his left that they were to advance. Consuela moved like a shadow among the remaining soldiers, readying them for a frontal assault on Revancha—for the freedom of their families and villages.

José had decided to carry out the attack in waves, which would shake up the Union resistance and give him the best chance of capturing the reactor. Now it was time for Consuela to inspire the guerrillas not only to fight but also to obey orders.

Too many were angry men and women who wanted only immediate revenge for the deaths of loved ones. Attack. They understood that. But to attack with purpose and retreat to lure the enemy into a trap? That required more faith on their part, even after they had seen it work repeatedly. But the one who concerned him most was Consuela. She had been strangely silent after their last talk about whether to chase down the monster rather than attacking Revancha. José suspected that her mind was still on the frightening creature she had reported seeing.

Until this week José's attacks had been typical of guerrilla action everywhere it had ever occurred. Attack and raid, harass and demoralize, then vanish back into the jungle, protected always by sympathizers in the towns and villages. Now, two entire patrols had been lost. It was a sign, a signal that it was time to become a soldier, not a guerrilla.

"Death to the Union oppressors," José said, loud enough for Consuela to overhear. She smiled weakly and gave him a more reassuring wink. The words rippled through their ranks, and the attack began.

José and Consuela took point, their squads ranging behind them as they moved out of the jungle toward the high chain-link fence surrounding the CANDU reactor. Dotting the knee-high grass were the round, machined-aluminum sensor heads designed to alert the guards of any attack.

José glanced at his watch. Gunther's squad should have engaged the Union guards at the front gate by now, drawing forces away from this section.

"Cut the fence," he ordered.

Consuela dropped to her knees and began using a laser cutter. The beam sizzled through several tough metal links before it hit a live wire, causing an explosion that knocked her back into the grass.

José instantly scooped up the laser cutter Consuela had dropped and began slashing furiously at the fence. He hit another live wire that delivered a jolt strong enough to jar his teeth. When he pulled back, dazed, another of his men took the cutter from his hands and finished the job. José knew that cutting the live wires in the fence would have triggered an alarm circuit. Speed was now of the essence.

"We did not know about this," he said quietly to Consuela, hands shaking in reaction to the electric charge that had scrambled his nerves. José gripped his Kalashnikov tightly to keep his temporary infirmity from being too apparent to the others.

"No," she said, "but we must expect more traps. At least we took out the sensor heads in the field to keep the enemy from tracking our movements." She gestured behind them, and José saw that while he had battled with the fence, his troops had systematically blown up the warning system. He had not authorized this—it wasted precious grenades and drew attention—but he wouldn't chastise Consuela for showing initiative. By now the soldiers inside the facility already knew they were under attack. They would defend the central building containing the reactor while broadcasting frantically for help from Diego.

Which he would be unable to provide, thanks to the Cyclops attack on El Manguito. José had found a use for the hideous mutations the Neo-Soviets had sent him: diversion. Let the abominations be chewed up and destroyed.

The first guerrillas through the hole in the fence started across the dirt perimeter of the compound. One of them stepped on an ordinary-looking patch of ground and was torn in half by an explosion that also caught two of his comrades. Land mine!

"Stop!" cried José. His remaining soldiers froze in place, staring at the carnage just within the fence. "Who has the map of the interior?"

"Here," Consuela said, handing it to him and squatting down next to him on the ground. He spread it out. The locations of mines had been marked with small red Xs.

"This area is not supposed to be mined," he said. "How long ago was this map stolen?"

"Last week," Consuela answered. "I—" She had to put out an arm to catch herself when another mine exploded fifty meters away.

"The mines must be remotely detonated," José said. "They put them here, expecting an attack!" If he had a traitor in his ranks, it hardly mattered now. It was too late to turn back—had been too late almost from the start. Even if they were expected, the guerrillas would do what they came for.

"Find their observers," he ordered. "Remove them!"

The soldiers fanned out doing what they did best. They melted into the landscape, and even José was hard-pressed to spot the guerrillas as they moved forward. They might stand out to IR equipment, especially if they fired their rifles, but they moved too quickly for detection to matter.

He hoped.

"Come on!" he cried, rushing forward. José wished now that he'd launched the attack before dawn, using the cover of darkness as an ally, infrared detectors or no. As he went, he tossed out IR flares, invisible to the eye but a burning, blinding spot to any electro-optical sensor. Confuse, then move in for the kill. It was all they could do against a superior force.

Sporadic firing told him his troops had found the Union observers. That they were on duty so early was one more sign of a traitor in his ranks. Or could Diego actually have guessed that Revancha was the real target? Had José grown so obvious that even Diego could anticipate his next move?

The garrison could not stay on alert endlessly. Its soldiers would tire and make mistakes after a day or two of back-to-back shifts. That meant Diego must have issued the orders only recently—probably with incentives of money, whiskey, and *campesino* women—to coincide with the El Manguito attack.

"He is smarter than I thought, my little brother," José murmured to himself.

"What did you say?" asked Consuela, dropping to one knee. She lifted her Kalashnikov, then squeezed off a three-round burst that took out an enemy soldier advancing on them.

"Nothing. They are coming out of their holes. Fight, *chica*, fight!"

José took his own advice without waiting for a response. The garrison commander risked much by sending his troops out to meet the guerrillas head-on. He might feel confident on his own territory, territory mined and waiting to kill unwary invaders, but he was wrong. José and his force now controlled the exterior of the CANDU.

"Report," he snapped into his radio. Now that their advantage of surprise was blown, maintaining radio silence no longer mattered. He had to know how the fight went elsewhere.

"No resistance," came Gunther's surprising report. "They drew back when we opened fire. We're inside the main gates."

"Watch out for mines, both remotely detonated and contact. They've been blocking our way over here. The Union soldiers are coming out to engage us directly," José said.

"Affirm—" Gunther's voice was cut off and lost in a haze of static as José's radio went dead. An alert Union comm officer must have sent out a high-powered burst that fried the radio's chips. Listening in might give some small tactical advantage, but removing the enemy's ability to communicate gave the greater edge to the defenders.

José tossed away the now-worthless radio unit. The Neo-Soviets knew nothing about building such devices anyway. He needed to steal a good Union-made one, with variable encryption and microburst capability.

He hit the ground at the corner of a warehouse near the reactor, skidded on his belly, and brought up his rifle. Meeting with no resistance, he pulled a grenade from his belt, triggered it, and tossed it through the open door of the warehouse. The resulting explosion a few seconds later was strong enough to take out any Union personnel lurking inside. The building would serve well as a staging and assault point for the final push toward the central reactor building. Consuela went in first, and José followed with a half dozen freedom fighters.

"Empty," Consuela said, looking around in confusion. "The entire warehouse is empty."

Her words echoed in the cavernous space, ordinarily piled with equipment and supplies. Despite the enemy's hasty withdrawal from the building, they had taken every piece of important equipment. It must have been well planned. Diego *had* warned his force at Revancha.

"They suspected we would attack and prepared for it," José said urgently. "To the reactor building. Quickly, or we will lose all chance of taking it!"

Nervous, but still determined, José's men formed up behind him as he ran for the back door of the warehouse, closest to the reactor. He had just reached it, Consuela close on his heels, when all hell broke loose.

Diego Villalobos leaned forward, studying the green ghost-spots darting across his battlefield display. He sucked in a breath and let it out, thumbed his comm unit, and said, "The guerrillas are at the outer fence. Prepare for assault. Repeat, all units prepare for assault."

The Pegasus whined, lifted, and shot forward. Diego had halted his forces almost a kilometer outside Revancha to keep from spooking José. The plan had worked. Just as he'd guessed, the guerrillas had struck with a shock squad hitting the front gate to pull Union defenders away from the back fence. Diego watched as the guerrillas rushed across the road he had ordered mined. Some died—not many, but enough to slow the attack.

The Pegasus kicked into high-speed approach. Diego saw the dots begin to merge on his screen and shifted to less detail on a larger area display. Two squads of guerrillas had taken cover in the warehouse he'd ordered abandoned.

"Major Hinojosa," Diego called over the comm to the Revancha commander. "Warehouse is occupied."

"Blow it, sir?"

"Blow it!"

The center of Diego's battle display blossomed with

the intense heat of detonating bombs. Any guerrilla in the warehouse was far past caring about the reactor now. He wondered with a brief pang if José had been caught in the blast. It was the position he would have taken, were he leading the guerrilla attack. Then Diego concentrated more on the ebb and flow of battle on other fronts. The guerrillas coming in the front gate fought like maniacs.

"Driver, get us around to the front gates. Trap the Zapatistas between the Revancha defenders and our guns." He extended one hand to brace himself as the Pegasus swung about and raced for the worst of the fighting. Diego felt the need to get into battle again.

He did not find the battle. It found him.

An RPG blasted out the side of the poorly armored Pegasus, sending it slewing to one side. Diego grabbed his Bulldog rifle and bailed out, hitting the ground and rolling until he could find a target. He squeezed off a round and took down a guerrilla. Then the survivors from his Pegasus added their fire to that of another Union squad.

He ordered his soldiers forward, squeezing the guerrillas between two deadly barrages.

"Sir, a few are escaping along the fence line," one of his men reported.

"Let them go," Diego said. "Attention, everyone, we're going to squash the guerrillas near the reactor the same way we did these. Take out as many as you can, but do not pursue. I repeat, do not pursue. We're here to defend the reactor."

Diego joined with the lieutenant commanding the company at the front gate. Together, with a force of more than fifty soldiers, they ran through the reactor complex toward the central building. Lacking his battle display, Diego almost overran the fighting. The guerrillas had been caught just short of the reactor.

"Stop them. The ones with the explosives," he shouted. He fired full-auto at a trio of Zapatistas trying to plant a bomb on the external wall of the reactor-pressure vessel. It was thick 401 stainless steel, and he doubted they could breach it, but why take a chance?

Shooting the three was an easy task for a full rifle company.

"Report," he demanded into his comm unit. "Where's the worst of the fighting?"

"At the reactor, sir," came Major Hinojosa's triumphant voice. "We've got 'em on the run everywhere else."

"Clean up the stragglers, Major, then swing around and form another line behind my position. That will trap the Zapatistas within two lines of our soldiers."

Diego worked harder to get his troops into position. He was glad that they had fought against the Cyclops, even with their severe losses. It had made them more confident going against mere humans—and turned the ground around the reactor into a killing field.

"Got the surviving Zapatistas cornered at the northeast corner of the reactor," Diego reported. "Not more than thirty or forty of them left. Everyone, check your charge levels, reload, and get ready. We're going in for the kill. No quarter, unless they surrender!"

Diego Villalobos slammed a new clip into his Bulldog, loaded a grenade in the launcher, then gave the order to attack.

"They're everywhere," Mary Stephenson said, injured and propped up against several fuel barrels—the only cover they had been able to find. "We got rat-trapped good and proper, José."

"You don't need to tell me." José was sick. He had barely escaped the warehouse before it blew. Nearly all of his men had been killed in the blast. Flaco had been shot dead in front of him by a Union rifle. He had lost contact with Gunther but recognized a few of his men struggling to reach the jungle and get away. Mary was severely wounded and unable to walk on her own. Consuela was covered in blood, most of it her own, and he had too many minor wounds to count. They had come close, very close, to the reactor—but not close enough. And now any chance they had had of capturing it was drifting away in the wind.

"They are closing in on us, like a noose about our necks." José took a deep breath and forced himself to calm down. He recognized some of the Union soldiers advancing on them as belonging to Diego's personal squad. Underestimating his younger brother had proved disastrous. Now it was time to salvage what he could.

"Can we at least get to the reactor and disable it?" The disheartened looks he got told him that road was closed. "What of the rail guns?"

"One left. Four RPGs with grenades," Consuela said.

José came to a swift decision. This was no time to be faint of heart. Diego would have him in a flash if he hesitated, and his capture would doom the Zapatista movement. The Consulta would be disbanded and hope for independence in Chiapas gone.

"Use the rail gun to take out a segment of the attackers directly north of us," he ordered. "Fire fast and fire often. Those of you with the RPGs, run for the jungle the instant you see the way open up. Then, from the jungle, use your grenades to cover the rest of us."

José reached over and squeezed Consuela's hand. "Only a few of us will escape, *chica*. I am sorry for this."

"No victory without daring," she said, smiling back at him with an effort.

The rail gun began spewing depleted-uranium ingots through the Union line. The wave of advancing Mexican Contribution Force soldiers rippled and fell back, giving the four Zapatistas with the RPGs their opening. The supporting fire José and the others laid down held open the narrow path to escape.

"Now, go, *chica*, go. Direct the RPG fire."

"José, you can't stay behind. You—"

"Consuela, go!" He shoved her in the direction of the jungle that had shielded them so admirably over the years. She ran, head down, while he fired his Kalashnikov into the Union ranks to cover her retreat. He turned to Mary, bent, and started to pick her up. Her legs were too damaged to walk.

"Don't be a fool, José," she gasped, swatting him away. "Go on. I'll keep 'em off your neck. Just promise me one thing. They beat us today. Don't let them win the final battle!"

"Mary," he said, putting his grimy hand to her equally grimy, bloody cheek. "With a dozen more like you, we would have won long ago."

She yanked the Kalashnikov from his hands, wiggled around, and started firing both her own rifle and his. José knew it was time to go. He followed the others, vaulting over those who had fallen, feeling the hot sting of lead singing past him. He had almost reached the cover of the jungle when the lower-pitched sound of Mary's Kalashnikov, easily discernible over the higher-pitched Pitbulls, fell silent. Just short of the protective greenery, José paused and looked back.

And locked eyes with his brother. Diego was standing near the barrels where José had so recently been crouched, his rifle raised and pointed in José's direction. Even at this distance, José could see him hesitate, then lower the gun. The two stared at each other a moment longer, and then José turned and dived into the safety of the jungle.

The four guerrillas with RPGs, under Consuela's able direction, had saved them. Many of his people had escaped under the covering fire. Even the one armed with the Harbinger rail gun had made it out of the deadly trap Revancha had become. But they were still few—pitifully few. Most of their comrades lay dead behind them. For them, the fighting was over.

"Explosives," José ordered. "Set bombs with proximity fuses, drop them, and then run like the devil himself is on our heels."

The devil did not follow, but Diego did.

18

I will see you court-martialed for this, Sergeant!" Alex Allen shouted, glaring at Suarez. "How dare you break comm silence against my orders?"

"That was the colonel's order, not yours," Suarez replied with carefully calculated insolence—just one hair's width this side of insubordination. "You've been pointing out for hours that you're the only one in charge now, and nothing Colonel Villalobos said is to be obeyed."

"I am the commander of the San Cristóbal garrison now," Allen said angrily. "Lieutenant Travis reports directly to me and to no one else. Is that clear?"

"You betcha," Suarez said. After a discernible pause, he added, "Sir."

Allen continued to glower at the stocky soldier, who stood, hands behind his back, legs planted solidly, completely unperturbed by the waves of hostility coming from his superior officer.

"What did Lieutenant Travis report from El Manguito?" Allen asked at length, annoyed that he had to ask—

finally. The glint in Suarez's eye told him the man thought he'd scored a point.

"The Cyclops are more difficult to eliminate than anticipated," Suarez said. "She reports four killed. There may be as many as three more still roaming the region. Lieutenant Travis wants to secure the port and be certain the civilian population is protected before she goes after the remaining mutants."

"The local garrison commander can tend to that. I don't like San Cristóbal being so . . . vulnerable," Allen said. What good was command if he had only twenty soldiers? That wasn't even platoon strength. He fretted, briefly weighing the advantages of having Lieutenant Travis's squads back at San Cristóbal versus the disadvantages of having the truculent officer here herself. He hadn't gotten the impression that she thought much of Diego Villalobos, but he suspected she thought even less of him. What he had in mind was too important to risk interference from a squat, stubborn mule of a woman.

"All right," he said at last. "Leave them where they are and let them assist the garrison commander in hunting down the remaining Cyclops." His mind made up, he turned his attention to the other potential threat to his command: Colonel Villalobos. He was hoping for a truly spectacular screwup at Revancha—maybe something along the lines of a massacre. Forty or fifty dead Union soldiers, and Allen would look even more appealing to the brass, once his version of Diego's incompetence was confirmed. That, plus the prize that lay out in the jungle, just waiting for him to come get it, would ensure his quick rise back in the ranks.

"While you were illegally using the comm equipment,

did you happen to pick up anything about Colonel Villalobos?" he asked Suarez.

"The colonel himself was unavailable," Suarez said, sounding disappointed. "I spoke to Major Hinojosa, who's in command at Revancha, and he reports a complete rout of the guerrillas. At least a hundred, maybe more, dead. Minimal casualties on our side. No damage to the reactor."

Allen drummed his fingers on the desk, irritated at this turn of events. But in the end, it would make little difference. From what he had gathered, the brass in Mexico City HQ hated Villalobos enough that they would seize on any excuse to get rid of him—one insignificant victory in battle would not be enough to change that. As long as he performed better than Villalobos, his command was safe. And he only needed to keep it long enough to get that meteorite.

"So where is the colonel?" he asked.

"He pursued the surviving guerrilla forces into the jungle," Suarez reported. "No word from him since."

With any luck, we'll never hear from him again, Allen thought, and then dismissed Villalobos from his mind. He had to stay focused on destroying that pit creature and getting his hands on the meteorite.

And asserting his authority over this sergeant. The man's insubordination was troubling. Allen had not thought any of Villalobos's soldiers had that much loyalty for their commander—*former* commander, he corrected himself. But Suarez had been nothing but trouble ever since Allen had taken over. The problem would soon spread to Suarez's men—unless Allen slapped him down now.

"See to patrolling the post perimeter, Sergeant," he or-

dered. "I want visual observation as well as electronic surveillance at all times."

"There aren't enough soldiers for that," Suarez replied
without inflection.

"For that, *sir!*" Allen snapped. "You will address your
superior officer in a military manner!"

"Put me in the guardhouse. You'd be down to one
sergeant and two corporals."

"I don't bluff, Sergeant."

"I don't either, Captain."

The two men locked eyes across the desk, but in the
end it was Allen who dropped his eyes first. As much as he
hated to admit it, he could do nothing to the senior enlisted
man. If he were to order Suarez placed under arrest, he had
no one to replace him. Worse, Allen was not entirely certain the other soldiers would obey such an order. Any sedi-
tion in such a small number would doom his command.

And his precarious position definitely ruled out any
expeditions to the crater. Even without the fact that such a
sortie would leave the garrison completely vulnerable to
attack, he wasn't certain he could depend on these ragtag
men and women to hold their ground against an alien creature so powerful and unpredictable. He knew that well
enough from his experiences in Alaska.

No, his original plan was best: a long-distance, surgi-
cal missile strike. Take out the creature, and the field was
wide-open. He could collect the meteorite at his leisure.

"The crater with this monster in it," Allen said. "The
one I found. Have the biotechs discovered anything about
the fragment I brought back?"

"Sir, you know that almost the whole garrison is in the
field," Suarez said with a hint of satisfaction. "The bio of-

ficer went with Lieutenant Travis to study the Cyclops in case he could get enough of a corpse to do it. The other biotechs have been busy keeping the post going. That hunk of crystal is still sitting in the isolation lab where you ordered it placed."

"The creature is a huge threat to Chiapas, much more than those guerrillas," Allen said. Suarez had not seen the crystalline thing; he had. He alone knew the menace it presented.

"I need a full inventory of long-range weapons capable of destroying a heavily armored main battle tank," he said. "Something powerful enough to take out a Subjugator class tank."

"All we have is a couple of SPEAR missiles," Suarez said. "And those are more useful against personnel."

Allen tapped his finger on one of the maps that littered Villalobos's desk. "The target I'm interested in is here," he said, pointing to the spot in the jungle where he had seen the monster.

Suarez leaned over the desk to study the map, interested in spite of himself. "Then we have a problem. SPEAR missiles have a fairly short range. That's too far to reach, unless we want to send out a man on an Aztec with a missile launcher."

"Can we do that?" Allen asked.

"Nope," Suarez said. "Lieutenant Travis has both working Aztecs with her at El Manguito."

Allen scowled, still staring at the map. He was so close to victory he could taste it, and once again his men were letting him down.

"We could try placing a homing beacon at the site,"

offered Suarez. "That could help the SPEAR home in on the target and maybe extend its range a bit."

"Do we have any?" Allen asked with growing interest.

"We have several. A scout unit could position the homing device and confirm the creature's location."

"That would do. The SPEAR is perfect for this type of assault." The SPEAR rained down cluster bombs and carpeted a wide area with enough destruction to take out a small army. The biggest problem was that one of the submunitions might destroy the radiant source at the bottom of the crater. Allen wanted the creature gone, but he also had to retrieve the meteorite to cement his position with the Union Command.

Handing an energy source of that power over to the Union's scientists would surely guarantee his promotion to major. Maybe he could even jump a couple of ranks. Colonel Allen sounded far better to his ears. That would make up for the time spent cooling his heels after the Alaska debacle.

"I can get the missile prepped and on a vehicle to take it into range of the crater in a few hours, but it will require at least ten techs."

"Not the crater," Allen said in exasperation, realizing he could not risk his little gift from space. But he dared not mention it to Suarez. Word would get around too fast that something worthwhile lay out in the jungle for the taking.

"I don't understand, sir. A minute ago you asked for—" Suarez fell silent when Allen glared at him.

"There are villages all around that area, you fool. They pepper the countryside. Where there aren't villages, there are fields with crops. Destroying those would be as terrible for the peasants as hitting a village. Instead of killing them outright, we'd be sentencing them to slow starvation. What's wrong with you, Sergeant?" Allen liked the way that sounded—as if he gave a damn about a few miserable villages—and he liked the way it snapped Suarez's mouth shut even better.

"I have nothing to say, Captain," the sergeant said, fuming.

"I thought not. I—"

The sudden blare of alarms cut him off. Allen spun around and looked at the battle display console near Villalobos's—his—desk. He switched it to local mode. "Something coming from the east. Slow. But massive. And energetic."

Suarez fiddled with the comm board, then looked up. "It might just be the creature you're talking about. The readings we're getting don't look like anything I've seen before. I guess you won't have to blow it out of the countryside. It's coming here."

"Do you have orbital recon?" asked Allen, not sure how to find what he needed on the battle display. It was a different model from the one he had used in Alaska.

"Negative," said Suarez. "Communications with the battle station are still out. Have been for several days."

Allen wondered if this might be due to the same meteorite he hoped to retrieve out in the jungle. But it did not matter now. He had to defend San Cristóbal.

"Get the SPEARS ready," he ordered Suarez. "Our unwelcome visitor is going to be in for a surprise."

"But we've got civilian population nearby, sir. You said—"

"Get the missiles ready. We might have to sacrifice a few civilians to stop this threat to all our lives!" Allen's voice rose shrilly. Suarez frowned, but left to prep the missiles while Allen tried to get a grip on himself. Staring at the battle display didn't help. The creature wasn't moving fast, but it was inexorably moving closer.

Why was it coming to San Cristóbal? An uneasy feeling grew until Allen felt as if fingers were tightening around his throat. He left his position in the command and control center and ran to the isolation lab. He pressed his face against the thick plastic observation port and stared at the crystalline growth he had brought back. The thrashing tendril in the bottle had changed dramatically. The questing tentacles had thickened to savage thorns poking their way through the bottle walls. If it continued to grow, it would soon rip the plastic apart.

What if the creature was coming here because it could sense this thing's presence? It had spawned the snaky globs from its own body, after all. Perhaps it had some way to communicate with them.

Perhaps it was a mother coming for her offspring.

Allen swallowed hard. The snake-thing might have helped him wrest command from Villalobos, but right now it seemed like bringing it to the base was a mistake. He rushed from the isolation lab to the first floor of the command center. Suarez was working on the consoles, getting the SPEAR missiles ready. Beside him labored a corporal, sweating buckets. The corporal looked up when he came in.

"Sir, what *is* that thing? Never seen its like before."

"Don't worry, Corporal. Just do your duty and all will be well." Allen hoped he wasn't lying. He entered the command codes into the control console—the codes for which he had risked so much—and stared at the visual display above the boards, which was trained on the edge of the jungle just outside the garrison. The creature had mutated even further since he had seen it struggling in the jungle crater. It was larger, but it moved more slowly, almost falling at every step. The growths all over its body had changed, some vanishing entirely.

But its face! That was enough to give Allen nightmares for the rest of his life. Medusa had nothing on this monstrous being. Crystalline snakes of all sizes and colors lashed about wildly, as if goading the creature to attack. The arms were clear of new growth, but from the waist down it was arrayed with grotesque extensions that writhed in the same manner as the piece he had imprisoned in the isolation lab.

"Get a Rottweiler pointed at it," he ordered. "Open fire when it gets in range."

"Sir, if the Rott doesn't take it out, there's no way we'll be able to use any kind of missile," Suarez protested. "It will be too close to our own position."

"Yes, yes, of course. All or nothing," Allen said. He, too, was sweating profusely, his uniform plastering itself to his body.

"Can't let it get much closer or the missile will be a no-go," the corporal said, seconding Suarez's warning.

"You can't fire, Captain," Suarez said firmly. "Carpeting that area with submunitions from a SPEAR will take out an unknown number of civilians."

"Collateral damage. Unfortunate but not unexpected. Fire the SPEAR. Target that . . . thing, and fire!"

"Sir, I protest!" cried Suarez. "There are civilians living at the outskirts of San Cristóbal who—"

Allen reached over and punched the firing button. For a

moment he worried that Suarez had not properly set up the SPEAR. Then the rush of missile exhaust echoed outside the C&C building. The display showed a burning exhaust trail, then the screen switched to high polarization to blank the brilliant detonation of dozens of powerful antipersonnel submunitions ripping apart the land around the creature. The building shook from the close-proximity detonation.

Dust rose in high columns outside the garrison, blocking the visual display. The corporal switched from one filter to another until he found a combination that cut through the curtain.

"Dead-on, sir," the corporal said. "Blew it into a million pieces."

"Not to mention the civilians," Suarez said with cold fury. "Corporal, go see how bad the casualties are. Offer them whatever medical aid we can provide."

Allen let the corporal go without protest. However many villagers might have been killed in the attack was inconsequential compared with the fact that the meteorite was now his for the taking. What were a few miserable peasants, weighed against the potential that tiny speck held for the Union?

And for him.

19

José Villalobos fell to his knees on the jungle floor, gasping for breath. He was in superb physical condition, but never before had he been forced to flee so far so fast. He strained to hear any sounds of pursuit over the roaring of blood in his ears and his own harsh panting. He wasn't certain, but he thought they might finally have succeeded in throwing off the Union troops who had pursued them like avenging Furies—led by his own brother.

The reprieve had come none too soon. The ugly, swirling orb of light in the sky that was the Maw was sinking slowly toward the western horizon. It would be dark soon, and José had not relished the idea of trying to fight his way through the jungle at night—not when so many of his guerrillas were wounded.

The few survivors of the disastrous raid on Revancha sat slumped around him, as exhausted and demoralized as their leader. Of the two hundred who had attacked the power plant, fewer than fifty remained, and none had escaped unscathed. Sweat, dirt, and blood gleamed on their downturned faces; their clothing was shredded and torn from their panicky flight through the jungle. José was glad to see that most had managed to hang on to their weapons, but with so little remaining ammunition, he didn't know how useful they would be.

His breathing was slightly calmer now, the roaring in his ears diminished, and he still could detect no signs of pursuit. For the first time in nearly twelve hours, José permitted himself to relax slightly.

He still could not believe how quickly it had all fallen apart. The attack on the reactor had been precisely planned down to the tiniest detail, and within minutes of their breaching the fence, disaster had struck. José had lost troops before, but never so many so quickly—and never so many that he counted as friends. He had seen familiar face after familiar face fall, covered in blood, cut down by the lethal chatter of automatic fire or the hot fury of grenades. The cheerful Flaco would drink no more bottles of tequila. Faithful, resolute Mary—his eyes stung at the memory of his last sight of Mary Stephenson: unable to walk, holding off the Union soldiers with a final burst of strength so her comrades could escape.

And for a time, it had looked as if her sacrifice would be in vain. In all his previous engagements with the Union, the enemy soldiers had feared to follow the guerrillas once they melted back into the jungle. The jungle was the guerrillas' home; they knew its twisted paths and dangerous heart better than any Union soldier ever could. The heavy vehicles and powerful armaments that gave the Union such an advantage in open battle became a liability in the close confines of the jungle. That was why José had started a guerrilla campaign in the first place; he knew he could never hope to defeat his former comrades by fighting on their terms.

But this time, perhaps emboldened by their over-whelming victory at Revancha, Diego's troops had pur-sued. The guerrillas, weakened, wounded, and demoralized, had been hard-pressed to evade them. For hours Diego had chased them, occasionally picking off one or two strag-glers with well-placed fire. As they moved deeper into the jungle, the Union vehicles became ensnared in the trees and undergrowth. Diego attempted to continue the pursuit on foot, but José and Consuela had sent the rest of the sur-vivors ahead, then slipped back silently through the jungle and caught unawares a few Union soldiers who had be-come separated from their fellows. The sight of their bod-ies, torn throats gaping bloodily as they lay on the trail, had convinced Diego that the fight was best left for another day.

Diego. José had always loved his younger brother—even after the disastrous raid three years ago that resulted in the deaths of so many innocents—but he had never re-spected him. It was José who'd had the brilliant mind, José who'd been top in his class, José who could plot dazzling strategies on the battlefield. Diego had always been the plodder, the methodical one. Competent, yes, but not par-ticularly creative, and try as he might, José could not help looking down on him for it.

He had seen no reason to change his opinion over the years he had opposed his brother. Time after time he had thwarted Diego's attempts to maintain order, had under-mined his authority in Chiapas, had sabotaged his supply routes and killed his men. Always José had been several steps ahead.

But this time he had underestimated his younger brother. José had to give him credit, even as he sat staring at the bloody aftermath of his handiwork. Diego had planned and executed perfectly what must surely have been a last-minute defense strategy. He had lured the guerrillas into a trap and sprung it at precisely the right moment. It had been a masterful stroke.

José thought back to that moment on the battlefield when he had locked eyes with his brother. It had been years since they had actually seen each other, and he had been shocked at how much older Diego looked. He wondered if Diego had thought the same about him. It was hard to know how to feel about his brother anymore—the love they had shared since childhood was now so tangled up with hatred and resentment and fear that there was no separating them.

Right now the fear was paramount. Diego had anticipated José's every move, had broken his forces, had made a shambles of all his carefully laid plans. Diego had done his work thoroughly—so thoroughly that now, as José looked around at the tattered remnants of his army, he had no idea what to do. Two of his most trusted lieutenants were dead, along with three-quarters of his force. It was a crushing defeat, the worst the guerrillas had ever suffered.

But it was more than the shock of defeat that kept José slumped on the ground, uncertain what to do. He had spent months planning for the attack on Revancha: gathering intelligence on the plant's defenses, raiding to build up a cache of ammunition and weapons, carefully plotting diversions to divide the Union forces. He had spent countless sleepless nights poring over maps and drawing up supply and troop lists. He had poured his entire being into the attack, and all those months of planning and obsessing over the smallest detail had been swept away in a few disastrous moments.

He had rested everything on victory at Revancha, and he had failed. But he had been thinking for so long in terms of the attack that now he could not think of anything else.

José did not look up from the ground as a pair of booted feet came into his field of vision. Then the owner of the boots squatted until a pair of brown eyes could look into his. Consuela.

"Your head is bleeding," she said in a brisk, practical tone. José absently touched his forehead, dully surprised to see that his fingers came away red.

"Here," Consuela said, holding out a bandage from a stolen Union medkit. When José failed to reach for it, she sighed, pushed his matted hair back from his forehead, and applied the bandage herself. She stood, moved out of his sight, and returned a few minutes later carrying a canteen.

"Drink," she said firmly, thrusting it at him. Automatically, José took the canteen and drained the little water it held in a few swallows. He had not realized until then how thirsty he was.

Consuela took the empty canteen back and stood looking at José, her expression a mixture of disapproval and concern. She said nothing, and a few seconds later she walked away. As always, Consuela saw what was, accepted it, and did what she could. José watched her as she moved among the guerrillas, dispensing bandages to some, water and food to others. As she worked to restore them physically, she also strove to renew their spirits: joking with one, lecturing another, commiserating with a third on the loss of a friend.

They had all lost friends this day, but José knew all those deaths would have been as nothing if he had lost Consuela. She was the glove to his hand, the rock against which he leaned, the earth beneath his feet. Without her, he was nothing.

José's view of Consuela was abruptly blocked. He looked up to see Gunther standing over him, his body taut, his features distorted almost unrecognizably by rage.

"This—this is your great victory?" he spat, waving at the pathetic remnants of José's force. "For years you have told us the Union is nothing, your brother is nothing! Is this the result of nothing?"

José was dismayed but unsurprised to see a number of the others nodding agreement with Gunther's words. They had never faced such a devastating defeat before, and their confidence in their leader had been shaken, if not irrevocably shattered. He couldn't blame them—at this moment he didn't have much confidence in himself either.

"We wasted ammunition, we laid down our lives, and for what?" Gunther shouted. "A handful of dead Union soldiers? We traded three of our people for every one of theirs! I did not join the Zapatistas to sacrifice my life for nothing—I joined to kill Union pigs. At this rate, the villages will be empty before the Union is finally driven out. There will be no one left to savor our victory. You have failed."

José said nothing. What was there to say? Gunther was right. Perhaps he had been too myopic, too focused on one goal. Revancha had lived in his thoughts for months. Perhaps that obsession had blinded him to the larger picture.

If he had kept some distance, some perspective, would he have seen the trap that Diego had laid? It was all his fault.

Made bold by José's lack of response, Gunther turned to face the assembled guerrillas. "Behold your leader. Is he not inspiring?" he said, his voice heavy with sarcasm.

"For too long we have pecked away at the Union," he continued, his voice rising to be sure all those present could hear. "We have been too timid, too afraid to risk all to gain all. This is the result. We need to go beyond minor raids or the deaths of one or two Union soldiers. We must fight until the earth runs red with their blood. Only then will they realize that the cost of conquest is too high and leave us in peace." He turned back to José. "And if our present leaders are unwilling to take the necessary risks, perhaps it is time we find leaders who are."

"And I suppose you have somebody in mind?" Consuela called mockingly from the back of the crowd. She pushed her way through to the front, the guerrillas parting quickly before her, until she stood just in front of Gunther, her fists planted on her hips, glaring up at him.

"I?" Gunther asked in mock surprise. "I bow to the will of the people. Of course, should they have someone in mind . . ." His gaze swept over the assembled crowd, and one or two of his squad members started to cheer, but fell silent when Consuela's oppressive eye fell on them.

"You bow to no one, unless it is to spit on their feet," Consuela said. Gunther's hands tightened their grip on his rifle, but he did nothing. Slowly, deliberately, she turned her back on him and addressed the guerrillas. "So this is what you think commitment to our cause means?" she asked scathingly. "To fall to pieces at the first defeat? How many battles has José brought us safely through?" She pointed at a battered man a short distance away. "You—did not José save you from a Union patrol that had you surrounded?" The man dropped his gaze, unable to meet Consuela's eyes.

"And you," she said, swinging around to face a female soldier. "Your village had been raided—did José not hunt down those responsible for killing your people and stealing your possessions?" The woman nodded reluctantly.

"Now, suddenly, we suffer one defeat, one setback, and you want to pick up your toys and go home? This is not a child's game we play. This is war. People die. Losses happen. Nothing worth fighting for has ever come easily. And I assure you, our freedom is still worth the fight. As long as I breathe"—she glared momentarily at Gunther—"I follow José. And so do you."

Gunther's face had been growing darker throughout her speech, but he could tell the tide of opinion had turned against him. The guerrillas were shifting awkwardly, embarrassed by their momentary lapse. Consuela did not give them an opportunity to change their minds again.

"We need time to rest," she said loudly. "Let us prepare to camp for the night so we can rest and bandage our wounds. The morning is time enough to decide where we go from here."

The knot of guerrillas broke up into a swirl of activity. Consuela circulated through them, assigning tasks and creating order out of chaos. When she was satisfied with their progress, she left them to their own devices and stalked over to José.

"Have you finished feeling sorry for yourself yet?" she hissed, keeping her voice low so that the others could not hear her.

"I—" José started, but she did not let him finish.

"What I just did, with Gunther—that was your job," she said. "He has made his challenge now, and he will not back down from it. One day soon, I think, you will have to kill him or be killed. Which will it be?"

"I just . . . I just don't know what to do," José said helplessly. He had never felt less competent.

"You are a leader," she snapped. "So lead. We have suffered a terrible defeat, yes, but that does not remove our responsibility to defend our people. We failed against the Union, but there is a greater threat out there that needs our attention: the crystal monster."

"Again with the monster!" José flared, a little energy returning to him. He gestured at the pitiful remnants of his army. "This is all we have. How do we fight a monster with that? We could not even defeat a pack of ill-trained Union soldiers. How can we hope to defeat an alien creature with the powers you describe?"

"I don't know," Consuela admitted, "but we have to try."

José let out a sigh, then finally levered himself to his feet. "In the morning," he said wearily. "We all need the rest. After we have slept, then we will begin to consider ways to kill this thing."

Consuela's taut expression eased. She touched him lightly on the shoulder, then turned and hurried off to supervise the others. José watched her go with a faint smile. She was right, as usual. He had a responsibility to protect his people from whatever threatened their safety—whether that was a Union soldier or a hideous crystal beast. He was a leader.

So he would lead.

20

The front gates of the San Cristóbal compound rose out of the dusk before them, and Diego grinned as a faint cheer came from the others also riding in the Pegasus transport. They were as exhilarated as he was, and less reserved about showing it. As their commander, he had to maintain a semblance of dignity, but inwardly he was just as adrenaline-soaked.

The battle at Revancha had gone even better than he had dared hope. The last-minute trap he'd laid, with the able help of Revancha's commander, had worked perfectly, drawing the guerrillas deep into the base and trapping them against the reactor. The guerrillas had lost around three-quarters of their force. That was a devastating blow, one that might even cripple the rebel movement permanently.

The one cloud hanging over his victory was that moment when he'd seen his brother. Diego had frozen when he realized who he had in his rifle's sights. Through the scope, José had looked so old, so defeated. Perhaps it was pity that had stayed his finger from the trigger. But deep within him he wondered if it was fear that had kept him from following through on the final confrontation with his brother at the crucial moment. Maybe BJ and his superiors were right—he had had the *cojones* to battle Viejo's men, but lacked the will to face his brother directly.

Viejo had always been a larger-than-life figure to him, with Diego following along in his shadow. José Villalobos had been the brilliant one, the leader of men, and Diego had plodded behind him, the competent commander. Now their roles were reversed, and Diego was unsure how he should feel about that.

But there would be time to worry about it later. Right now he had to concentrate on relieving the skeleton crew he had left to man the garrison, seeing to his few wounded, and composing a report to his superiors in Mexico City. His astounding victory notwithstanding, Diego knew he could give them no room to criticize his actions. If he could present them with a fait accompli, perhaps they would ease off on their pressure slightly.

The Pegasus rumbled through the gates of the post and glided to a stop. Diego was the first one out of the troop carrier's hatch, and he gave the gate guards a jaunty salute. They returned the courtesy, but seemed strangely reluctant to meet his eyes. Diego didn't give it much thought. Perhaps they were annoyed that they'd been left behind. They would recover.

His men spilled out of the Pegasus behind him, laughing and talking among themselves. He turned to them and held up his hands for silence.

"Good work, everyone," he said, pride evident in his voice. "Those of you who were injured, get yourselves checked out in the infirmary. The rest, report to your barracks and get cleaned up. I'll have duty assignments for you in a little while. Until then, relax and enjoy yourselves. You've earned it."

His soldiers let out another heartfelt cheer and scattered, some to their barracks while others helped their injured comrades toward the infirmary. There were few injuries, thankfully, and those were minor. Only a handful of his people had been killed, most of them in the jungle during their abortive pursuit of José.

Diego strode toward the command building. A subdued air hung over the post. The few soldiers he encountered hurried past him, also refusing to meet his eyes. No one spoke. Diego was at a loss to explain it; even the troops left behind should be sharing in the excitement of victory. Instead they seemed almost . . . embarrassed?

He snagged a passing soldier by the arm. "Where is Lieutenant Suarez?" he asked.

The soldier jerked a thumb toward the command building and hurried away. Diego was starting to get a bad feeling about this situation, but he headed toward his office anyway. After his people got squared away and his report to HQ was made, he needed to start planning the final strike against José. The guerrillas had been all but broken at Revancha. Diego knew he had to follow up on his advantage and finish them off quickly. But first, he needed to find out what was going on here at San Cristóbal.

He walked into his outer office, where Private Murdo ordinarily reigned, and was shocked to see Suarez sitting behind his orderly's desk, face downcast.

"What's going on here, Lieutenant?" Diego asked forcefully. Suarez looked up wretchedly and opened his mouth to answer, but was forestalled by the door to Diego's office opening.

"Ah," said Captain Allen, beaming, his voice virtually dripping with insincere bonhomie. "I thought I heard you out here. Come in, come in. I need to debrief you on the battle at Revancha. How did that go?"

Diego stared at him in disbelief, rage building swiftly inside him. This man had disappeared when his superior officer had needed him, and now here he was acting as if he owned the garrison.

Diego's voice, when he spoke, was dangerously quiet. "Debrief *me*?" he asked. "In case you've forgotten, this is my post. In fact, this is my office. I'm glad to see you've returned safely from wherever it was you disappeared to without permission, but right now, get the hell out of my sight before I have you thrown in the brig."

"Actually, *Colonel*, it's you who should be worried about the brig," Allen said smugly. "Assuming General Ramirez doesn't just have you shot on the spot."

He held out a sheet of hardcopy to Diego, who ignored it, continuing to glare at him.

"My orders," Allen said, unfazed by Diego's reaction. "I had HQ in Mexico City send them over, just to clear up any confusion. They were quite perturbed about your abandoning the post and leaving the garrison virtually unprotected. They were so upset, in fact, that they relieved you of command. I'm in charge now, so perhaps you should start getting ready for your court-martial. I rather imagine the general will want to schedule it as soon as possible."

Diego finally took the sheet of paper Allen was persistently holding out and gave it a cursory scan. It confirmed what Allen had said: for abandoning his post, he had been relieved of duty pending an inquiry and possible court-martial. He felt curiously unsurprised—numb, even. This had been coming for years, ever since José had turned against the Union. Ramirez hated him for that, convinced that where one brother could go rogue, the other might follow.

Diego had known Allen was trouble the minute he'd shown up. Admittedly, he hadn't expected the man to snake his command out from under him. But what else could he have done? Between Ramirez continually stealing away his best soldiers and José with his cursed Neo-Sov mutants, Diego had been backed into a corner. He knew that going to Revancha had been the right choice—and even now, if it came down to it, he would do the same thing all over again.

Diego forced himself to look back up at Allen, who had clearly been enjoying his silence. "I trust everything is clear now?" Allen asked with false courtesy. Diego nodded, not trusting himself to speak.

"Then if you'll come into *my* office," Allen said, "I'll have that report on the action at Revancha now."

Diego glanced at Suarez, who was staring down at the top of the desk, clearly unwilling to witness Diego's humiliation. He gritted his teeth and walked past Allen into his office.

Allen closed the door behind him, walked behind Diego's desk, and sat in Diego's chair. While Diego remained standing, Allen stretched his legs out ostentatiously and got comfortable, rubbing in the reversal in ranks as much as he could.

"So?" Allen asked, raising an eyebrow.

Diego gave him an abbreviated version of the battle at

Revancha, choosing his words carefully. He had seen Allen's type before—clever and quick to take every advantage, but greedy. They always overextended themselves and tripped up. He would simply have to bide his time and wait for that to happen—and hope that it didn't come too late for him to finish off the rebels before they could build their strength back up.

Allen sat nodding and smiling condescendingly throughout Diego's report, until the part about calling off the chase through the jungle. Then he sat up. "You mean you didn't pursue?" he asked incredulously. "You had them on the run and you failed to finish them off?"

"With all due respect," Diego said insincerely, "they knew the terrain much better than we did. Pursuing them any farther would have carried unacceptable risks. Their back was broken at Revancha. We should be able to eliminate what's left of them without much difficulty."

"It sounds like your gamble largely paid off," Allen said magnanimously. "But I still think you could have finished the job properly. Why, while you were gone, with only the handful of men you left me, we managed to defeat a far worse threat."

Diego came to full attention. "An attack on the post?" he asked, shocked. "Here? Was it the Cyclops? Did they get past Travis at El Manguito?"

"Negative," Allen said, enjoying Diego's discomfort. "Travis repelled the attack at El Manguito, but she's still chasing the last Cyclops through the jungle—she doesn't want to risk it attacking another village. No, what attacked us was something much worse than a mutant."

He swiveled in his chair and tapped a few keys on the

comm console. A picture blossomed in midair above the desk, and Diego leaned forward to get a better look.

What he saw defied description. The video had obviously been taken from one of the observation towers on the garrison's perimeter, but the creature it had captured was like nothing he had ever seen. It looked like walking crystal, hung all over with globules and tentacles of glass. It staggered as it came toward the post, looking like it was injured. The video had no sound, so he couldn't tell if it was making any noises as it came.

Then the monster, and the surrounding terrain, vanished in a blaze of light. The video abruptly cut off. Diego stood disbelieving in his office, the blood pounding in his ears. As if from a distance, he heard himself ask, "What ordnance did you use?"

"SPEAR missile," Allen replied smugly.

Diego stared at him in shock. "You used a SPEAR this close to the post?" he asked. "That thing was right outside the perimeter! What about the villages nearby? Did you even stop to think about collateral damage?"

"Of course I thought about it," Allen snapped. "I decided that the civilian losses would be acceptable."

All the rage Diego had been holding back finally boiled over. "Acceptable losses!" he raged. "No civilian casualty is acceptable! It's our duty to protect these people, if you've forgotten. But I imagine your only duty is to yourself!"

Allen was on his feet in an instant, fists on the desk. "You are out of line, Colonel!" he shouted back.

Diego's lip curled. "Out of line for wanting to protect the citizens of Chiapas? Out of line for finally telling you the truth about yourself, you bloated, backstabbing wind-bag?"

"Maybe some time in the brig would make you rethink your position," Allen threatened.

"You're welcome to try," Diego answered, "if you don't mind having your arms ripped off." Both men were now leaning across the desk, noses practically touching as they exchanged insults.

Allen pulled back slightly. "This is still the Union military," he said icily. "There is a chain of command. I am in charge here—I decide what's necessary. I decide what are acceptable losses. And I decide what you do—unless you plan to turn traitor. Like your brother."

The words hit Diego like a dash of cold water in the face. He slowly straightened, tugged down the front of his uniform, and sank into the chair in front of the desk. And glowered at Allen.

"I didn't give you permission to sit, soldier," Allen said deliberately. Diego simply looked at him, and Allen seemed to realize he had pushed Diego as far as he could. He sat down himself, cleared his throat, and began shuffling through the stacks of papers on the desk.

"Well," Allen said with strained casualness, both men tacitly agreeing to pretend the shouting match had never taken place, "I'm sure Ramirez will be getting back to you soon enough about your final disposition. But in the meantime, we need to find something for you to do." He pulled out a sheet of paper from the stack he held.

"Just the thing," he said. "Since you're so concerned about the local peasants"—he smiled meanly—"we've had some scattered reports coming in about attacks on several villages. Apparently a few people have disappeared or something—no one's been quite clear on the matter. Some of them have been babbling about demons in golden armor—frankly it sounds like utter nonsense, but I'm sure it's just up your alley." He tossed the report across the desk to Diego. "Take a squad and find out what's going on. But there's no hurry—I imagine you're rather tired. Get a good night's sleep and set out in the morning."

"Aye, sir," Diego said through his teeth. He got up abruptly and left without waiting for permission. One more minute in that office with that preening ass and he would have gone over the desk for the man's throat. He knew this mission was simply scutwork to keep him out of the way. And he knew more than that: his career was over. He had gambled everything, and he had lost. He had saved the reactor, and possibly the Union's hold on Chiapas, but he had given Mexico City the excuse it needed to get rid of him.

He could resign now—that would be the dignified way out of the situation, rather than waiting to be court-martialed. But there was Allen to consider—he simply couldn't walk away and leave the locals in that man's care. His lack of concern for the people he was supposedly sent to protect had been made abundantly clear with his use of the SPEAR so close to their homes. He shuddered to think of how it must have been for them, to suddenly have death raining down on their uncomprehending heads from a clear sky.

No—they needed him. Their safety was more important than his pride.

At that moment, Diego felt closer than he ever had to understanding why José had done what he did. Both brothers had dedicated their lives to the Union military, and both had been poorly repaid for their sacrifices. José had chosen to walk away, but poor, duty-bound Diego once again had no choice. He had to act to protect his people, and no matter what José thought, he could do that best from within the military.

His thoughts had carried him through his outer office and out into the compound. But now he vaguely heard someone calling after him. He turned and saw Suarez hurrying toward him.

"Sir, I'm so sorry," the lieutenant said, his words tumbling over each other. "It happened before I knew anything about it, there was nothing I could do, I know you left the post in my hands and I failed. I—"

Diego held up a hand to stop him. "It's all right, Lieutenant," he said reassuringly. "This has nothing to do with you—it's something that's been building for years. It just happened to spill over now. Not your fault."

"I couldn't help overhearing you," Suarez said. "Please take me with you tomorrow. I want to help somehow—and frankly, if I have to stay in that office much longer, I'm going to punch that *gringo* right in the nose."

Diego stifled a smile and clapped him on the shoulder. "Come on, then," he said. "Let's see what we can do. And don't worry—it'll all work out somehow."

Back in what had been Diego's office, Allen was pleased. He had consolidated his position—and, more important, he had Villalobos's troops back. Now that he had the manpower, he could begin planning his expedition to the crater to retrieve his meteorite. That tiny fragment was his ticket to higher things—much higher than command of some rinky-dink little post, no matter how much value an unimaginative officer like Villalobos might place on it.

He reached for the comm console and began barking

orders. By this time tomorrow, the meteorite would be in his hands—and his career would at long last be back on track.

21

The Death Priest picked his way cautiously through the jungle. The riot of vegetation was difficult enough to cope with in the daylight hours; without the brilliant white light of the Vorack to illuminate his way, it was even more hazardous.

But the priest had no time to waste. He had detoured briefly to check on the Slayer's work at the *Destroyer for the Faith* and been pleased with the progress. He still regretted the loss of his control-room slaves; they had been painstakingly trained, and work went slower with these primitives, who were still adjusting to their new life of glorious service to the God-king.

However, with enough . . . persuasion, they could be made to effect the repairs under the enthusiastic supervision of the Slayer. The immense Pharon warrior was beginning to chafe under the restrictions the priest had placed on him. Slayers were trained for one thing only—battle— and all this enforced waiting was alien to the killer's nature. But soon the time for secrecy would be at an end.

Soon the priest would have his hands on the bit of Vor-stuff, and then the Maelstrom would tremble under the might of the God-king. And the priest would be there, standing at his side. The Death Priest trembled in anticipation of the glory that would be his.

But if that magnificent day were ever to come to pass, the priest would have to hurry. Time worked against him. The mote was becoming more unstable with each passing hour, and the slaves he had working on retrieving it insisted on dying. None could survive close proximity with the deadly beams emitted from the fracture in the crystalline globe for more than a few minutes at a time before they died a second death, crisped by the radiation beyond the ability of the life-support packs to repair the damage.

Therefore, the priest was abroad in this cursed jungle yet again, in search of more slaves. And he had to hurry—if he tarried too long, the last of the slaves toiling at the crater would expire, and work would cease completely. The time for secrecy was finally past—speed was of more importance now.

The Death Priest paused as the jungle suddenly gave way to an expanse of open fields. Beyond the open space was the largest habitation he had yet seen on this world: several massive buildings, strung with lights that made the compound bright as day even in the darkness of the night, which was usually lit only by the planet's lone satellite and the few pinpoints of light that could be seen in the sky of the Maelstrom.

The priest activated his phase generator to conceal his presence from the primitives scurrying around the complex and studied the scene. A battle had obviously taken place here recently—the signs of destruction were everywhere.

Charred craters indicated the use of explosives, while the walls around the place were scarred with pockmarks—no doubt caused by the projectile weapons the primitives seemed so fond of.

That explained why there was so much activity here, while the other, smaller settlements he had passed had been dark and quiet, their inhabitants asleep. Whoever resided in this complex was still recovering from the effects of a skirmish. That meant their defenses would be chaotic and disorganized, making it easier for the priest to slip in among them undetected.

And where there was battle, there would be bodies.

The priest studied the scene a while longer and decided to avoid the main gate. Most of the activity seemed to be concentrated there, and while he was confident he could get past their feeble defenses, he would prefer not to raise any alarms. There must be another way into the compound where he could infiltrate them undetected.

Keeping to the fringes of the jungle, the priest circled the place until he found what he was looking for. At the rear of the walled perimeter, there was a spot where the metal wire of the fence had been cut and hastily repaired. He studied the ground between where he stood and the weak spot in the fence. There were a number of detection devices, but those were easily neutralized. He started across the open field toward the fence, his phase generator making it seem as if he was simply flickering in and out of existence. He reached the fence without being detected, and one blast from his energy weapon fried the sensors in the fence as it melted its way through the flimsy barrier.

Once inside, the priest proceeded with even more caution. The ground was seeded with explosive devices that had to be identified and avoided, and an occasional guard trotted past. The priest evaded detection; they were potential slaves, true, but he had his sights set on a greater goal.

Somewhere in this compound was the source of a stench of death so powerful the priest had been able to detect it from outside the perimeter. The recent battle had clearly inflicted great losses on its participants—losses that could be turned into gains for the priest, and for the God-king.

The priest slipped past the burned-out remains of what had been a large building and paused. A slight sigh of pleasure escaped his creased and rotted lips. In front of him stretched row after row of black bags, laid out on the ground like cordwood. The shiny fabric of the bags outlined the unmistakable shape of native bodies. Dozens, perhaps even hundreds of them. Here at last was the supply the priest had been seeking. These would ensure that he would have an ample supply of bearers for the Vor-stuff, with enough left over to man the ship for the long flight back to the Pharon homeworld.

The priest knelt behind the first bag in the front row and gently, almost lovingly, unfastened it to reveal the body of a woman, her slight form still twisted in its death throes. She had once been small and delicate-looking, but now her legs were crushed and her chest gaped wide with the wound that had brought her death.

The Death Priest cared about none of that. As long as the body was intact, it could serve the God-king, regardless of how terrible its injuries had been in life. Placing his bandage-wrapped hand over her face, he began the ceremony that would restore life to the lifeless form before him.

As he completed his invocation to the God-king, the woman began to stir slightly. He quickly reached behind him for one of the life-support tanks he had brought with him and rolled her over, as she struggled feebly, to fit it to her back. The hoses plunged into her torso and began feeding her the nourishing fluids made from the remains of others of her kind that would sustain her in her life-after-death.

The priest rocked back on his heels and waited. It always took slaves some time to adjust to their new existence. He watched as this one struggled to her feet and began taking a few tentative steps on her twisted legs. Her gait was a terrible, jerking parody of a human walk, but it would suffice. Had the priest cared to look, he might have noticed the look of unmitigated horror in the sunken eyes peering out from that ruined, blood-flecked face. But he did not.

When he judged she was steady enough on her feet, he issued her instructions. "Go back to the ship," he told her, placing one hand on the side of her face and mentally guiding her to its location deep in the heart of the jungle. "Bring back tanks for the others."

The slave bowed stiffly and began a slow, shambling walk toward the fence. The priest did not bother to watch her go; he had already turned to the next bag in the row. He had brought enough tanks with him to continue his work until the slave returned with the rest. If he hurried, he could finish his work here and be back at the crater before dawn—all without the stupid primitives in this compound being any the wiser to his presence. He would even have enough to send some to the Slayer to assist with the repairs to his spacecraft.

Within a few short hours, he would be returning to his ship, his prize firmly in hand. And then nothing—not these humans, not the Shard, not the power of the Maelstrom itself—would be able to stand in his way.

22

José swore under his breath as a dangling vine swatted him in the face. He had grown up in and around the jungles of southern Mexico—they were his home—but he was beginning to feel as if his life was one endless march after another through the sweltering vegetation. His days were beginning to blur together; he could no longer remember how long it had been since their successful raid on Puerto Madero or their agonizing defeat at Revancha.

He paused and squinted up through the foliage toward the sky. The sun—or what passed for the sun ever since the Change—had only been up for an hour or two, and already it was broiling.

He looked back at the ragged column of guerrillas struggling along behind him. From the imposing army of two hundred that he had commanded a few short days ago, his followers now numbered less than fifty. He was proud of all of them—they might not have the faintest idea what they were doing hiking through the jungle, on their way to a confrontation with some mythical beast, but there they all were, trying gamely to keep up.

But José was a realist—he knew his grasp on them was tenuous at best. Their faith had been shaken by the devastating defeat at Revancha—he could see it in the way their gaze slid away from his, in the set of their shoulders, and their dragging step. He could see, too, Gunther making his way from soldier to soldier, pausing for a few words of whispered conversation with each before moving on to the next one. It worried him, but he didn't know what to do about it. All he could do was keep going and hope Consuela was right.

He quickened his pace and caught up with his sturdy lieutenant a few paces down the trail. "How much farther is it?" he asked, keeping his voice low to keep from being overheard. He couldn't afford to appear anything less than supremely confident in front of his soldiers just then.

"Only a few kilometers more," Consuela said. "Soon you will start seeing burned vegetation—that will be the sign that we are close."

José chose his next words carefully—he did not want to alienate Consuela, but he had to be sure of what they were doing. "*Chica*, you must know that I do not doubt your judgment," he said, stealing a sidelong glance at her. She kept walking, eyes steady on the trail in front of them. "But I must be certain of what we will find. Have you told me everything? Is it possible you have exaggerated the danger of—"

"No," Consuela interrupted, her voice stony. José kept his eyes on her, and after a few more paces she relented. "José," she said softly, "I know what I have told you is un-believable, but it is true. You know me, and you trust my abilities." She took her gaze off the trail long enough to look him in the face. "This thing that I saw—it is worse, far worse, than anything we have faced thus far. I led that stupid Union officer there so that I could test its strength, and it took everything he could throw at it without flinching. We must stop it. I do not know how, but we must."

José nodded and clapped her on the shoulder. "All right, *chica*," he said. "When we get there, we will figure out what to do."

"Assuming we find anything there at all," came Gunther's mocking voice. He had come up behind them unheard, and his eyes as he looked at José were scornful. "Admit it, José—there is no monster. This is just a fantasy you have seized upon to avoid going up against our true enemy—the Union."

Consuela halted so abruptly José bumped into her. She whirled on Gunther. "This is no fantasy!" she hissed, as angry as José had ever seen her. "You are so obsessed with the Union that you fail to see the greater threat in front of you. If you—"

José held up a hand, and both combatants fell silent. They had heard it almost at the same moment as he had: the small, stealthy sounds of someone moving quietly toward them on the trail. Hands went to guns, but seconds later all three relaxed as they recognized one of their advance scouts.

The woman hurried up, her face set. "Sir, we've got mass movement up ahead," she reported.

"Union patrol?" José asked, worried.

"Unknown. I didn't wait around to get a closer look."

"Diego?" Consuela asked.

"Possibly," José said grimly. He turned to the guerrillas behind him and gave a low whistle to attract their attention. When he was satisfied he had it, he gave the hand signal to go to earth.

To an untrained observer it might have looked as though they had all simply melted into the ground. Guerrilla warfare depended on the ability to strike at the enemy from hiding, and José's troops were very good at hiding. Some slipped into the dense undergrowth on the sides of the trail; others concealed themselves behind fallen logs or tangled bushes, their faded clothes blending seamlessly with the dappled foliage.

Several climbed trees and stretched out along high branches, their rifles at the ready to attack, sniper-style. José sincerely hoped his brother had not renewed his pursuit. Being caught between two enemies—the Union soldiers here and whatever was at the jungle crater—was not a position he relished. He had hoped the casualties he and Consuela had inflicted in their earlier pursuit would have discouraged Diego, but he knew this was his brother's best opportunity for victory since assuming command at the San Cristóbal garrison. Diego had never been this aggressive in the past, but perhaps the victory at Revancha had encouraged him.

Wanting to get a better view of the coming conflict, José scrambled up an almond tree that bent precariously under his weight. He stopped at the first large limb and peered through the foliage as the first of their opponents came into view.

He crossed himself when he saw who it was—or, rather, what it was.

Now he knew what had happened to his missing patrols.

He heard a small gasp from Consuela, but he could not tear his eyes away from the shambling, decayed parodies of humanity that lurched into view on the trail. Shreds of their uniforms hung off their twisted limbs, the wounds that had killed them clearly visible through the rags. Hoses from the dull metallic tanks on their backs circled their tortured bodies and entered their chests in several places.

"The dead have risen from the grave," he breathed.

"José!" came Consuela's horrified voice. "Do you see what I do?"

José had been a soldier for many years; he had foolishly thought he was inured to any vision of horror. Now he knew how wrong he was as yet another walking dead woman lurched into view: Mary Stephenson. Or what had once been Mary. Her legs were twisted and crippled, yet she walked. Her chest gaped from her death wound, yet she lived. A wicked curved knife gleamed in her hand, and it did not seem that death had dulled her lethal combat skills.

"What are we going to do, José?" Consuela cried, frantic. "We cannot leave her!"

"That is not the Mary we knew," José said from his aerial perch. He aimed the Kalashnikov he had commandeered from one of his soldiers in Mary's direction but could not fire. What good would it do? She was already dead. Obviously.

José forced himself to look from the abomination that had been one of his finest soldiers to the others coming from the green veil of the jungle. He recognized many of the guerrillas who had gone with him to Revancha and not returned—now somehow restored to this shambling mock-

ery of life. Had Diego found some way of resurrecting the
dead to use against their former friends?

But no. He knew Diego. Never would his brother use
such evil technology, even if the Union were capable of it.
Unlike his older brother, who loosed Neo-Sov mutants on
his enemies.

Below, there was a sudden commotion as one of his
guerrillas burst from hiding and ran into view. José's heart
sank. After his first glimpse of the hideous zombie creatures that had once been his friends, he had hoped to remain hidden and let them pass. How did you fight
creatures that were already dead?

But the sight of one of the zombies had galvanized the
man into action. He skidded to a stop in front of one of
them, a woman. "Ana," he pleaded. "Do you not know me?
What have they done to you?"

José recognized the woman—she and the man had
been lovers before the explosion of the warehouse at Revancha had torn them apart. Now she stared at her former
lover from flat, uncomprehending eyes. He reached out a
pleading hand to her. In response, her arm whipped out
quicker than José's eyes could follow and left a red, gaping wound where the man's throat had been.

With a look of blank surprise on his face, the man fell,
dead before he hit the ground. There was a moment of
frozen suspension, and then José's guerrillas attacked.

With a roar, several dozen guns opened up from their
hiding places. The bullets staggered the zombies, but did
not kill them. As one, the army of rotting corpses rushed
forward, wielding wickedly sharp steel knives and bars.

José reflexively ducked as a ricochet tore through
leaves above his head—a bullet had bounced off a metal

backpack and went zinging into the jungle. He brought his rifle up, ready to fire—and then froze as he saw something new emerge from the jungle onto the trail, something that winked in and out of sight like a poorly remembered dream. And fast! It moved with the speed of an attacking jaguar—faster.

Even from across the clearing, the stink of the monstrous being caused José's nose to wrinkle. He had been in many cemeteries, but this was worse than the simple stench of death. This was the odor of centuries of corrupted flesh.

From the glimpses he caught of it, this creature wore far more elaborate gear than José's former comrades. Clad in interleaved metallic armor, it danced about, almost in sight and then vanishing, only to appear elsewhere. If Mary and the others were dangerous, this creature was utterly deadly.

The fighting had dislodged several guerrillas from their hiding places, and one unwary woman strayed into the monster's field of vision. From some sort of peculiar energy weapon the creature carried lanced out a ball of green lightning that engulfed the unfortunate woman in a field of crackling electricity. She screamed as her body stiffened and her limbs began a spasmodic dance. The lightning dissipated, and she crashed to the ground, still twitching involuntarily. From a distance, her eyes found José's, high in his tree, and her trembling lips formed the word "Please."

His heart aching with horror and pity, José unclipped a grenade from his belt, armed it with a quick twist, and lobbed it toward her. The grenade hit the ground next to her, bounced once, and detonated with a roar. José ducked against the trunk of the tree to avoid the worst of the blast, his ears ringing. When his vision cleared, he looked down at the sad remnants of what had once been a soldier, and his throat tightened. At least the putrid creature would not be able to resurrect her into a pseudolife of slavery.

This had to be the *chupacabra* that Flaco had spoken of and that José had so casually dismissed. Poor, jolly Flaco—who was jolly no longer. He watched in horror as the shambling wreck that had once been his trusted lieutenant aimed a crushing blow at an opponent's head, sending the man crashing to the ground. José lifted his Kalashnikov and sighted on the armored creature when it flickered back into view next to the downed guerrilla. It knelt and donned a knobbed gauntlet. Its victim never flinched as a long needle penetrated his chest; he simply withered to an empty husk.

José lowered his rifle. He could not shoot and be certain he could kill, because he was not sure whether this tall, commanding monster was not already dead, like the humans with it. Its head was wrapped in greasy rags. Sticking up from the top of its backpack was a bullet-ridden set of lenses, possibly a weapon or a solar collector. This creature had been in battle.

And had survived.

José lifted his rifle straight up and fired into the air to gain his soldiers' attention.

"Retreat!" he shouted. "Disengage!" He slithered down from the tree, nearly falling in his haste, and collided with Gunther on the ground. The man's eyes were so wide that white showed all the way around the edges.

"Get your squad together and get them out of here,"

José ordered. "We cannot fight these things now. Get them away!"

Dazed, Gunther nodded, then visibly shook himself and began shouting orders. One by one, then by twos and threes, the guerrillas abandoned their former friends and stumbled into the jungle. The zombies seemed to lose interest once their opponents were no longer immediately before them.

From his hiding place crouched in the bushes, José watched as the tall monster in golden armor gathered its obscene flock back to it. For a time they stood quietly as the creature issued instructions to them in a strange, hissing language. When it had finished, a half dozen zombies turned and lurched into the jungle. The creature herded the rest of its slaves down the trail in the direction of the crater. José watched as they passed, and for a long time after they had disappeared from sight, he remained, staring at nothing.

He flinched as he felt a tentative touch on his shoulder, but it was only Consuela. "Was that the thing Flaco spoke of?" she whispered.

"It was not the creature you saw at the crater?" he asked.

"No," she said, her eyes wide. "This was something new. And the things with it . . ." She shuddered.

José crawled out onto the trail and stood silently as the other guerrillas crept back to him. Only a few had been lost in the brief, abortive battle, but all were pale and shaken by the horrors they had just witnessed. Even Gunther was uncharacteristically silent, clutching his rifle to him like a talisman.

"All right," José said, then had to pause and clear his throat. "We need to decide what we're going to do."

"Decide?" Gunther asked hoarsely. "There is no decision necessary. We must destroy that thing."

For once, José was in complete agreement. "Don't worry, Gunther," he said, meeting the man's eyes. "That monster cannot be allowed to live. But we must plan our attack carefully. You saw what happened when we fought without a strategy. If we are to have a hope of defeating it, we must be very careful."

Gunther nodded reluctantly. José turned to Consuela. "I have a special task for you, *chica*," he said. "I need you to follow the zombies who split off from the main group. We need to know where they are going and if there are more of them elsewhere in the jungle."

Consuela nodded and melted into the trees, wasting no words.

José turned back to the remainder of his force. "Come," he said. "We follow the monster to its goal, and there we will find the means to stop it."

The guerrillas nodded as one and prepared to follow José. They were all on board now—anxious to stop the horror that had enslaved their friends and relatives. José only wished he had the faintest idea how to do it.

23

Diego Villalobos had never seen such destruction. The village of Portillo had been burned to the ground, and then the ashes had been turned into the thin soil by some kind of laser beam. Hurricanes routinely destroyed property and killed *campesinos*, but such complete devastation was unheard of.

The village was gone. Too many of the *campesinos* remained. Diego had seen combat and its resulting death and injuries. But his gorge still rose when he stared at the head-high pile of bodies.

"All the old folks, Colonel," Lieutenant Suarez said in a choked voice. "Small kids, too, the ones under seven or eight."

"But what happened to the rest of them?" Diego wondered.

"Unknown, sir," Suarez said. "They're gone without a trace. And whoever did this didn't leave anyone alive to tell us what happened."

Diego stared at the devastated village. This was the

second settlement his squad had visited this morning. The first had lost only a few people—nothing on this scale of destruction. And the remaining *campesinos* had reported seeing a tall golden creature appear out of nowhere to steal their friends and relatives away.

It was the sort of tale Diego might ordinarily dismiss, if not for two things. First, he had seen the video of the crystal alien with his own eyes. Where he had seen one monster, he was prepared to believe in others. And second, the villagers he had spoken to were deeply frightened. People who ordinarily would have been hostile now crowded around him, eager to talk, anxious for the well-armed Union soldiers to protect them.

Looking at the pile of bodies before him, he understood why. It was almost enough to take his mind off the wreckage of his career. Allen had not even bothered to see them off—Suarez had told him the scheming captain had left even earlier than they had on some mysterious errand. He was probably off making up more lies to feed General Ramirez. Diego should have been warier when Allen showed up, but he had simply been juggling too many burdens to pay too much attention to the man.

That was a mistake, but he had no time to brood. The Union might have betrayed and abandoned him, but he was going to carry out the duty he had signed up for many years ago: protect its citizens.

"Sir!" A voice from across the village square broke his concentration, and he looked up to see BJ Travis waving at him. Her battered face was split in a fierce smile, and the men behind her looked tired but contented.

Diego saluted her as she hurried up to him, and she returned the courtesy, looking happier to see him than she had in a long time. Perhaps a couple of military victories against the guerrillas had finally reassured her as to his loyalties.

"Didn't expect to see you here, sir," she panted as she skidded to a stop next to him. "If you've come to lend a hand with the mop-up, you're too late—we tracked down and killed the last Cyclops just a few hours ago."

"Negative, Lieutenant," Diego said. "This"—he gestured at the sad mound of bodies—"is what brings me here."

BJ's face tightened. "We've gotten reports from other villages that have been attacked, too," she said in a subdued voice. "Nothing on this scale, though. That's why we're here, in fact. We figured as long as we were here, we might as well look into it. But now that you're here . . ."

"Stay," Diego commanded. "I may be able to use your help."

"Sir, what's going on back at the post?" BJ asked. "I got some weird message yesterday that made it sound as if Allen ruled the roost. I figured he was just being bullheaded and ignored the comm."

"He is in charge now," Diego said. This time the anger could not be suppressed. "HQ in Mexico City decided I had abandoned my post by taking my men to defend Revancha, and General Ramirez has relieved me of command pending an inquiry. So Captain Allen sends me out here to investigate the attacks on the villages."

"What kind of utter—"

"Lieutenant," he said to cut off her explosion, "I have my orders, and so do you."

"Bull—"

"Lieutenant," Diego snapped, "stay out of this. It's political, and you'll be ground up and spat out if you get caught in the middle."

"I take my orders from you," BJ said forcefully, "not some preening peacock from up north. If Allen doesn't like it, he can court-martial me right alongside you."

"Is there any doubt Captain Allen would recommend it?" Diego asked.

"Didn't like the son of a bitch from the minute I set eyes on him," BJ grumbled. "What's he want us to do?"

"Carry on, protect the villages, and don't give him any static," Diego said. "I've been demoted to nothing more than squad leader, but at least he didn't strip me of rank—he just took me out of the chain of command."

"That's crazy, even for someone like Allen," BJ snorted.

"I appreciate your support, Lieutenant, but right now what's happening here is more important," Diego replied.

"What could be causing this?" she asked, her expression bleak as she stared at the carnage surrounding them.

"Did you get the report on the creature that attacked San Cristóbal?"

BJ nodded. "Didn't understand much of it. You think it might be behind this? Didn't Allen blow the thing apart with a SPEAR?"

"It might not be the only one, or there might be some other kind of alien roaming the countryside," Diego said. "Whatever it is, we have to target and destroy it."

"You and what flight of neutron bombs are going to do this?" BJ asked.

Diego said nothing. He commanded a partial squad of four men, none of them—apart from Suarez—veterans or even fully jungle-trained. They carried Pitbulls, a few grenades, and nothing more. If he encountered the golden alien, or even a guerrilla force of any strength, he could not hope to prevail. Diego knew that was what Allen expected—the man was secretly hoping he might die in combat and avoid the potential messiness of a hearing.

"How many men do you have with you, Lieutenant?" Diego asked, his mind racing as he recalculated his odds.

"Unfortunately, not many," BJ said. "I sent most of 'em back to San Cristóbal after we dispatched the last Cyclops and just kept a squad of eight soldiers to investigate the village attacks. I did keep the Aztec cycles with us, though I don't know what good that will do us if we can't find whatever's doing this."

"Lieutenant Suarez," Diego called. The man, who had tactfully moved a few meters away during this conversation to give them some privacy, hurried up.

"Let's gather our squad and Lieutenant Travis's men and hit the next village down the line," Diego ordered. "Maybe if we can plot the pattern of attacks, we can figure out where they're coming from."

"I think you should take a look at this first, sir," Suarez said, scowling down at his equipment. "I'm getting some anomalous readings here—power surges like nothing I've ever seen. See these spikes?"

"Guerrillas?" Diego guessed.

"Not unless they've gotten their hands on a fusion generator," Suarez said. "That's the closest I can come to these readings—but even that's not quite right."

The two men's eyes met, and each knew what the other was thinking. An unknown force attacks a village. An unknown power source is operating in the jungle not far away. Coincidence? Improbable.

Diego peered over Suarez's shoulder at the readings. Something out in the jungle was pushing the instrument readouts orders of magnitude above their usual levels, yet in such a way that he doubted space or aerial recon would reveal the source. The power leakages came out parallel to the jungle floor, as if being deliberately hidden.

"It's only about fifteen klicks due west of here, sir," Suarez pointed out. "We could take the Hydra there— there's room for Lieutenant Travis's squad as well—and see what's up. It might be a major Neo-Sov invasion force or some kind of secret guerrilla base that's stayed hidden from us until now."

Staring at the readouts, Diego came to a speedy decision. "We'll take the Hydra to within a kilometer and then go to ground and investigate on foot," he said. "If somebody's got the tech to hide that much power, they've probably got electronic nets scattered around to pick up something as large as a Hydra.

"Get the men loaded up, Lieutenant," Diego ordered. "This is going to be it. I feel it in my bones."

Diego, Suarez, and two other soldiers slipped into the jungle away from the Hydra, which had powered down and was virtually concealed by the thick undergrowth. BJ and the rest of the men had been ordered to stay by the Hydra while Diego's squad did a preliminary recon. Diego hesitantly kept to a newly cut trail, although he was worried they might be walking into a trap. Suarez had point and kept up a constant chatter, warning of possible snares. They found nothing, but Diego felt the hair rising on the back of his neck as they approached the site identified as the energy nexus. He slowed, then motioned his scouts off the trail.

"Colonel," whispered Suarez, "my readings are sky-high now. Whatever's there is a thousand times more powerful than I thought."

"What do you mean?"

"They are blanketing emissions. What I picked up before is just the leakage. This might be a weapons complex capable of defending the entire planet from space attack."

That meant the Neo-Sovs were not involved. Diego might have had some training problems, but such huge amounts of ordnance could never have been moved into the jungle without his men discovering it. José might have accumulated some energy weapons over the years, but nothing on this scale.

If not the Neo-Soviets or José, then who?

He fastened the latches on his body armor, loaded a grenade into the Bulldog, and began a quiet advance. Standing around asking questions he couldn't answer was not the way to go. Seeing the energy source up close was. Suarez and the other two spread out, moving on cat's feet through the vegetation. They moved so quietly all Diego heard was the soft wind in the high leaves of the jade jacaranda trees.

The jungle ended abruptly, crisped by what looked like laser burns. Diego went to his belly and eased his rifle ahead of him. Using the Bulldog's scope, he studied the new clearing stretched out in front of him. He gasped when he finally figured out what it was.

"A spaceship," he said into his mike. "Suarez, do you copy that?"

"Copy that, sir," the lieutenant reported. "That's the source of the energy."

Diego slowly scanned the length of the ship, wondering at the construction. He knew the configuration of every Neo-Soviet and Union space vessel. This wasn't any of them.

He studied the craft, finding a pair of large cargo-bay doors, now closed, and the forward weapons. Extrapolating from what he could see, the ship mounted no fewer than fifty laser cannons of incredible size and destructive capacity. If there had been any possibility that this was a peaceful trading vessel, that erased it entirely.

"Sir," came the voice of one of his scouts, working her way toward the far side of the spaceship. "Airlock opening. People coming out."

"Patch through a video feed," Diego ordered. It was dangerous using broadband comm so close to a technically superior enemy, but he needed to see what was going on.

He recoiled when the picture popped up just a few centimeters in front of his face. He adjusted his battle helmet and studied the scene, going cold when he saw the "people" emerging from the spaceship.

"What are they, sir?" asked the scout, her voice turning shriller as she spoke.

"Dead," was all he could say. He recognized one or two of them as they trudged out—guerrillas killed during the Revancha attack. Diego had demanded that every Zapatista killed be identified so their families could be notified. He had flipped through the files, every picture burning itself into his brain.

"That one's Mary Stephenson," said Suarez. "I recognize her from a couple of raids she led. That's one of

Viejo's top lieutenants! We've found the main Zapatista base!"

"No, Lieutenant, not that," Diego said grimly. Stephenson moved awkwardly because of a battered metal pack on her back. It unbalanced her, but she seemed not to notice. Fumes vented and hoses ran around her thin body to vanish into her belly and chest. She herded the others, similarly outfitted, toward a spot on the spaceship hull that appeared to need repair.

Stephenson was still acting like a lieutenant, but Diego doubted it was for José. The others obeying her orders all wore the hissing, venting backpacks, too. And all were in various stages of decay. Some were largely intact. Others, like Mary, had begun to decompose badly.

"What's going on, sir?" asked Suarez. "They . . . they look like corpses."

"Get all the readings you can, Lieutenant," ordered Diego. "I don't know what we've found, but it isn't any Zapatista base."

"But Stephenson!" protested Suarez.

"Dead. I saw the report. I *verified* the report." Diego scanned back and forth across the spaceship and the zombie workers making what seemed the last of extensive repairs.

"I . . . look at that!" Suarez exclaimed.

Diego thought he had seen everything during his career in Chiapas. He was wrong. His finger tightened on the trigger of his Bulldog, but he hesitated to fire. He hardly believed his eyes, yet what both scouts and Suarez fed him through his battle-helmet monitor confirmed it. Coming out of the spaceship was the most horrendous creature he had ever seen. At first he thought it was only a mirage caused by the intense afternoon heat.

But it was nothing of the sort, not with the other three reporting the same hideous sight. Tall, thin, wearing heavy interleaved armor, it had a more elaborate pack on its back than those worn by the humans—by the dead humans. Was this *thing* dead, too?

Diego and his squad watched in silent horror as the monster approached a group of slaves working to repair one of the ship's tailfins. Then, from a few meters away came a tremendous clatter as another of the hapless slaves dropped the piece of machinery it was laboring to fix.

The alien monster's head jerked around at the noise, and Diego could hear a hideous metallic clacking noise as it opened and closed the mammoth claw attached to its left arm. Before Diego could even blink, the creature had taken two huge strides toward the unfortunate group of enslaved humans—or what had once been humans—and whipped up the energy weapon in its other hand. One burst of the green beam, and the entire group of slaves fell, smoking and dead, to the ground.

The creature hesitated briefly, staring at the results of its handiwork, then turned back to the rest of the workers busily repairing the ship. It waved an arm, clearly issuing instructions, then gestured curtly at the group by the tailfin and headed out of the clearing, followed by a half dozen zombies. Diego held his breath as the horrific group passed so close to his hiding position that he could have reached out and touched the monster's beautifully engraved armor, had he been of a mind to do so. But they passed him by unnoticed, and after a few moments he could feel his heartbeat returning to normal.

He found his voice and activated his comm mike. "Lieutenant Travis," he broadcast softly.

"Here, sir," came the instant response.

"Have you been picking up our video feed?" Diego asked.

"Yes, sir. What the hell are those things?"

"I don't know. But we need to find out what they're up to. My squad will pursue on foot; I want you to get the rest of our soldiers loaded into the Hydra and remain on standby. When we find out what their target is, we'll notify you."

"And we'll come a-running," BJ said crisply.

Diego waited a few moments for Suarez and the others to work their way around to his position without alerting the monstrosities still toiling away in the clearing. When the four had reunited, Diego led them cautiously along the trail left by the alien and its slaves. He had no idea what he would do when they caught up with their prey, but he knew he would have to think of something.

24

Forward!" José shouted, wiping the blood from his eyes in a futile attempt to clear his vision. A bullet had hit the tree trunk he was using for cover and sent splinters of wood flying into his forehead. But many of the men and women fighting with him had suffered much worse.

The battle at the crater was not going well. José had waited until most of his former comrades were toiling at the bottom of the pit under the golden monster's direction before attacking, hoping to gain the advantage of surprise. But there were still plenty of other zombies willing to defend their master with every bit of unnatural strength they possessed. No matter what José's guerrillas tried, they refused to die.

And throughout the battle stalked the glowing form of the creature that had raised them from the dead. It carried an ornate cube in one hand, from which deadly lances of blue energy licked out; when they touched a person, that person died.

But they had to try. José was determined that not another *campesino* would fall victim to the alien monster's depredations. He took aim at another zombie and fired. The thing lurched as the bullet tore through one of the hoses cruelly plunged into its torso, spilling noxious fluids everywhere, but it kept coming.

José backpedaled frantically, striving to stay out of range of the wicked knife it wielded. The zombie slashed and slashed again, and each time José just barely evaded it. The creature was too close for José to fire, so in desperation he swung his Kalashnikov like a club and hit the tank strapped to the zombie's back with a resounding clang.

The zombie staggered back a few paces, and purely on instinct José leveled his rifle and fired directly at the tank. The top of the metal pack exploded in a shower of fluids, and the zombie collapsed like a puppet with its strings cut. José stared at it, scarcely daring to believe, and then raised his voice, shouting to be heard over the din of the melee.

"The tanks!" he cried at the top of his lungs. "Target the tanks!"

A few of his soldiers heard him, and a few more zombies fell. But their sense of loyalty continually worked against them. When faced with the reanimated corpses of their former comrades, many of the guerrillas were reluctant to fire, and that reluctance was deadly. Only Gunther killed without hesitation—killed once or killed twice, friend or foe, it was all the same to him.

José aimed carefully and took out two more zombies, but the battle was going against them. As long as the golden alien continued to wield its deadly energy beam, the guerrillas were fated to lose. José began concentrating his fire on the creature, hoping that since it wore a tank on its back as well, puncturing it would have the same effect. But the thing was impossible to hit—it seemed to flicker in and out of existence, disappearing from one part of the battlefield to reappear with deadly effect in another part. One lucky shot spanged off a round metal disk at the top of the monster's tank, staggering the thing but otherwise having no effect.

José slammed one of his few remaining clips into his Kalashnikov and swore heartily. Wherever she might be, he hoped Consuela was having better luck than he was.

The scent of burning vegetation made Consuela's nose twitch long before she heard the sounds of fighting coming from the village of Hermosilla, which lay just ahead. She tightened her grip on the Kalashnikov she held at the ready. Following the zombies that had split off from the main group being herded along by that monster had been easy; they had never even noticed her slipping along silently behind them. She had stayed hidden at the edge of the jungle as the zombies had reported to yet another of those hideous creatures. Shortly thereafter, the thing had headed off in the direction of this village.

Now she quickened her pace as the sounds of fighting grew louder. She had feared this might come to pass—the zombies were attacking another village, determined to create more of their kind from the hapless *campesinos*.

Consuela burst out of the jungle and into the outskirts of Hermosilla. Her rifle was up and firing on full-auto before she was even conscious of reacting, cutting the legs out from under a zombie that was menacing two huddled villagers with a wickedly sharp knife. Crippled but not discouraged, the zombie began clawing its way toward Consuela. She fired another burst into the tank on its back, and it abruptly collapsed to the ground and ceased moving. But now two more zombies had rounded the corner of the building and were advancing on the villagers.

"Go!" Consuela shouted. "Get to the jungle!" The frightened *campesinos* stared at her uncomprehendingly for a moment, then dashed for the safety of the enshrouding jungle. Consuela slammed a fresh clip into her rifle and fired a burst into the two approaching zombies, checking their advance long enough for her to do the only sensible thing: turn and run.

She skidded to a halt in the center of the village, appalled at the sight that greeted her. Across the dusty square stalked the monster she had seen by the alien ship, its huge clawed hand red with human blood, the energy weapon it held in its other hand sending out deadly green beams. Consuela looked around frantically. There was a knot of women and children crouching next to one of the houses, but the monster would undoubtedly see them in a few moments. She gave a low, carrying whistle to attract their attention and gestured for them to get into the village meeting hall behind her. In there, they would have more cover and might be able to hold the things off. For a little while.

She laid down a long burst of fire to cover them as they ran for the dubious shelter of the hall, then dived in after them.

Only to find herself face-to-face with a squad of Union soldiers, led by none other than Diego Villalobos himself.

Consuela instinctively leveled her rifle at him. "I should have known," she said coldly. "Are you in league with those things outside? Is this how the Union treats its people?"

"In league?" Diego asked incredulously. "We came here to stop them—whatever they are." He and Consuela both ducked as the alien's energy beam cut through the building overhead with a sizzle of frying wood.

"Look, we can continue this conversation some other time," Diego snapped. "Right now, we've got a job to do— saving these people. Are you going to help, or are you just going to stand there?"

"Help?" Consuela asked in disbelief. But Diego, oblivious to the rifle she still held pointed at him, had already moved past her to one of the windows and had begun firing out of it, joined by his three soldiers.

Consuela looked past them and saw a zombie outlined in the open doorway. She fired a burst at it to force it backward, slammed the door, and leaned against it. The door shook with the heavy pounding of the creatures outside, and she knew it wouldn't hold for long.

"Suarez!" Diego called, ducking as answering fire from the alien cut through the air. "We've got to get these people out of here. I want you to lead them out the back and into the jungle. Use windows, whatever you need to. Blow a hole in the wall if you have to. We'll try to hold these things off."

One of the Union soldiers nodded and raced to the back of the building, urging the dozen or so villagers huddled there up and out through the back door. Consuela braced herself as a renewed attack shook the door.

"We can't hold them for much longer," she gasped.

"I know," Diego said grimly. He released his grip on his Bulldog long enough to fumble at his belt. "Grenades," he said, showing one to her. "We draw them inside and blow the building. That ought to slow them down long enough for us to get these people out, at least."

He motioned to the other two soldiers, and they began to retreat toward the back of the building, dropping grenades as they went. Consuela stayed put, holding the door as long as she could against the zombies' assault. She flinched as a putrefied arm came through the window next to her and a zombie began to clamber into the building.

"Go!" Diego shouted to her from outside the hall, and Consuela leapt away from the door and ran full out toward him. She had barely cleared the doorway when Diego shouted, "Fire in the hole!", leveled his Bulldog, and began lobbing grenades into the building. For a second, Consuela thought nothing had happened. Then the blast came, powerful enough to knock her and the Union soldiers off their feet. Dazed, her ears ringing, she crawled back upright. The explosion had leveled the building, trapping a number of zombies in the wreckage.

"Come on," Diego said, touching her arm. "We need to take cover."

She looked him directly in the eyes, liking the way he met her gaze without flinching. So many years she had fought against this man, and this was the first time they had ever met face-to-face.

"Why?" she asked.

"Why what?" Diego said.

"You saved the *campesinos*. And you also risked your life to save me, when you knew I was a Zapatista."

"The rules have changed, in case you hadn't noticed," Diego said. "It's human against alien now—and at the moment the aliens seem to be trouncing us."

Consuela stood a moment longer, looking at him, then turned and slipped into the jungle without another word. By the time Diego's soldiers had reached the spot where she had disappeared, she was far away from them, headed back to José to tell him of what she had found. And of what she had learned.

"Captain Allen, you won't believe what we saw," the scout said, his eyes wide.

"What?" Allen asked impatiently. His expedition had taken far too long to reach the crater. He chafed at the delay and had sent two scouts to reconnoiter the position. He knew he had to make certain there were no more crystalline monstrosities lurking at the crater—and from the looks of this pair, he wasn't going to like what they told him.

"Dozens of them!"

"What?" Allen came out of his reverie. "What did you say? Dozens of what?"

"Creepy, Captain," the first scout replied. "All these men and women, looking like they'd been dug up fresh out of their graves, working for this tall . . ." The private's words trailed off as he struggled to describe what he'd seen.

His companion chimed in. "It was a monster. Shiny armor, holding some kind of box, with this green beam . . ."

"I don't understand what you're saying," Allen said. "These dead people are walking around following orders from some creature with a box?"

"And they all wore backpacks that hissed and creaked and had hoses running into their guts," said the first scout.

"Even the creature had one, except its equipment was a lot more complicated. It was even beautiful, fancy gold inlay, shiny steel . . ."

"They were just taking those guerrillas apart," said the second scout.

"Guerrillas?" Allen asked, his voice rising. "What guerrillas?"

The two scouts exchanged glances. "The ones at the pit," the first scout finally said. "The ones we told you about earlier. Weren't you listening? Sir?"

If Allen had been listening before, he wasn't now. He was consumed by a rapidly building fury. Had the guerrillas—those stinking, dirty peasants—actually beaten him to the meteorite? Were they actually digging up his ticket back north and out of this hellhole?

He was torn about what to do. He had only brought along ten soldiers, leaving the remainder of his command in the post at San Cristóbal. He had tried to get General Ramirez to send reinforcements before venturing out, but the MCF commander in chief had hedged, saying his troops were otherwise occupied and could not be spared for garrison duty.

Allen knew how tenuous was his hold on San Cristóbal. He had to prove to Ramirez how capable he was, and he was not about to make the same mistake Diego Villalobos had. But at the same time, he dared not let anyone else—or *anything* else—steal his treasure.

The armored personnel carrier had settled to the ground about five hundred meters from the crater. The soldiers with him carried the heaviest arms he had been able to find in the San Cristóbal armory. Two struggled along with a Harbinger rail gun and the depleted-uranium ingots it fired, another

had a Rottweiler, and the rest had been outfitted with Bulldog rifles to give them grenade-launching capability. He had
considered bringing along the one remaining SPEAR missile, but the Aztec cycles that usually carried them were with
Lieutenant Travis, wherever the hell she was. His ten soldiers boasted the firepower of an entire company.

That ought to be enough. Hadn't he already destroyed
the crystal monster? Whatever was trying to muscle in on
the monster's domain at the pit should fall quickly to such
firepower, without the need to use the remaining SPEAR
missile.

"Advance," Allen ordered, hefting his rifle. The going
was easier now because he was traveling in the APC instead of slogging through the thick jungle, sweating his
brains out. That would make any skirmish easier to win because he and his men were rested, even if it was the hottest
part of the afternoon. Not that he thought the scouts' report
about dead soldiers was anything but superstitious clap-
trap. They had probably seen some of the guerrillas
dressed in rags and mistaken them for dead men. This was
going to be a cakewalk.

"Captain, you hear that?" asked one of his men.
"Sounds like quite a fight."

Allen cocked his head to one side and frowned. He
heard nothing. He kept moving toward the crater, though,
and a few minutes later he heard what the sharper-eared
man already had. His heart skipped a beat when he thought
of something happening to his meteorite.

"Forward. Gunners, prepare your weapons. Especially
you with the Rott and the Harbinger." He took a deep
breath, gagged on the heavy jungle odors and stifling heat,
then took point. Allen wanted to be first at the site. What

terrible luck had let those guerrillas stumble on his discovery? He had to retrieve the meteorite immediately, before the entire population of Chiapas discovered the crater.

He stepped from the jungle to the glassy plain surrounding the crater and stopped, mouth agape. The two scouts had not exaggerated. Everywhere was chaos, a swirl of battling guerrillas and walking dead. The overpowering stench of freshly spilled blood and rotting human flesh almost made Allen lose his breakfast. He leveled his Bulldog but wasn't sure where to point it.

Then he saw the armored creature, hovering near the pit where the meteorite—his meteorite—lay, its brilliance dimmed. This one looked nothing like the crystalline monster he had killed earlier, but it was obviously after the same thing Allen was. This was the real threat, not the ragtag guerrillas fighting around it.

Its allies were dead humans. This—whatever it was—shared nothing but death with them.

"Fire!" cried Allen, locking his laser sights in on the armored monster. The Bulldog recoiled in his grip as a grenade sailed forth, followed by heavy slugs ripping toward the alien creature.

The grenade blew up a few meters in front of the monster, but at least one of Allen's steel-jacketed rifle rounds hit the armored zombie.

"Get it! Concentrate your fire on it!" he shouted. Some of his squad had vanished into the jungle, too spooked to fight. Those remaining opened up with their weapons. He heard the deep chatter of the Rottweiler begin, but the gunner was taking out the dead humans and the guerrillas, not the demon Allen had identified as the real danger.

From the armored form came a beam of energy that

cut through two of Allen's soldiers, silencing the Rottweiler.

"Rail gun, fire! Give it all you've got!"

His command went unheeded. The man lugging the Harbinger, as well as his loader, had turned tail and fled. Allen had just three riflemen left, and they shifted their aim to the creature at his order. Several guerrillas died, caught in the cross fire, but Allen barely noticed. All his being was concentrated on getting to the crater that held his prize, his mind filled with only one thought: mine.

The creature laid down its energy cube and replaced it with some sort of projectile weapon. Fléchette darts whizzed past Allen, every striking dart exploding. Another soldier died.

The creature shouted orders at its undead army, and a number of them broke off their struggle with the guerrillas and attacked Allen's surviving soldiers. The area around the pit was total chaos, as soldiers and undead alike blindly attacked anything that moved, no longer able to distinguish friend from foe. Allen loaded another grenade into his Bulldog and fired, taking out three of the dead humans. They fell, the hoses to their back tanks severed and hideous fluids spilling out over the hard ground.

Allen kept firing, working his way deeper into the battle step by step, struggling to get closer to the crater. The monster had left off its attack, content with its slaves' progress, and now turned its attention to the thing at the bottom, intent on some alien equipment it held in its hands.

Allen briefly froze as a luminous glow rose above the lip of the pit. It appeared to be a crystalline globe, encased in what looked like some sort of force field, its awesome energy swirling turbulently inside. Several slaves were carrying it in a rough sling. Even as Allen watched, one fell, crisped by the devastating radiation that burned through the containing force field. Another took its place.

Allen swelled with rage. That creature was stealing his meteorite! Heedless of the danger, he began forcing his way roughly through the battling men and women toward the crater. Dimly behind him, he could hear his few surviving men calling to him to wait, but he ignored them. The guerrillas, even the animated corpses were nothing. Only the orb mattered.

A bullet whined past his right ear. Another clipped the shoulder of his uniform. It missed the flesh, but the tug on his clothing pulled Allen from his self-absorption, and he realized abruptly how foolhardy he was being. Promotion and acclaim would do him little good if he were dead. He whirled around frantically, looking for cover—and ran smack into a thin guerrilla who looked at him with a killer's eyes. Even before Allen had time to react, the man raised his gun and clubbed him to the ground. Dazed, blood trickling down his face, Allen looked up at the guerrilla.

The man leaned down. "My name is Gunther," the soldier said confidingly.

Even barely conscious as he was, the incongruity of the introduction struck Allen, and his lips struggled to form words.

"I just wanted you to know who is going to kill you," the man—Gunther?—said. He leveled his rifle, pointing the barrel directly between Allen's eyes.

"Wait!" Allen cried desperately. "I am a friend to your people. I know a peasant girl—her name is Consuela. She can vouch for me!"

Gunther laughed. "I know her well," he said mockingly. "When I report back to her, I will send her your regards."

Allen froze. That tiny girl who had led him to his prize was a guerrilla? Impossible. How could he have miscalculated so badly?

He never heard the report of the bullet that killed him. But as it tore through his skull and into his brain, his eyes fixed despairingly on the glowing form of the orb. And one last thought took him into the final darkness: mine.

25

José Villalobos slumped against the trunk of a jacaranda tree, panting for breath. The days since the Revancha defeat had tested him—and his guerrillas—more severely than he could ever have expected. In the past, his war had always been waged from hiding, with snipers and booby traps. It had been a war fought by taking one life at a time, especially if it frightened a dozen more of the enemy soldiers. He had hoped to carry the war to the next level with his disastrous strike on Revancha, but Diego had anticipated his every move and decimated his forces.

Now, he was beset by enemies at every turn. He had escaped his brother's pursuit only to be attacked by the re-animated corpses of his own soldiers. Consuela's mysterious crystalline monster had seemingly vanished, only to be replaced by the walking dead, commanded by the putrefied alien the *campesinos* had dubbed a *chupacabra*. Everywhere he turned, he found only violence and death, and his forces were dwindling man by man, woman by woman.

The battle against the zombies in the jungle had cost him several soldiers; at the pit he had lost a dozen more.

For a while it had seemed as if the fight near the crater would finally hand him the victory he had sought for so long. Once José and the others had begun targeting the mysterious tanks carried by their undead foe, the tide of battle had begun to turn in their favor. But then that idiotic Union soldier had burst into the middle of the fight and destroyed everything. Faced with enemies from both sides—the corpses of friends at their fore and the Union soldiers firing from behind—José's guerrillas had panicked and broken ranks.

And he could not blame them. It was hard enough staring into the flat, dead eyes of people they had once called comrades, friends, even lovers, and seeing only enemies. His people had been pushed to the brink of their endurance by the events of the past few days, and the surprise attack from the rear had been the final straw. He looked at them, slumped nearby, and did not know what to say to them. They were exhausted, wounded, discouraged—stretched thin. And somewhere behind them lurked the monster that was enslaving their people—and José had no idea what he could do to stop it. He had lost almost 90 percent of his force; they were now down to a few dozen soldiers. How could such a tiny remnant hope to defeat such a powerful force as they had witnessed at the crater?

His hand went to his battered Kalashnikov when he caught movement out of the corner of his eye, but he relaxed when he saw it was Consuela. She had returned from her mission, but he couldn't imagine what intelligence she could possibly provide that would give them even a fighting chance. The golden-armored alien was simply too powerful to resist.

"What happened?" Consuela asked in a shocked tone, looking at the remnants of their army.

"We could not win," José said, almost too tired to form the words. "The alien is too strong. We thought we had a chance for a time, but then a Union force surprised us and caught us between the alien and their guns. We had no choice but to retreat. We accomplished nothing, except to lose another dozen of our people."

"We have lost more than that," Consuela said, her expression somber. She told him of the carnage she had witnessed in the village. "No matter how many of our people they enslave, it never seems to be enough for them. They will not stop unless we stop them."

"How are we to do that?" José asked her. "This"—he gestured at the demoralized guerrillas around them—"is all we have to fight with. I feel for the *campesinos* as much as you do, but I have nothing left to give them. The most we can do at this point is comfort the survivors and try to hide as many as we can."

"There is one other thing we could try," Consuela said hesitantly. José raised an eyebrow inquiringly, and Consuela paused, choosing her words carefully. But before she could tell him what she had in mind, José was nearly sent sprawling by a blow to his shoulder. He caught himself and turned to glare at his assailant.

Gunther had stormed up and was towering above the seated José. The guerrilla glowered down at his leader, his hatred hotter than the stifling afternoon air around them, and José saw that Gunther's rage had built to unmanageable levels. The man had been briefly shaken by the sight of their dead comrades—as they all had—and had gone along with the attack on the crater readily enough. But the fresh taste of killing had gone to his head, and their defeat did not sit well with him.

"You are scared, Viejo," Gunther said accusingly, each word etched in acid.

"Never," José said coldly, rising until he could look the man in the eye.

"Really? I never could have known that from the way you ran from our enemies." Gunther looked around at the other guerrillas, seeking an appreciative audience, but they were too tired to pay much attention.

"And where were you?" José asked pointedly. "I did not see you volunteering to stay behind. We were outnumbered and flanked by enemies on both sides. Retreat was our only option."

"We should not have been there in the first place," Gunther snapped. "The alien is dead. The people it uses to fight with are dead. We should concern ourselves with the living. Our true enemy is the Union. We should be planning our next attack on them, not wasting our time in the jungle fighting with corpses."

"You are wrong, Gunther," Consuela said, coming to stand next to José. "For years we have fought the Union, yes, but there are worse enemies out there. This alien thing is the greatest threat we have ever faced. We must defeat it before we can hope to free our people from the Union. What good is winning the people's freedom if they are dead?"

"I would expect you to defend him," Gunther sneered. "But how can we fight them? Look at what our brilliant leader has done. More than half our people are dead, our battles lost. We lost fighting this creature you are so frightened of, and we lost at Revancha. The attack was poorly executed. I wonder if brother Diego knew of our plans in advance. Perhaps the two of you are working against us."

"That's absurd!" Consuela flared. "No one has done more for the Zapatista cause than José."

"Spoken like his lapdog. Or is that his whore?"

Consuela started for him, and José held up a restraining hand. "Gunther," he said quietly. "Now is not the time to tear ourselves apart. We must stand united, regroup, and plan how to fight another day. Should we kill each other instead of our enemies?"

"You have gone soft, Viejo," Gunther taunted. "Old and soft in the heart and head. You take us away from the battle. That is cowardly. Like I would expect from your brother."

José merely stood looking at Gunther with a mild expression on his face that he knew would drive the man wild. Gunther had obviously decided the time had come for the Zapatistas to acquire a new leader—himself. The man was trying to goad José into a fight so he could assume leadership. Which would be disastrous. Gunther would get all of the guerrillas killed within days, and that would mean the death of the Zapatista movement. Gunther lacked everything a leader needed—especially a way to hold his murderous nature in check.

"This is not the place to decide such important matters," José said finally. "We are too exposed."

"Yes," Gunther said. "You are exposed. For a liar and a coward. You are no better than your brother."

José had fought Diego for years and considered him an enemy. Gunther was not saying anything he himself had not thought a thousand times. But for some reason it stung hearing Gunther brand Diego as craven.

"José is not a coward, and neither is his brother," Consuela said fiercely. "I saw him with my own eyes, fighting to save the *campesinos* from one of those mummy creatures. Where were you while he was risking his life?"

"I was killing one of his officers," Gunther boasted. "That foolish man who attacked us at the crater—he will not live to kill any more of our people."

"So while he fights to save people, you fight to destroy them," Consuela said with contempt. "This is indeed a great day for our movement."

"You saw Diego, *chica*?" José asked in surprise.

"I fought beside Diego," she replied. "I had not thought him to care so much for the people as to risk his life defending them. I think we have been wrong about him in the past, José. I think perhaps he is a man beside whom we could fight with honor."

"He is my brother—I cannot trust my own judgment about him," José admitted. "But I trust yours. What are you suggesting?"

"That we join forces," Consuela said. She hurried on before anyone could interrupt her. "Alone, neither of us can hope to defeat these monsters. They are too strong— you saw that at the crater, I saw it at the village. But together, we might stand a chance. Your brother said it himself—it is human against alien. It is our responsibility to put aside our past differences now. It is the only way we can save our people."

José hesitated, torn. Deep down, he knew Consuela was right. But he had spent too many years thinking of his brother as the enemy. It was hard to change that now.

Gunther had been growing steadily more enraged during their conversation. He hated being ignored—now he interrupted. "I cannot believe you are considering this!" he shouted. "That man is our enemy—we cannot trust him. Unless I was right, and you have been working with him all along!"

"Do you really think we can depend on him, *chica*?" José asked Consuela, paying no attention to his furious lieutenant.

"He could have killed me in the village. He did not. I think if he will agree to work with us, we can respect his word," she replied.

José hesitated a moment longer, then nodded. "Do it," he ordered curtly, inwardly quaking but outwardly showing no doubt. A leader had to appear confident before his followers. "Go to Diego and propose an alliance—a *temporary* alliance," he emphasized. "We will work together until we have driven off this menace, and then we will see where we stand."

Consuela nodded, relieved. José calmly turned back to face his troublesome lieutenant.

"I was right," Gunther spat. "You are a traitor!"

Without a word, José punched him so hard in the face that Gunther stumbled backward and fell heavily to the ground. The other guerrillas stared, shocked.

"I am the leader of this army," José said, speaking as much to them as to Gunther. "If you disagree with my decisions, you are free to leave. But I will not brook mutiny."

"Traitor!" Gunther shrieked, losing the last shred of self-control. He clawed for the pistol at his waist, but before it even cleared his holster, José had dived for his Kalashnikov on the ground beside him and shot him point-blank in the chest. Gunther died without another word, a look of surprise on his face, the front of his fatigues quickly reddening with his heart's blood.

There was dead silence from the others—none would look up to meet José's eyes. But Consuela did, and her gaze held warm approval and confidence.

"It was bound to happen sooner or later," she said quietly. "You did what had to be done."

"It is time for all of us to do what we have to do," José said, then raised his voice. "Zapatistas! Assemble and follow Consuela. We will go to Diego and see whether he will agree to an alliance. And if he does, we will fight together to defeat this menace. But we will not give in, and we will not give up hope."

Slowly, the guerrillas began to rise and gather their weapons and equipment. They still would not meet his eyes, José was saddened to see, but they would obey. For now, that was the best he could hope for.

He took a deep breath, and for the first time in three years, he prepared to meet his brother face-to-face

"That's all the firepower we can deliver?" Diego said, swallowing hard at Lieutenant Travis's report. "Only one SPEAR missile?"

"Allen used the only other SPEAR on that crystal thing," BJ replied. "Dropped it right on our doorstep. Killed a bunch of the locals, too, the bastard."

Diego compressed his lips. After seeing the destruction the other alien had wreaked on the village, he could not entirely blame Allen for his actions. He hated to give the man too much credit, and his heart ached at the thought of the civilian casualties, but it was entirely possible that letting the creature continue its rampage would have resulted in even more deaths.

"This spaceship," BJ said, interrupting his train of thought. "You want us to target it?"

"What kind of range do you have with ordnance already warmed up and ready to fly?"

"Not much. We've got the missile launchers on the Aztec cycles, but that's about it. We've been short on ordnance since . . ."

"I know," Diego said, silently cursing General Ramirez for the thousandth time. Chronically undermanned, undertrained, and underequipped—it was a wonder the entire region hadn't fallen by now, either to the Zapatistas or to whatever these things were that were attacking the *campesinos*.

At least the undead thing had finally left the village, taking an undetermined number of residents with it. Diego and BJ were standing in the ruins of the town, surrounded by burning buildings, rubble, and bodies. Diego had never seen destruction on this scale, not even in the worst of the guerrilla campaign. And he had no idea how to stop its cause.

"Sir!" called Suarez, hurrying toward the pair from across the village square, passing a squad of BJ's soldiers who were laboring to put out the worst of the fires. Others were trying to find and identify the bodies so they could determine how many were missing.

"Sir," the lieutenant panted, skidding to a halt next to them. "I just received a report from Private Murdo back at San Cristóbal. He tells me Captain Allen has been killed."

"Killed?" Diego said blankly. Beside him, BJ tried hard to repress a wide grin at the news.

"Yes, sir. Apparently he led some kind of expedition out in the jungle, and he ran into a group of guerrillas," Suarez said. "Shot dead."

Diego could not say he was sorry to hear of the man's death. His mind was already racing, trying to decide how best to take advantage of it.

"Lieutenant," he said, "as the ranking officer in Chiapas, I'm temporarily assuming command of the garrison at San Cristóbal."

"What about Ramirez?" BJ asked.

"Unfortunately, we're having trouble with communications," Diego said, staring hard at her to be sure she got it. "We'll ask General Ramirez for his orders as soon as they're restored."

"Aye, sir," she said, no longer able to suppress her grin. Suarez was smiling as well, and Diego felt a sudden rush of affection for them both.

"Suarez," he said, "I want you to take one of the Aztecs and get back to the garrison ASAP. I want a full inventory of all available weapons. I have a feeling we're going to need every one of them if we're going to have a prayer of killing that thing."

"Yes, sir," Suarez said with feeling. He had just turned to go when a commotion at the other end of the village caught all their attention.

"I'm here to see Colonel Villalobos!" a voice was shouting, and with a shock Diego realized it was Consuela Ortega, José's lieutenant. Diego had not expected to see her again when she disappeared so quickly after the alien's attack. But here she was, walking boldly into the village as if she owned it, seemingly without fear of the Pitbulls pointed in her direction.

"Hold your fire!" Diego shouted hastily, hurrying over to where the small woman stood, surrounded by very nervous Union soldiers. Consuela gazed at him over the rifle muzzles, unsmiling.

"I didn't expect to see you again," Diego said. "Not alive and kicking, anyway."

"And under ordinary circumstances, I never would have come," she said. "But as we both know, these circumstances are far from ordinary." She gestured at the devastated village.

"Agreed," Diego said ruefully.

"We have big trouble," Consuela said. "You and José and everyone else in Chiapas."

"It's been that way for years," Diego said, his exhaustion beginning to catch up with him. Only a day earlier, he would have been overjoyed that his patrol had captured one of José's best. Now it seemed almost insignificant.

"But never like this," she replied. "You have seen the same monster I have—you know how dangerous it is. How many of our people it has killed. You do not seem to be having much luck fighting it."

"I suppose you've done better?" Diego asked, raising an eyebrow.

"No," Consuela said simply. "There is another one, at a crater deep in the jungle. We tried to kill it, but it was much too strong for us."

"At a crater?" Diego said, his interest quickening.

"The aliens seem to be after an object that fell from the sky," she said. "It is a deadly glowing orb—I call it *el corazón del infierno*."

"Hell Heart," Diego murmured. He looked up. "What do they want with it?"

"I do not know," Consuela said. "But it does not matter. They have killed and enslaved many *campesinos* to get it. For all our sakes, we have to stop them."

"Agreed," Diego said again. "What exactly did you have in mind?" His soldiers were beginning to shift uneasily, unsure why their commander was chatting so casually with one of the enemy.

"We must not fight one another," Consuela said earnestly. "We must work together to fight these creatures!"

"Together?" Diego asked skeptically.

"I have no experience trying to end wars," Consuela admitted. "But now we have a bigger enemy, one more dangerous than the Union or the Neo-Soviets. And time is running out."

"Old habits die hard," Diego said. "Has José agreed to an alliance with his younger brother?"

"Yes," Consuela said, and Diego stared at her, stunned. He knew deep in his gut that this was no Zapatista trick, as much as he might want to believe it. He had seen the destruction the alien creatures were capable of, and it was far beyond anything humans could create. But ally himself with José after so much bad blood? What help could José possibly provide that would be worth the risk?

"I have two ag cycles, the Hydra, and dozens of soldiers," Diego told Consuela bluntly. "We have Pitbulls and Bulldogs and missiles. What could you supply that we do not already have?"

"We know the jungle," she said. "You may have the better weapons, but we have the knowledge you need to use them. And if we are not dividing our forces by fighting each other, we stand a much better chance of defeating those monsters."

Diego found himself nodding, slowly, unwillingly. BJ, standing at his elbow, hissed, "You can't be serious, Colonel! Team up with these criminals?"

A few days ago, Diego would have felt the same way. But since then, he had been betrayed by his superiors, lost his command, and watched innocent civilians murdered before his eyes. He was closer to understanding José's point of view than ever before, even if he still disagreed with his brother's methods.

"It's worth the risk," Diego abruptly decided. "If José's willing to meet, I'm willing to talk to him."

"Colonel . . ." BJ protested.

"Lieutenant?" Diego asked, the tone of his voice making it clear his mind was made up. She subsided, but the set of her jaw told him there would be further discussion— later.

"Bring José to me," he said to Consuela. "We can talk and decide where we should go from here."

"Done," said Consuela with a half smile. From behind her, in a dozen different places, guerrillas appeared. Diego stared, openmouthed. The guerrillas had concealed themselves so well along the edge of the jungle that he'd had no idea they were there until they revealed themselves.

The guerrillas gathered in a half circle behind Consuela. They were filthy and exhausted-looking. Nearly all of them wore streaks of blood from minor injuries; several had to be supported by their colleagues. More continued to file out of the jungle and assemble in the clearing on the edge of the village. The last one to emerge from the sheltering vegetation was José. He looked even wearier and thinner than he had on the battlefield at Revancha. Diego absently wondered whether his own appearance was as bad.

José stopped at Consuela's side, and the two men stared at each other warily, each unsure how to feel about the other.

Finally, José broke the silence. "Diego," he said, his voice raspy with exhaustion.

"Viejo," Diego said, hardly trusting his own voice. They looked at each other for a few moments longer.

"You look well, brother," José said.

"You look like hell," Diego replied.

José's face split in his old, familiar grin, and Diego found himself smiling back at him.

"True," José said, and then his smile disappeared. "We will all of us look worse before this is over," he said, serious again. "Shall we begin?"

"After you," Diego said, stepping aside and making a sweeping gesture toward the center of the village. José strode past him confidently, followed by Consuela and the rest of the guerrillas. Diego's men fell in behind them, still wary but willing to follow their commander's lead.

Diego only wished he had as much confidence in himself as they seemed to have. But as he walked behind his brother, the two of them preparing to go into battle as in the old days, he found that, against all odds, he was happy.

26

Satisfaction.

The Pharon Death Priest felt the warm glow of accomplishment as he checked his sensor readings one more time. After hours of labor at the crater where the Vor-stuff had plunged to earth and countless trips through the putrid vegetation of this world to replenish his constantly dwindling supply of slaves, he had finally achieved the goal he had sought for so long.

He glanced proudly over his shoulder at the grim procession behind him. Following at a safe distance back struggled the slaves carrying the crudely rigged sling containing his prize. The speck's intense light was slightly muted by the force field the priest had constructed with such effort, but it was still too bright to look at for longer than a few seconds.

If looking at it from a distance was painful to the Death Priest, being in close proximity to it was proving deadly to the hapless slaves. It required three of them to bear the sling with the trapped mote, and these three were already showing signs of deterioration. Where their hands held the sling, the flesh was slowly crisping and turning black. In several places, the white gleam of bone showed through the devastated flesh. Hideous sores were erupting on their limbs and faces, and the farther they walked, the slower their steps became. The priest barked at them as one staggered, nearly upsetting the delicate balance of the litter and sending the Vor-stuff crashing to the ground. The Pharon was certain the force field would survive the impact, but a spill would delay him further, and he had waited quite long enough for his moment of triumph.

There was a hideous gurgle from the slave supporting the front end of the litter, and its legs finally gave way, sending it collapsing to the packed earth of the jungle trail. It twitched a few times before succumbing to death, its body blackened and twisted by the hellish radiation emanating from its burden. The priest snapped an order, and another slave hurriedly took the dead one's place, rescuing the sliding litter before it could unbalance completely.

The priest blew out a sigh of exasperation. There were already far too many of the pathetic, charred corpses littering the trail behind him. He was still kilometers from reaching *Destroyer for the Faith*, and his supply of slaves was quickly dwindling. The natives of this world were proving alarmingly fragile; despite the dozens the priest had discovered lined up at the compound, his supply might run out before completing the long trek to the ship. Something about the radiation of the Vorack-stuff had a rapidly deteriorating effect on the delicate chemistry of the revivified corpses. The priest was shielded from the worst effects of the radiation by the complex field of his phase generator, but the slaves had no such protection.

The Death Priest glanced at the procession of slaves that trailed behind their glowing burden, mentally toting up their numbers and not pleased with the result. He had hoped to save some to serve as replacement crew members on the long trip back to the Pharon homeworld, but at this rate they would all be charred bodies by the time he got back to the ship.

Ah, well, he told himself, he would just have to hurry. He barked another order at the primitives struggling along behind him, and with an effort they quickened their pace. The priest strode along the trail, happy for the first time in days. Soon the ordeal would be over, and he would return in glory to the presence of the God-king.

"We are running out of time," Consuela said, sounding a bit desperate. "From what José saw at the crater, the mummy creature had almost retrieved the Hell Heart. It must surely have succeeded by now."

"And it is probably on its way back to its ship," Diego mused. He, José, Consuela, and BJ were all crammed into the back of the Hydra for an impromptu war council. BJ was still eyeing the erstwhile guerrillas with deep suspicion, but José and Consuela ignored her obvious hostility.

Tensions were no less thick outside the ag transport. Diego's soldiers and José's guerrillas kept to opposite sides of the small plaza at the center of the village, all clutching their weapons tightly to themselves and glaring at one another with deep mistrust. Diego had ordered Lieutenant Suarez to stay outside and keep an eye on the situation. He didn't want another shooting war erupting anytime soon—

not when they had far worse enemies to worry about than a handful of moth-eaten guerrillas.

He himself was sufficiently unnerved by the situation. Here he was, in the back of a Hydra, looking across at his brother. His sense of déjà vu was intense; how many times had they sat like this in the old days when they were still fighting on the same side? Back then José wouldn't have been asking Diego's advice and listening to his suggestions. It was an odd feeling to be fighting together after being enemies for so long. Diego was not sure, but he thought he liked it.

"It has a ship?" José asked now, interrupting Diego's reverie. "You have seen it?"

"My expedition discovered it a few klicks from here," Diego answered. He nodded to BJ, who obediently called up the vid Suarez had recorded at the alien spaceship. A muscle worked in José's jaw as he studied the remains of his comrades working around the huge, beached form of the ship, under the direction of one of the mummy creatures. Diego had studied the recording several times, and he was still appalled by the contrast between the beauty of the ship, covered in intricate tracings and swirls of engravings and plated with gorgeous, glimmering metals, and the hideous, shambling, undead things that swarmed over it, effecting repairs.

"Note the openings in the hull here," BJ said, indicating what looked like the muzzles of laser cannons. "We've counted nearly fifty of the damn things, each of unknown capacity and power. If they work, I don't know what kind of attack we could mount against them."

"It looks formidable," José agreed thoughtfully. "But

it appears their crew is largely outside, working on repairing the damage. That makes them vulnerable."

"It also looks like they're almost finished," Diego said. "Perhaps if we just let it take off . . ." He didn't finish the thought, knowing it could never be. The disgusting creatures had brought too much death for that to be possible. If they escaped, they would be going away with the knowledge that they had slaughtered and enslaved without being punished.

"It has victimized the *campesinos*," Consuela said fiercely.

"We cannot let it leave. It or others of its kind will return and continue what they've started here," Diego finished.

"The aliens are the true threat, and as far as we know there are only two here: the one we fought at the crater and the one you faced in the village," José said, steering the conversation back to the main topic at hand.

"The human slaves are a big enough threat," Diego said wryly. "When we met up with them at Hermosilla, they just wouldn't stop fighting. I must have pumped a dozen rounds into one of them without even slowing it down. We did manage to cut their mobility by targeting the legs, but even that didn't kill them; it just made them move slower. I mean, how do you kill something that's already dead?"

"I may have a solution to that," José answered. "During our battle at the crater, we found that if we targeted the tanks strapped to their backs, here"—he indicated several of the undead slaves in the still-playing recording—"it took them out. Something in those tanks is what sustains their unnatural life. Destroy them, and you destroy the enemy." Then, half under his breath, he added, "And send our people at last to a peaceful grave."

"The tanks—of course!" Diego exclaimed. Then he sobered. "But look at them—there must be dozens of them at the ship. How many did you say you saw at the crater?"

"Perhaps a hundred," José said somberly. "We are outnumbered at least three to one, and our ammunition is almost gone."

"We can provide that," Diego said, "but not much more. We still have one SPEAR missile, but maybe even a SPEAR wouldn't make a dent in that thing."

"How many troops can you supply?" Consuela asked.

"What you see is pretty much what you get," Diego said. "Reinforcements are out of the question."

"HQ again?" José asked with understanding.

"Affirmative," Diego said. "General Ramirez . . . doesn't exactly know I'm in charge here."

"My brother the rebel," José said with a poker face, surprising both Diego and BJ into a snort of laughter. The two brothers grinned at each other, the first tension-free moment either of them had enjoyed in years. But the feeling quickly passed, and José's smile faded as he turned his attention back to the recording.

"There are too many to fight," he said finally. "Even if we snipe at the tanks from the safety of the jungle, we will still be vulnerable to those cannons. We have to assume they are functioning. I don't know how we can . . ."

Diego held up a hand, and José trailed off. Diego almost had something—it was glimmering just at the edge of his memory . . . Then he had it.

"We do have one weapon we could use against them," he said. José raised an inquiring eyebrow.

"The green goo," Diego said, with just a touch of smugness.

"Of course!" Consuela exclaimed.

"You know what effect it had on our Ares," Diego told her. "I saw some of those tanks close up, and I'm certain they're made of metal. Ditto for the ship. It would almost certainly have the same effect on the aliens—assuming you have any of the stuff left."

José nodded reluctantly. "There are two more canisters, hidden in the jungle," he said. "I have been unwilling to use them—some weapons are too dangerous to risk. But if it will stop these aliens from killing our people . . ."

"One problem," Consuela said. "The spray is a short-range weapon. We would have to get it up close to the ship for it to have any effect, and anyone carrying it would be killed long before we could get there."

"What if we used the SPEAR missile to carry it?" Diego asked, liking the idea better and better as he spoke. "I don't know if it would work, but if we could rig one of the warheads to carry a canister instead of the explosive—"

"I think it could be done, sir," BJ interrupted. "But we'd need to get it here and experiment."

Diego looked at José. "How soon could you get the canisters here?" he asked.

"They are hidden not far from here," José replied. "We can have them here within a half hour."

"Do it," Diego said. "I'll take one of my men and get back to San Cristóbal to retrieve the SPEAR. In the meantime, we need to see if we can come up with a backup plan—just in case this doesn't work."

"It will work," Consuela said confidently.

"I hope so," Diego said under his breath. He and José

stood up simultaneously, he to find Suarez and José to fetch the cylinders. He just hoped it wasn't already too late.

Diego and Suarez rode the crimson-and-gold Aztec cycle into the post at San Cristóbal just after dusk. They had made good time from the village along deserted, dusty roads. Frightened by the carnage of the past few days, the *campesinos* were staying hidden indoors, and while their fear saddened Diego, it also made his job easier for the moment.

Diego was disturbed when no sentry challenged him. He knew the post was currently guarded by a only a skeleton crew, but security had clearly grown lax under Allen's "command." He would have to work hard to restore discipline—assuming any of them lived beyond the next few hours.

Diego dropped off the ag cycle, followed in short order by Suarez. "Find a weapons tech and get the SPEAR loaded into the missile launcher," he ordered his lieutenant. "And make it quick. We haven't got much time."

"Where is everyone, Colonel?" Suarez asked, pushing back his visor and squinting as the bright light from the security lamps shone directly on his face.

"We don't have time to worry about it now. Get over to the launch center," Diego repeated. "While the tech is preparing the missile, check the Ares suits. See if they were cleaned and if we can use them."

The last report Diego had seen wasn't too promising, but even if the suits were ruined, knowing how much damage they had sustained from José's lethal bioweapon would still be useful. It might give them a better idea of what effects the goo could have on the alien ship, not to mention the wheezing life-support systems worn by the undead human slaves.

"Colonel?" came Suarez's voice over Diego's helmet commlink.

"Here, Lieutenant," he said, hastily activating his mike.

"There's not even a puddle left of those fancy assault suits. The acid chewed them up pretty well. A few spare parts survived, but that's all."

"Understood. See to the Aztec," Diego said, and signed off. He gazed at the ruins of his command—how had Allen managed to wreak so much havoc in so short a time?

No sentries had been posted, but Diego knew the post was still occupied. He strode to a barracks and kicked open the door. Three men on their bunks jumped guiltily on seeing his insignia shining in the bright light and scrambled to get to their feet and stand at attention.

"Who's in command of this post?" Diego asked coldly.

The three exchanged looks, and then as one shrugged and shook their heads. Diego could hardly believe that Allen had left the garrison without passing along command to someone. If he'd already run through his entire roster of officers, he should have breveted a couple of sergeants and let them run the place till he got back. But to abandon it!

Allen had put the post at extreme risk. If the man were still alive, Diego thought he just might have killed him personally.

With difficulty, he swallowed his anger. He had no time to spare on recriminations. The best he could do now was to act to protect the post and hope it was enough.

"How many soldiers do we still have in fighting condition?" he asked, none too surprised when the soldiers could not answer.

"Secure the perimeter, if you can," he ordered. "If you can't, fall back and fortify the command and control center. Roust all the troops you can find and concentrate on defending it."

"Who's going to pay attention to us?" one man protested.

"You're all promoted to sergeant," Diego said with exasperation. "Pass along my orders to any other noncom you can find, and if there aren't any, you three are in charge. Any questions?"

The first soldier blanched, his mouth opening and closing like a fish washed up on the ocean shore. "We're supposed to hold the entire post? Even if the guerrillas attack?" he asked.

"I don't think that's going to happen," Diego said, amused in spite of himself. From outside the barracks, he heard the high-pitched whine of the Aztec. Suarez must have finished rigging the missile.

"Defend as much as you can," he said curtly. "Carry on."

Diego did a smart about-face and left, hollow inside. He hated to leave his post in such inexperienced hands, but he had done the best he could. His job was to try to deal with the alien menace—everything else would have to wait until later.

If there *was* a later.

The Death Priest emerged finally from the jungle into the clearing with a feeling of overwhelming relief. There before him lay the beautiful silhouette of his ship, the *Destroyer for the Faith*, outlined in artificial light to counter the growing dark. Nearly all the damage had been repaired, and he could see the dark bulk of the Slayer outlined against the shining surface of the ship, barking orders backed up by the menacing hum of his ever-present energy weapon.

The Pharon strode forward confidently, gesturing impatiently for his slaves to follow. They did, slowly, staggering under their burden. Far too many twisted, pathetic remnants littered the trail for kilometers behind them, but they had succeeded in their mission. Millions of them could die, for all the priest cared. He had the Vor-stuff!

He would need to keep the sphere outside, still held in abeyance by his force beams, until he was certain the cargo hold's force shields were in place and operational. One failure could tear the entire ship apart, and take everyone aboard with it.

But in a matter of hours, he would have left this accursed planet behind forever—or at least until the Pharons saw fit to conquer it for the glory of the God-king. Once they had harnessed the power of the Vorack, this world, and every other world in the Maelstrom, would be easy pickings.

"Slaves, assist the others on the repairs," the priest ordered. He had a headache from urging the almost-mindless slaves along the trail. He longed to return to the homeworld, where the slaves were less recalcitrant and did not require constant supervision.

Still, at least they obeyed, even if too slowly. The few survivors stumbled toward the ship and began working on the last of the hull damage.

The Pharon ordered the swaying slaves holding the litter to set it down—gently. With the last of their strength, they complied—and then simply disintegrated from the force of the radiation. Ordinarily that would have exasperated the priest, but nothing could perturb him now. Escape from this noisome world was imminent. By the grace of the God-king and decent repairs, the Death Priest could be in court with his magnificent tribute before the ninety-first anniversary of the God-king's ascension.

He could hardly restrain his anticipation.

27

S ir, we're detecting movement along the perimeter defenses," came BJ's sharp report. "You want us to fire when we acquire a good target?"

Diego glanced at the battle display and saw that the four approaching blips were making no effort to hide. He checked heat signatures and made a preliminary ID.

"Weapons down," he ordered. "It's Viejo."

Within another few minutes, the four figures came into view. José and Consuela led the way, carrying a large plastic cylinder between them. Following were two more guerrillas bearing a similar canister. They carried the cylinders gingerly, as if afraid of their contents. And with good reason, thought Diego, remembering with a shudder what just one of those cylinders had done to his Ares suits.

"Were you able to get us the SPEAR?" José asked Diego, setting the cylinder carefully on the ground and stretching as if his back hurt.

"Affirmative," Diego answered, gesturing to the Aztec now outfitted with his last SPEAR missile.

"Then we may have a chance," José said.

"Sir!" BJ called from by the battle display. "We're picking up a significant surge of energy from the alien ship. It looks like they're powering up—maybe getting ready to take off."

"Suarez!" Diego instantly snapped. "Get to work on fitting one of those cylinders into the warhead. We don't have much time—let's make the best of what we've got. And be careful."

Suarez and two Union soldiers edged past the guerrillas and gingerly picked up José's cylinder from the ground.

"Anything they need to know?" Diego asked.

"You probably know more about it than I do," José answered. "The Neo-Sovs weren't particularly forthcoming with details. What about the creature? Your officer said it is ready to take off?"

"About five klicks away. I sent out RPVs with cameras for recon, but the mummy-things snuffed out every one as they got close. I finally started lofting message rockets with cameras. They give us only a quick look, but Suarez is good at interpreting what they see."

"And what *have* they seen?" Consuela asked. She had followed Suarez and the Union soldiers over to the Aztec and was watching with interest as they retrofit the missile.

"The last one we sent up wasn't good," Suarez told her. "It looks like they've just about finished repairs on the ship's hull. That probably means it won't be long before they're ready to take off."

"And taking our people with them," José said grimly.

Diego knew how he felt. Seeing the *campesinos* turned into grotesque, undying slaves was horrifying enough; the thought of them being stolen away to some alien world to labor for the rest of their unnatural lives in the service of those monsters—that was not to be borne. They had to stop the alien ship before it took off and sent those poor people to their final rest.

Diego strode over to the ag cycle and peered into the guts of the missile payload. Wires dangled everywhere as Suarez labored to squeeze the Neo-Sov aerosol sprayer into a space not designed for it. If the cylinder ruptured, it would kill them all.

Suarez was beginning to look uncomfortable about his commanding officer breathing down his neck, so Diego backed off to give him room to work. Suarez knew how important his task was; hovering would accomplish nothing.

"Diego," José said in a low voice, "have you considered that if we blow up the ship with that energy ball inside, the explosion might destroy much of the jungle?"

"And take countless *campesinos* with it," Consuela added.

"We thought of that," Diego said. "I've got BJ targeting the area directly outside the ship. Hopefully that will spread the green mist far enough to disable the ship and kill the aliens, but won't hit with enough force to destroy whatever is holding that thing in check. I've got no interest in finding out just how powerful it is."

"We're as ready as we'll ever be, sir," Suarez reported, powering down his handheld laser and backing away from the Aztec. The jury-rigged missile looked crudely assembled, but it would probably hang together long enough to reach the ship and do what needed to be done.

"BJ, launch another message rocket. We need to see what we're targeting," Diego ordered. The stocky lieutenant complied, and the tiny rocket soared into the air, carrying a surveillance camera with it. The people on the ground squinted to follow it as it disappeared into the dark night sky. A few seconds later, BJ reported, "Target achieved."

"Suarez, what did we get?" Diego asked.

"We've got about a dozen zombies outside the ship," Suarez said. "Both of the alien things are outside, too. The globe is nowhere in sight—looks like they've already loaded it into the ship."

"That's as much luck as we can hope for," Diego said, and José nodded in agreement. "Suarez, launch the missile."

Everyone backed away to a safe distance. Suarez made one last check of the weapon, and then took a deep breath and punched a button on the battle console. With a roar that set the ag cycle trembling, the SPEAR missile shot into the air, carrying their best hopes with it. Diego traced the outline of his crucifix and sent a quick prayer after it, and for a moment he thought he saw José doing the same.

In a few seconds, they would know whether they had succeeded or failed. Diego sincerely hoped it was the former. Failure at this stage meant death.

The Death Priest worked at the controls of the force-beam equipment, intent on the slightest power variation, the merest hint that something might fail. Painstakingly precise, he moved the speck of virulent matter into the center of *Destroyer for the Faith*'s hold. The slaves had finished the hull repairs. The ship's engines were in decent condition, and once the Vorack mote was secured in the hold, the priest would be in command of more power than any other Pharon in history.

"For the glory of the God-king," he murmured as he manipulated the globe into the hold's acceleration dampers. The crystalline sphere surrounding the mote continued to crack and leak out energy at distressingly high levels. The Death Priest wasted no time turning on the internal force shields once the valuable mote was in place.

Giving a silent thanks to the God-king, the priest at last shut down his makeshift console. He had isolated the power source for the hold's force shields from the rest of the ship. In case any of their hastily made repairs failed on the way back to the homeworld, he did not want the force field around the Vor-stuff failing as well. He was not interested in witnessing a supernova from the inside. The hold's generators were now entirely self-contained within the force field. The priest was confident it would withstand even a catastrophic hull breach or a complete power failure.

"Slaves," ordered the priest, "into the ship. Take your positions." They obeyed, but with maddening slowness. He felt the pressure of time wearing on him. Too many natives of this world had seen him, and he had already wasted far too much time battling their primitive efforts to stop him. He wanted no more delays. He was so close to escaping this noxious place he could almost taste his anticipation.

"Slayer!" the priest called, and the huge warrior hurried over to him.

"Orders, holy one?" he asked.

"Gather the remainder of the slaves into the ship and prepare for takeoff," the priest ordered. "We are ready to leave this cursed world behind."

The Slayer clacked his enormous battle claw with pleasure at these words. "At once, holy one," he said in his hideous, ruined voice.

He hurried off to collect the few remaining slaves, and the priest turned to enter the ship. He needed to get to the control room and supervise the efforts of the slaves there. He was dissatisfied with the level of training he had been able to give them, but had lacked the time for much more. Once safely back on the Pharon homeworld, he would see to it that they were disciplined properly.

Suddenly, a droning shriek split the air, and the priest whirled clumsily in the hatchway to see a pinpoint of light descending from the sky. Reflex took over, and the priest dived through the hatch, which slammed shut just as the missile impacted.

The explosion as the missile hit could be felt even five kilometers away, where Diego and the others stood.

"Report!" Diego snapped.

Suarez was busy at the battle console, intently studying the display. "Dead on target, sir!" he said, satisfaction evident in his voice. "The SPEAR hit just outside the ship. Readings indicate the bioweapon is spreading throughout the clearing."

"Do we know yet how many casualties?" Diego asked.

"Looks like . . . yes! The readings on the slaves indicate the bioweapon is disintegrating their life-support tanks. At least a dozen have ceased movement."

"What about the monsters?" Consuela asked urgently.

Suarez's smile disappeared. "We scored one hit," he reported somberly. "But it looks like the other one made it inside the ship before the missile impacted."

Diego swore under his breath, and Suarez looked up from his displays. "Don't worry, sir," he said. "That ship isn't going anywhere. The green goo is starting to eat away at the hull. In a few minutes, it won't be spaceworthy, and I wouldn't be surprised if it ate out the propulsion systems as well. There's enough metal there to keep the goo busy for quite a while. Eventually, it'll eat its way into wherever the other alien is hiding, and that will be that."

"But we don't know what kind of damage that creature can do in the meantime," José said warily.

"Colonel!" BJ called urgently from her position at the battle console, and Diego went quickly over to where she stood.

"What is it, Lieutenant?" he asked, not sure he wanted to hear the answer.

"We've got some new power readings coming from the ship." She looked up at him, her expression filled with dread. "I think it's powering up the laser cannons. At this range, those weapons could rip all the way through the jungle and cut us down where we stand. We haven't got anything that can stand up to that kind of power."

Diego cursed again. "All right. Immediate evac!" he called, and the clearing erupted with a swirl of activity. "We've got to get out of range before those lasers reach full power."

"We'll never make it, sir," BJ said quietly.

Diego turned to her, and their eyes met with complete understanding. "I know," he said in an undertone. "But we have to try."

He whirled and strode toward the Hydra, shooing soldiers and guerrillas in front of him as he went. He had just gone through the doorway when he heard the whine of ag lifters coming from one of the Aztecs. He spun, ready to rush back out, but stopped dead in his tracks when he saw Consuela standing just inside the door, tears running down her cheeks.

"What's wrong? Where's José?"

"He told me to give you this," she said shakily, holding out José's crucifix. "He asked that you keep it for him until he comes back."

Slowly, Diego reached out and took the crucifix, then looped it around his neck where it rested atop his own. The chain felt cool against his skin. He listened hard as the ag whine died away. José was headed directly for the alien ship, the final cylinder of green goo undoubtedly loaded on the back of the Aztec.

"He shouldn't have gone off alone," Diego said, then pushed past Consuela to the battle display so he could follow his brother's progress. José piloted audaciously, but there was so little time. The power emissions from the ship were rising at an alarming rate. The alien could fire at almost any moment.

Behind him, the bustle of a hurried evacuation continued, but Diego was oblivious to it, all his being concentrated on the tiny blip that represented his brother—the blip that represented their only real hope of survival.

28

José Villalobos drove the Aztec with reckless abandon. He had always been a hot-rodder, the one to risk everything on a single throw of the dice. Unlike his little brother.

Now José felt that not only the lives of his remaining guerrillas—including his beloved Consuela—and his brother hung in the balance, but the fate of the Earth as well. This monster could not be allowed to live. More would surely follow, and Chiapas, Mexico, the Union, the entire planet would be at risk. He had already lost far too many of his people to the undead creature—he wasn't going to let it finish the job.

José slewed the Aztec to one side to avoid a giant jacaranda tree, and the cylinder lashed hastily to the back of the ag cycle slid precariously. José ignored it. So what if it went off prematurely? It would take several minutes before it could eat through enough metal to disable the cycle, and he was within seconds of the clearing that held the alien spacecraft.

Veering to one side, he scraped past a mahogany tree, then rebounded and emerged into the burned-out area around the ship. He could see the initial burn marks of its landing in the center of the clearing, lit clearly by the bright lights streaming from the ship. The alien had enlarged the area—undoubtedly to provide space to repair its craft.

It had used *campesinos* murdered and enslaved by its evil technology. He could see their corpses now, lying scattered like leaves around the ship, their life tanks melted and destroyed by the Neo-Soviet bioweapon. Among them lay one of the alien creatures. One mammoth arm was still outstretched as if reaching for the safety of the ship, but its beautiful engraved back tank had disintegrated, the hoses still pumping the tank's obscene fluids into the packed earth around the ship.

José could see that the ship itself was beginning to disintegrate. Green moss sprouted everywhere, and holes were beginning to appear in the craft's formerly shiny surface as the goo slowly ate through the skin of the hull.

José skidded to a stop near the ship's tailfin. He cut the ag lifters, and the cycle fell heavily the last few centimeters to the ground. He jumped off the seat and fumbled with the cylinder, working to attach the sprayer-nozzle assembly to the cylinder. Already he was choking on the fumes released by the goo as it dissolved the alien metals.

Hefting the heavy cylinder and breathing as shallowly as he could, José began circling the ship, looking for a way in. He passed under several of the laser cannons, their throaty whine lending extra incentive to his search. Soon, he knew, they would fire, and when they did, his brother and all his remaining guerrillas would die.

He would not let that happen.

There. Above him was an airlock. He could tell it had once been sealed, but the goo had eaten a hole in the doors that was large enough to admit him. He clambered up onto the ship with some difficulty, still lugging the heavy cylinder, and gingerly entered the airlock. Green tendrils brushed along his face and shoulders as he ducked through the hole, and he shuddered at their clammy touch. But they found no purchase on his clothing, and their questing tendrils sought out and then ignored the plastic cylinder.

José had scarcely taken two steps inside the foul darkness when a sudden shift in the air currents warned him of an imminent attack. He ducked just as a razor-sharp knife cut the air where his head had been an instant before. His finger tightened reflexively on the spray trigger, and the green goo began spewing forth onto the attacking slaves. As it settled over their shoddy life-support units, they began keeling over. José kept his finger on the trigger until the last of them had collapsed to the floor.

"I do not kill you, my *amigos*, my countrymen," he said softly. "You are dead. I am only restoring grace after you have lost it."

He finally released the trigger and stepped gingerly over their devastated corpses, the floor underfoot made slippery by the fluids spewing from their ruptured tanks. He was in a narrow corridor with barely enough light to see. The junctures of ceiling, wall, and floor all seemed slightly off. There wasn't a single right angle in the place. That and the dim lighting made progress extremely difficult, and he had to concentrate on placing his feet carefully with each step.

Another slave attacked as he passed a side corridor, and he took a nasty slice on his upper arm before he could respond with the sprayer. His attacker collapsed and died like the others, and he continued deeper into the ship.

The assaults by slaves grew more frequent as he grew closer to what must be the heart of the ship. Everywhere he saw evidence of hasty repairs: bare wires sticking out of walls, patches on the inner hull, empty places where equipment had been cannibalized to effect repairs elsewhere.

The stench of death, which had seemed overpowering when José had entered the ship, now clustered so thickly that he could feel it burning at the back of his throat. He had to be close now.

He ducked as he caught a hint of movement out of the corner of his eye, and barely missed having his head taken off by a wickedly sharp scythe. But the sudden movement overbalanced him on the dangerously slick floor, and he tumbled heavily to the deck. Only a last-minute twist saved him from falling on the cylinder and rupturing it.

Dazed, he looked up and saw the emaciated form of Mary Stephenson—or what remained of her—standing over him, her weapon raised for a killing blow. José braced himself for the impact, cursing himself for a failure.

The blow never came. Barely seen in the gloom of the alien ship, her lips moved, forming words he could hardly make out.

"Please, José," the sorry remains of his faithful lieutenant breathed, the words emerging with difficulty from decayed vocal cords.

Slowly, José got to his feet, and Mary lowered her weapon until they stood face-to-face.

"There is one thing more I have to do, Mary," he said gently.

She stared at him a moment longer, then lifted a ravaged hand and pointed to a dim corridor behind him. "There," she whispered, and José nodded his understanding. Then he lifted the nozzle of the cylinder and pulled back on the trigger.

Mary Stephenson seemed to collapse inward on herself as the greenish mist ate into the tank sustaining her unnatural life. She looked up at him from ruined eyes, speech beyond her capability, and struggled to form one last word. But then the light faded from her eyes, and she dropped to the floor with a sigh, her thoughts forever beyond his knowing.

"Rest in peace, my friend," José said softly, then turned to enter the corridor she had indicated. Somewhere in its depths, he knew, was the monster he had come to kill.

José emerged, panting, into a huge space that he instinctively knew was the control center of the ship. He was bleeding from half a dozen wounds sustained while battling his way past what seemed like an endless horde of zombies infesting the place. Every square centimeter of surface was covered by display screens and control consoles, manned by yet more slaves. And in the center of the room, in a thronelike chair, sat the being responsible for the deaths of so many of his countrymen.

José had seen it at the crater, of course, but never this close up. As it turned to glare at him and rose slowly from its seat, José could see clearly the dead gray color of its skin and the greasy, filthy bandages wrapping its body, contrasting horribly with the beauty of its golden armor. It was taller than he had thought.

Then he was too busy to study it further, as the creature snapped out a word in some alien tongue, and its undead crew attacked. José fended them off almost absently, all his attention concentrated on the monster commanding them. Step by step, he fought his way toward the monster. He dimly felt the sharp pain as the slaves' weapons sliced into his flesh, but he ignored it and his growing weakness as he battled his way across the control room, slaves collapsing in his wake as he hosed them with the green goo. The cylinder cradled in his arms felt alarmingly light, its contents almost depleted.

But there was enough left to do what he had come for. As the last slaves fell, their lives gurgling away onto a floor awash in fluids, the alien creature unsheathed the long scythes hung at its waist with a lethal whisper. José circled it warily, wanting to make sure he had a clear shot at the elaborate life-support tank on its back. He dodged one slash from the scythes and then another, each time getting a little closer. Blood ran in a dozen rivulets from his wounds, but he ignored it as he finally saw his opening.

José pressed the trigger, and the deadly spray misted out and enveloped the tank. The monstrous creature roared as the mist began eating away at its life-support system. Fluids began to leak from a half dozen holes, and José could see in the monster's small, dark eyes the knowledge of its death.

With the last of its strength, the creature made one

desperate lunge at the man who had killed it, and José looked down in dim surprise at the razor edge of the scythe that had sliced cleanly all the way through his chest. Then his knees gave way, and he and the monster collapsed together to the floor. He felt his vision going dim, and the last thing he saw as he slipped into the darkness was the unseeing eye of the alien as it accompanied him into death.

Epilogue

_____

H ow do you explain it, Colonel?" asked Lieutenant Travis.

"I don't," Diego said as the two of them left the command and control building and walked slowly across the garrison. "I leave the explanations to the scientists."

"Well, have they figured anything out yet?" BJ grumbled.

"Not that I know of," Diego admitted, as they strolled along, enjoying the pleasantly warm day. Chiapas had never seen this much attention from their masters up north. The goo had barely finished eating its way through the alien spaceship two weeks ago before Union scientists had begun swarming over it, taking samples of everything. The remains of the two aliens had been removed for further study up at Union HQ in Cheyenne Mountain, as had the strange crystalline fragment Captain Alex Allen had found at the crater and the remains of the Ares suits destroyed by José's bioweapon. Diego had learned that the Neo-Sovs were making a new incursion farther north, using the goo and something that looked like the Cyclops. Naturally, the Union was eager to find a counteragent to the deadly stuff.

The only thing the scientists hadn't carried away was the cause of the whole thing: the glowing meteorite that had fallen to earth and brought with it so much destruction. The Hell Heart, as Consuela had dubbed it, sat hovering in midair among the melted ruins of the alien ship, entirely encased in a sphere of force beams. It had been the only thing to survive the destruction José and Diego had wreaked on the ship. The scientists and military were still circling it gingerly, afraid to do anything to it for fear of destroying the force field and unleashing its terrible power. The potential that lay within that glowing orb was tremendous, but Diego personally doubted they would ever find a way to harness its energy without destroying themselves—and most of the planet—along with it.

He and BJ walked past a knot of soldiers working to make repairs to one of the Hydras. Most of his soldiers were busy on maintenance in one way or another, working to get the San Cristóbal base back into operational condition. Those who had survived, anyway—nearly twenty percent of his soldiers had been killed.

One-fifth. For a few days, the commlink to MCF headquarters in Mexico City had hummed with denunciations of his command abilities. But even General Ramirez quieted down after Union Command let it be known that they considered Diego Villalobos the hero of the hour. Diego had not yet seen their official report, but rumor had it he had been recommended for a medal—even, perhaps, a promotion. He had lost 20 percent of his command, true, but he had also saved 80 percent, when the potential for total devastation throughout Chiapas had been extreme. He had held off a Cyclops invasion of El Manguito, protected the Revancha reactor, fought off an alien incursion, and broken the back of the Zapatista movement.

Which was not to say the Zapatistas were gone entirely. Diego had received several informal reports from Consuela, who had taken over after José's death. Their relationship remained tense, but he had hopes that perhaps they would be able to work together on the problems facing the people of Chiapas, rather than wasting their energies fighting an unwinnable war. She was not a bad sort, and she was extraordinarily competent. He could see why José had valued her so highly. Lieutenant Suarez was serving as his liaison to the guerrillas, and if he was reading correctly between the lines in Suarez's reports, the young officer liked Consuela even better than he did.

"If you'll excuse me, sir," BJ said, interrupting his reverie, "there are some things I should see to."

"By all means, Lieutenant," Diego said. "Dismissed." He watched the stocky officer fondly as she hurried off, already barking orders into her commlink. Her promotion to captain should come through soon. If it didn't, he could always threaten to resign—that carried some weight now.

Diego strolled slowly toward the main gate, saluted the sentries on duty, and walked out into the ravaged countryside.

The jungle would take years to heal. Huge black gashes showed where various indignities had been heaped on the land. Worse, from his perspective, were the graves that stretched across the denuded fields. He had tried to get a head count of those who were still alive, and had failed. Their best estimate was more than a thousand dead, including the sad corpses of the people the mummy creatures had enslaved. Diego's squads had worked overtime finding the bodies, which were scattered over kilometers of jungle, and had given them a proper burial. Among those interred in the earth was Captain Alex Allen—in one final irony, laid to rest in the land he had so despised.

Once the toxic goo had finished eating its way through the alien spaceship, they had done the same for the dead there, including José. Diego's fingers traced the outline of the single crucifix hanging around his neck. He had given its twin to Consuela. She would bear José's legacy well.

His steps carried him through the raw graves dug into the ground to a two-meter-tall concrete pylon towering in the center of the makeshift cemetery. The pillar held only a brass plaque with a single name engraved on it: José Villalobos. As the Maw sank into the west, its white light touched the plaque and made the name glow.

It was a cruel irony that José had been taken from Diego so soon after they had found each other again. But Diego knew his brother had died doing what he wanted most: saving his people. The Hell Heart had brought so much death and destruction to Chiapas. It was a piece of the Maw that hung over the Earth like a deadly sword. But this time they had triumphed over it—he and José, together at last. The way it was meant to be.

Diego Villalobos turned and walked back to his post in the setting light of the Maw, renewed in body and soul for the long, hard task ahead of him.

ROBERT E. VARDEMAN is the author of forty fantasy novels and eighteen science fiction novels, in addition to numerous westerns under various pen names, three mysteries, spy books and a high-tech thriller. Recent titles include the fantasy *Dark Legacy*, an original novel set in the MAGIC: The Gathering "Dark" era. Short fiction includes "Dragon Debt" in Fred Saberhagen's *Armory of Swords* anthology. Currently being serialized at http://crimsonskies.com is *The Great Helium War*, flying in the dangerously exciting skies of FASA's *Crimson Skies*.

Vardeman was born in Mineral Wells, Texas, down the street from the Crazy Water Hotel, and is a long-time resident of Albuquerque, graduating from the University of New Mexico with a B.S. in Physics and an M.S. in Materials Engineering. He worked for Sandia National Laboratories in the Solid State Physics Research Department, tended bar, and sold fish heads before becoming a full-time writer.

A 1999 New Year's Resolution to set up a home page, astoundingly, has been fulfilled: http://ourworld.compuserve.com/homepages/vardeman

WATCH FOR
VOR: OPERATION SIERRA-75

by Thomas S. Gressman
author of *BattleTech®: Dagger Point*

Sent to find the survivors of a crash landing on an unexplored planet, a company of Union Marines and medics are trapped on a hellish world of enigmatic ruins, where they find themselves hunted by an unknown enemy. But when space and time begin to warp, weapons and equipment vanish, and strange, murderous creatures haunt the Marines' every move, a simple rescue mission becomes a desperate death march . . .

coming in January 2001
from Warner Aspect

ASPECT®

VISIT WARNER ASPECT ONLINE!

THE WARNER ASPECT HOMEPAGE
You'll find us at: www.twbookmark.com then by clicking on Science Fiction and Fantasy.

NEW AND UPCOMING TITLES
Each month we feature our new titles and reader favorites.

AUTHOR INFO
Author bios, bibliographies and links to personal websites.

CONTESTS AND OTHER FUN STUFF
Advance galley giveaways, autographed copies, and more.

THE ASPECT BUZZ
What's new, hot and upcoming from Warner Aspect: awards news, bestsellers, movie tie-in information . . .